"A BURST WITH ACTION."
—*Los Angeles Times*

"AS ROUSING AND STRAIGHTFORWARD AS A
STRETCH DRIVE TO THE WIRE."
—*Newsweek*

REFLEX

Longtime jockey Philip Nore is no hero. But when he begins to suspect that a racetrack photographer's fatal accident was really murder, he sets out to discover the truth and trap the killer. Slowly, he unravels some nasty secrets of corruption, blackmail, and murder—and unwittingly sets himself up as the killer's next target . . .

"Moves with the free-loving speed of a racehorse in stride." —*The Philadelphia Inquirer*

"A stunning shocker . . . A wonderful mix of suspense story and psychological drama." —*Booklist*

A Main Selection of the Book-Of-The-Month® Club

continued . . .

RAVE REVIEWS FOR DICK FRANCIS

"It's either hard or impossible to read Mr. Francis without growing pleased with *yourself*: not only the thrill of vicarious competence imparted by the company of his heroes, but also the lore you collect as you go, feel like a field trip with the perfect guide."
—*The New York Times Book Review*

"One of the most reliable mystery writers working today . . . Francis's secret weapons are his protagonists. They are the kind of people you want for friends."   —*Detroit News and Free Press*

"[Francis] has the uncanny ability to turn out simply plotted yet charmingly addictive mysteries."   —*The Wall Street Journal*

"A rare and magical talent . . . who never writes the same story twice . . . Few writers have maintained such a high standard of excellence for as long as Dick Francis."
—*The San Diego Union-Tribune*

"Each Francis novel seems to be his best."
—*The Sunday Oklahoman*

"[The] master of crime fiction and equine thrills."   —*Newsday*

"Few things are more convincing than Dick Francis at a full gallop."
—*Chicago Tribune*

"Francis just gets better and better…It can't be as easy as he makes it look, or all mystery writers would be as addictive."
—*The Charlotte Observer*

"After writing dozens of thrillers, Dick Francis always retains a first-novel freshness."   —*The Indianapolis Star*

"He writes about the basic building blocks of life—obligation, honor, love, courage, and pleasure. Those discussions come disguised in adventure novels so gripping that they cry out to be read in one gulp—then quickly reread to savor the details skipped in the first gallop through the pages."   —*Houston Chronicle*

"Dick Francis stands head and shoulders above the rest."
—*Ottawa Citizen*

Fiction by Dick Francis

DEAD HEAT	TWICE SHY
UNDER ORDERS	REFLEX
SHATTERED	WHIP HAND
SECOND WIND	TRIAL RUN
FIELD OF THIRTEEN	RISK
10 LB. PENALTY	IN THE FRAME
TO THE HILT	HIGH STAKES
COME TO GRIEF	KNOCKDOWN
WILD HORSES	SLAY RIDE
DECIDER	SMOKESCREEN
DRIVING FORCE	BONECRACK
COMEBACK	RAT RACE
LONGSHOT	ENQUIRY
STRAIGHT	FORFEIT
THE EDGE	BLOOD SPORT
HOT MONEY	FLYING FINISH
BOLT	ODDS AGAINST
BREAK IN	FOR KICKS
PROOF	NERVE
THE DANGER	DEAD CERT
BANKER	

Anthology

WIN, PLACE, OR SHOW

Nonfiction

A JOCKEY'S LIFE
THE SPORT OF QUEENS

REFLEX

DICK FRANCIS

BERKLEY BOOKS, NEW YORK

THE BERKLEY PUBLISHING GROUP
Published by the Penguin Group
Penguin Group (USA) Inc.
375 Hudson Street, New York, New York 10014, USA
Penguin Group (Canada), 90 Eglinton Avenue East, Suite 700, Toronto, Ontario M4P 2Y3, Canada
(a division of Pearson Penguin Canada Inc.)
Penguin Books Ltd., 80 Strand, London WC2R 0RL, England
Penguin Group Ireland, 25 St. Stephen's Green, Dublin 2, Ireland (a division of Penguin Books Ltd.)
Penguin Group (Australia), 250 Camberwell Road, Camberwell, Victoria 3124, Australia
(a division of Pearson Australia Group Pty. Ltd.)
Penguin Books India Pvt. Ltd., 11 Community Centre, Panchsheel Park, New Delhi—110 017, India
Penguin Group (NZ), Cnr. Airborne and Rosedale Roads, Albany, Auckland 1310, New Zealand
(a division of Pearson New Zealand Ltd.)
Penguin Books (South Africa) (Pty.) Ltd., 24 Sturdee Avenue, Rosebank, Johannesburg 2196,
South Africa

Penguin Books Ltd., Registered Offices: 80 Strand, London WC2R 0RL, England

This is a work of fiction. Names, characters, places, and incidents either are the product of the author's
imagination or are used fictitiously, and any resemblance to actual persons, living or dead, business
establishments, events, or locales is entirely coincidental.

REFLEX

A Berkley Book / published by arrangement with G. P. Putnam's Sons

PRINTING HISTORY
G. P. Putnam's Sons edition / March 1981
Ballantine edition / April 1982
Jove mass-market edition / April 2003
Berkley mass-market edition / October 2005

ISBN: 0-425-20695-5

BERKLEY®
Berkley Books are published by The Berkley Publishing Group,
a division of Penguin Group (USA) Inc.,
375 Hudson Street, New York, New York 10014.
BERKLEY is a registered trademark of Penguin Group (USA) Inc.
The "B" design is a trademark belonging to Penguin Group (USA) Inc.

PRINTED IN THE UNITED STATES OF AMERICA

10 9 8 7 6 5 4 3 2

My thanks to the photographers
Bernard Parkin
and
David Hastings
and especially
Ron Massey
who made me the puzzles

1

Winded and coughing, I lay on one elbow and spat out a mouthful of grass and mud. The horse I'd been riding raised its weight off my ankle, scrambled untidily to its feet and departed at an unfeeling gallop. I waited for things to settle: chest heaving, bones still rattling from the bang, sense of balance recovering from a thirty-mile-an-hour somersault and a few tumbling rolls. No harm done. Nothing broken. Just another fall.

Time and place: sixteenth fence, three-mile steeplechase, Sandown Park racecourse, Friday, November, in thin, cold, persistent rain. At the return of breath and energy I stood wearily up and thought with intensity that this was a damn silly way for a grown man to be spending his life.

The thought itself was a jolt. Not one I'd ever thought before. Riding horses at high speed over various jumps was the only way I knew of making a living, and it was a job one couldn't do if one's heart wasn't in it. The chilling flicker of disillusion nudged like the first twinge of toothache, unexpected, unwelcome, an uneasy hint of possible trouble.

I repressed it without much alarm. Reassured myself

that I loved the life, of course I did, the way I always had. Believed quite easily that nothing was wrong except the weather, the fall, the lost race ... minor, everyday stuff, business as usual.

Squelching uphill to the stands in paper-thin racing boots unsuitable for hiking I thought only and firmly about the horse I'd started out on, sorting out what I might and might not say to its trainer. Discarded "How do you expect it to jump if you don't school it properly?" in favor of "The experience will do him good." Thought better of "useless, panicky, hard-mouthed, underfed dog," and decided on "might try him in blinkers." The trainer, anyway, would blame me for the fall and tell the owner I'd misjudged the pace. He was that sort of trainer. Every crash was a pilot error.

I thanked heaven in a mild way that I didn't ride often for that stable, and had been engaged on that day only because Steve Millace, its usual jockey, had gone to his father's funeral. Spare rides, even with disaster staring up from the form books, were not lightly to be turned down. Not if you needed the money, which I did. And not if, like me, you needed your name up on the number boards as often as possible, to show you were useful and wanted and *there*.

The only good thing, I supposed, about my descent at the fence was that Steve Millace's father hadn't been there to record it. George Millace, pitiless photographer of moments all jockeys preferred to ignore, was safe in his box and approximately at that moment being lowered underground to his long sleep. And good riddance, I thought uncharitably. Goodbye to the snide sneering pleasure George got from delivering to owners the irrefutable evidence of their jockeys' failings. Goodbye to the motorized camera catching at three-and-a-half frames per second one's balance in the wrong place, one's arms in the air, one's face in the mud.

Where other sports photographers played fair and shot

you winning from time to time, George trafficked exclusively in ignominy and humiliation. George was a natural-born dragger-down. Newspapers might mourn the passing of his snigger-raising pictures, but there had been little sorrow in the changing room the day Steve told us his father had driven into a tree.

Out of liking for Steve himself, no one had said much. He had listened to the silence, though, and he knew. He had been anxiously defending his father for years; and he knew.

Trudging back in the rain it seemed odd to me still that we wouldn't actually be seeing George Millace again. His image, too familiar for too long, rose sharply in the mind: bright clever eyes, long nose, drooping moustache, twisted mouth sourly smiling. A terrific photographer, one had to admit, with an exceptional talent for anticipation and timing, his lens always pointing in the right direction at the right moment. A comic, too, in his way, showing me less than a week ago a black-and-white glossy of me taking a dive, nose to ground, bottom up, with a caption written on the back: "Philip Nore, arse high to a grasshopper." One would have laughed but for the genuine ill will which had prompted his humor. One might have at least tolerated his debunking approach but for the cruelty sliding out of his eyes. He had been a mental thrower of banana skins, lying in wait to scoff at the hurt; and he would be missed with thankfulness.

When I finally reached the shelter of the verandah outside the weighing room, the trainer and owner were waiting there with the expected accusing expressions.

"Misjudged things pretty badly, didn't you?" said the trainer aggressively.

"He took off a stride too soon."

"Your job to put him right."

No point in saying that no jockey on earth could always get every horse to jump perfectly, and particularly not a badly schooled rogue. I simply nodded, and smiled a shade ruefully at the owner.

"Might try him in blinkers," I said.

"*I'll* decide about that," said the trainer sharply.

"Not hurt, are you?" asked the owner timidly.

I shook my head. The trainer brusquely stamped on this humane jockey-oriented enquiry and wheeled his money-source away from the danger that I might say something truthful about why the horse wouldn't jump when asked. I watched them go without rancor and turned towards the weighing-room door.

"I say," said a young man, stepping in front of me, "are you Philip Nore?"

"That's right."

"Well . . . could I have a word with you?"

He was about twenty-five, tall as a stork and earnest, with office-colored skin. Charcoal flannel suit, striped tie, no binoculars, and no air of belonging where he stood, in the business-only section of the racecourse.

"Sure," I said. "If you'll wait while I check with the doctor and get into something dry."

"Doctor?" He looked alarmed.

"Oh, routine. After a fall. I shan't be long."

When I went out again, warmed and in street clothes, he was still waiting; and he was more or less alone on the verandah, as nearly everyone else had gone to watch the last race, already in progress.

"I . . . er . . . my name is Jeremy Folk." He produced a card from inside the charcoal jacket and held it out to me. I took it, and read:

Folk, Langley, Son and Folk.

Solicitors. Address in St. Albans, Hertfordshire.

"That last folk," said Jeremy, pointing diffidently, "is me."

"Congratulations," I said.

He gave me an anxious half-smile and cleared his throat.

"I've been sent . . . er . . . I've come to ask you to . . . er . . ." He stopped, looking helpless and not in the least like a solicitor.

"To what?" I said encouragingly.

"They said you wouldn't like . . . but well . . . I've been sent to ask you . . . er . . ."

"Do get on with it," I said.

"To come and see your grandmother." The words came out in a nervous rush, and he seemed relieved to be rid of them.

"No," I said.

He scanned my face and seemed to take heart from its calmness.

"She's dying," he said. "And she wants to see you."

Death all around, I thought. George Millace and my mother's mother. Negative grief in both cases.

"Did you hear?" he said.

"I heard."

"Now, then? I mean, today?"

"No," I said. "I'm not going."

"But you must." He looked troubled. "I mean . . . she's old . . . and she's dying . . . and she wants you . . ."

"Too bad."

"And if I don't persuade you, my uncle . . . that's Son . . ." He pointed to the card again, getting flustered. "Er. Folk is my grandfather and Langley is my great-uncle, and . . . er . . . they sent me . . ." He swallowed. "They think I'm frightfully useless, to be honest."

"And that's blackmail," I said.

A faint glint in his eyes told me that he wasn't basically as silly as he made out.

"I don't want to see her," I said.

"But she is dying."

"Have you yourself seen her . . . dying?"

"Er . . . no . . ."

"I'll bet she isn't. If she wants to see me, she would

say she was dying just to fetch me, because she'd guess nothing else would."

He looked shocked. "She's seventy-eight, after all."

I looked gloomily out at the nonstop rain. I had never met my grandmother and I didn't want to, dying or dead. I didn't approve of deathbed repentances, last-minute insurances at the gates of hell. It was too damned late.

"The answer," I said, "is still no."

He shrugged dispiritedly and seemed to give up. Walked a few steps out into the rain, bareheaded, vulnerable, with no umbrella. Turned around after ten paces and came tentatively back again.

"Look . . . she really needs you, my uncle says." He was as earnest, as intense, as a missionary. "You can't just let her die."

"Where is she?" I said.

He brightened. "In a nursing home." He fished in another pocket. "I've got the address. But I'll lead you there, straight away, if you'll come. It's in St. Albans. You live in Lambourn, don't you? So it isn't so terribly far out of your way, is it? I mean, not a hundred miles, or anything like that."

"A good fifty, though."

"Well . . . I mean . . . you always do drive around an awful lot."

I sighed. The options were rotten. A choice between meek capitulation or stony rejection. Both unpalatable. That she had dished out to me stony rejection from my birth gave me no excuse, I supposed, for doing it to her at her death. Also I could hardly go on smugly despising her, as I had done for years, if I followed her example. Irritating, that.

The winter afternoon was already fading, with electric lights growing brighter by the minute, shining fuzzily through the rain. I thought of my empty cottage; of nothing much to fill the evening: of two eggs, a piece of cheese and black coffee for supper; of wanting to eat more and not doing so. If I went, I thought, it would at least take my mind off food, and anything which helped with the perennial fight against weight couldn't be wholly bad. Not even meeting my grandmother.

"All right," I said, resignedly. "Lead on."

The old woman sat upright in bed staring at me, and if she was dying it wasn't going to be on that evening, for sure. The life force was strong in the dark eyes and there was no mortal weakness in her voice.

"Philip," she said, making it a statement and looking me up and down.

"Yes."

"Hah."

The explosive sound contained both triumph and contempt and was everything I would have expected. Her ramrod will had devastated my childhood and done worse damage to her own daughter, and there was to be, I was relieved to see, no maudlin plea for forgiveness. Rejection, even if in a moderated form, was still in operation.

"I knew you'd come running," she said, "when you heard about the money." As a cold sneer it was pretty unbeatable.

"What money?"

"The hundred thousand pounds, of course."

"No one," I said, "has mentioned any money."

"Don't lie. Why else would you come?"

"They said you were dying."

She gave me a startled and malevolent flash of the eyes and a baring of teeth which had nothing to do with smiling. "So I am. So are we all."

"Yeah," I said, "and all at the same rate. One day at a time."

She was no one's idea of a sweet little pink-cheeked grannie. A strong stubborn face with disapproval lines cut deep around the mouth. Iron gray hair still vigorous, clean and well shaped. Blotchy freckles of age showing brown

on an otherwise pale skin, and dark ridged veins on the
backs of the hands. A thin woman, almost gaunt; and tall,
as far as I could judge.

The large room where she lay was furnished more as
a sitting room with a bed in it than as a hospital room,
which was all of a piece with what I'd seen of the place
on the way in. A country house put to new use: hotel with
nurses. Carpets everywhere, long chintz curtains, armchairs for visitors, vases of flowers. Gracious dying, I
thought.

"I instructed Mr. Folk," she said, "to make you the
offer."

I reflected. "Young Mr. Folk? About twenty-five? Jeremy?"

"Of course not." She was impatient. "Mr. Folk, my
solicitor. I told him to get you here. And he did. Here you
are."

"He sent his grandson."

I turned away from her and sat unasked in an armchair.
Why, I wondered, had Jeremy not mentioned a hundred
thousand pounds? It was the sort of trifle, after all, that
one didn't easily forget.

My grandmother stared at me steadily with no sign of
affection, and I stared as steadily back. I disliked her certainty that she could buy me. I was repelled by her contempt, and mistrusted her intentions.

"I will leave you a hundred thousand pounds in my
will, upon certain conditions," she said.

"No, you won't," I said.

"I beg your pardon?" Icy voice, stony look.

"I said no. No money. No conditions."

"You haven't heard my proposition."

I said nothing. I felt, in fact, the first stirrings of curiosity, but I was definitely not going to let her see it.
Since she seemed in no hurry, the silence lengthened.
More stocktaking on her part, perhaps. Simple patience
on mine. One thing my haphazard upbringing had given

me was an almost limitless capacity for waiting. Waiting for people to come, who didn't; and for promises to be fulfilled, that weren't.

Finally she said, "You're taller than I expected. And tougher."

I waited some more.

"Where is your mother?" she said.

My mother, her daughter. "Scattered on the winds," I said.

"What do you mean?"

"I think she's dead."

"*Think*!" She looked more annoyed than anxious. "Don't you *know*?"

"She didn't exactly write to me to say she'd died; no."

"Your flippancy is disgraceful."

"Your behavior since before my birth," I said, "gives you no right to say so."

She blinked. Her mouth opened, and stayed open for fully five seconds. Then it shut tight with rigid muscles showing along the jaw, and she stared at me darkly in a daunting mixture of fury and ferocity. I saw, in that expression, what my poor young mother had had to face, and felt a great uprush of sympathy for the feckless butterfly who'd borne me.

There had been a day, when I was quite small, that I had been dressed in new clothes and told to be exceptionally good as I was going with my mother to see my grandmother. My mother had collected me from where I was living and we had traveled by car to a large house, where I was left alone in the hall, to wait. Behind a white-painted closed door there had been a lot of shouting. Then my mother had come out, crying, and had grabbed me by the hand, and pulled me after her to the car.

"Come on, Philip. We'll never ask her for anything, ever again. She wouldn't even see you. Don't you ever forget, Philip, that your grandmother's a hateful *beast*."

I hadn't forgotten. I'd thought of it rarely, but I still

clearly remembered sitting in the chair in the hall, my feet not touching the ground, waiting stiffly in my new clothes, listening to the shouting.

I had never actually lived with my mother, except for a traumatic week or two now and then. We had had no house, no address, no permanent base. Herself always on the move, she had solved the problem of what to do with me by simply dumping me for varying periods with a long succession of mostly astonished married friends, who had been, in retrospect, remarkably tolerant.

"Do look after Philip for me for a few days, darling," she would say, giving me a push towards yet another strange lady. "Life is so unutterably *cluttered* just now and I'm at my wits' end to know what to do with him, you know how it is, so darling Deborah . . . (or Miranda, or Chloe, or Samantha, or anyone else under the sun) . . . do be an absolute *sweetie*, and I'll pick him up on Saturday, I promise." And mostly she would have soundly kissed darling Deborah or Miranda or Chloe or Samantha and gone off with a wave in a cloud of Joy.

Saturdays came and my mother didn't, but she always turned up in the end, full of flutter and laughter and gushing thanks, retrieving her parcel, so to speak, from the left luggage office. I could remain uncollected for days or for weeks or for months: I never knew which in advance, and nor, I suspect, did my hosts. Mostly, I think, she paid something towards my keep, but it was all done with a giggle.

She was, even to my eyes, deliciously pretty, to the extent that people hugged her and indulged her and lit up when she was around. Only later, when they were left literally holding the baby, did the doubts creep in. I became a bewildered silent child forever tiptoeing nervously around so as not to give offense, perennially frightened that someone, one day, would abandon me altogether out in the street.

Looking back, I knew I owed a great deal to Samantha,

Deborah, Chloe, *et al*. I never went hungry, was never ill-treated, nor was ever, in the end, totally rejected. Occasionally people took me in twice or three times, sometimes with welcome, mostly with resignation. When I was three or four someone in long hair and bangles and an ethnic smock taught me to read and write, but I never stayed anywhere long enough to be formally sent to school. It was an extraordinary, disorienting and rootless existence from which I emerged at twelve, when I was dumped in my first long-stay home, able to do almost any job around the house and unable to love.

She left me with two photographers, Duncan and Charlie, standing in their big bare-floored studio, which had a darkroom, a bathroom, a gas ring and a bed behind a curtain.

"Darlings, look after him until Saturday, there's a sweet pair of lambs ..." And although birthday cards arrived, and presents at Christmas, I didn't see her again for three years. Then when Duncan departed, she swooped in one day and took me away from Charlie, and drove me down to a racehorse trainer and his wife in Hampshire, telling those bemused friends, "It's only until Saturday, darlings, and he's fifteen and strong, he'll muck out the horses for you, and things like that ..."

Cards and presents arrived for two years or so, always without an address to reply to. On my eighteenth birthday there was no card, and no present the following Christmas, and I'd never heard from her again.

She must have died, I had come to understand, from drugs. There was a great deal, as I grew older, that I'd sorted out and understood.

The old woman glared across the room, as unforgiving and destructive as ever, and still angry at what I'd said.

"You won't get far with me if you talk like that," she said.

"I don't want to get far." I stood up. "This visit is pointless. If you wanted to find your daughter, you should have looked twenty years ago. And as for me ... I wouldn't find her for you, even if I could."

"I don't want you to find Caroline. I dare say you're right, that she's dead." The idea clearly caused her no grief. "I want you to find your sister."

"My ... *what*?"

The hostile dark eyes assessed me shrewdly. "You didn't know you had a sister? Well, you have. I'll leave you a hundred thousand pounds in my will if you find her and bring her here to me. And don't think," she went on caustically, before I had time to utter, "that you can produce any little imposter and expect me to believe it. I'm old but I'm far from a fool. You would have to prove to Mr. Folk's satisfaction that the girl was my grandchild. And Mr. Folk would not be easy to convince."

I scarcely heard the acid words, but felt only a curiously intense thrust of shock. There had been only one of me. One single fruit of the butterfly. I felt an unreasonable but stinging jealousy that she had had another. She had been mine alone, and now I had to share her: to revise and share her memory. I thought in confusion that it was ridiculous to be experiencing at thirty the displacement emotions of two.

"Well?" my grandmother said sharply.

"No," I said.

"It's a lot of money," she snapped.

"If you've got it."

She was again outraged. "You're insolent!"

"Oh, sure. Well, if that's all, I'll be going." I turned and went towards the door.

"Wait," she said urgently. "Don't you even want to see her picture? There's a photograph of your sister over there in the chest."

I glanced over my shoulder and saw her nodding towards a chest of drawers across the room. She must have seen the hesitation that slowed my hand on the doorknob because she said with more confidence, "Just look at her, then. Why don't you look?"

Without positively wanting to but impelled by undeniable curiosity I walked over to the chest and looked. There was a snapshot lying there, an ordinary postcard-sized family-album print. I picked it up and tilted it towards the light.

A little girl, three or fours years old, on a pony.

The child, with shoulder-length brown hair, wore a red and white striped T-shirt and a pair of jeans. The pony was an unremarkable Welsh gray, with clean-looking tack. Photographed in what was evidently a stable yard, they both looked contented and well fed, but the photographer had been standing too far away to bring out much detail in the child's face. Enlargement would help to some extent.

I turned the print over, but there was nothing on the back of it to indicate where it had come from, or who had held the camera.

Vaguely disappointed I put it down again on the chest, and saw, with a wince of nostalgia, an envelope lying there addressed in my mother's handwriting. Addressed to my grandmother, Mrs. Lavinia Nore, at the old house in Northamptonshire where I'd had to wait in the hall.

In the envelope, a letter.

"What are you doing?" said my grandmother in alarm.

"Reading a letter from my mother."

"But I—that letter shouldn't be out. Put it down at once. I thought it was in the drawer."

I ignored her. The loopy extravagant extrovert writing came freshly to me off the paper as if she'd been there in the room, gushing and half laughing, calling out as always for help.

That letter, dated only October 2, was no joke.

Dear Mother,
I know I said I would never ask you for anything

*ever again but I'm having one more try because I
still hope, silly me, that one day you might change
your mind. I am sending you a photograph of my
daughter, Amanda, your granddaughter. She is very
sweet and darling and she's three now, and she
needs a proper home and to go to school and everything, and I know you wouldn't want a child around
but if you'd just give her an allowance or even do
one of those trust things for her, she could live with
some perfectly angelic people who love her and
want to keep her but simply can't afford everything
for another child as they've three of their own already. If you could pay something regularly into
their bank account you wouldn't even notice it and
it would mean your granddaughter was brought up
in a happy home and I am so desperate to get that
for her that I'm writing to you now.*

*She hasn't the same father as Philip, so you
couldn't hate her for the same reasons, and if you'd
see her you'd love her, but even if you won't see
her, please, Mother, look after her. I'll hope to hear
from you soon. Please, please, Mother, answer this
letter.*

Your daughter,
Caroline

Staying at Pine Woods Lodge,
Mindle Bridge, Sussex.

I looked up and across at the hard old woman.

"When did she write this?"

"Years ago." She shrugged irritably. "I can't remember."

"And you didn't reply," I said flatly.

"No."

I suppose it was no good getting angry over so old a
tragedy. I looked at the envelope to try to see the date of
the letter from the postmark, but it was smudged and un-

decipherable. How long, I wondered, had she waited at Pine Woods Lodge, hoping and caring and desperate? Desperation, of course, when it concerned my mother, was always a relative term. Desperation was a laugh and an outstretched hand—and the Lord (or Deborah or Samantha or Chloe) would provide. Desperation wouldn't be grim and gritty, but it must have been pretty deep to make her ask her own mother for help.

I put the letter, the envelope and the photograph in my jacket pocket. It seemed disgusting to me that the old woman had kept them all these years when she had ignored their plea, and I felt in an obscure way that they belonged to me, and not her.

"So you'll do it," she said.

"No."

"But you're taking the photograph."

"Yes."

"Well, then."

"If you want ... Amanda ... found, you should hire a private detective."

"I did," she said impatiently. "Naturally. Three detectives. They were all useless."

"If three failed, she can't be found," I said. "There's no way I could succeed."

"More incentive," she said triumphantly. "You'll try your damnedest, for that sort of money."

"You're wrong." I stared bitterly at her across the room, and from her pillow-piled bed she stared as unsmilingly back. "If I took any money from you I'd vomit."

I walked over to the door and this time opened it without hesitation.

To my departing back she said, "Amanda shall have my money ... if you find her."

2

When I went back to Sandown Park the following day the letter and photograph were still in my pocket but the emotions they had engendered had subsided. The unknown half-sister could be contemplated without infantile rage, and yet another chunk of the past had fallen into place.

It was the present, in the shape of Steve Millace, which claimed everyone's attention. He came steaming into the changing room half an hour before the first race with drizzle on his hair and righteous fury in his eyes.

His mother's house, he said, had been burgled while they were all out at his father's funeral.

We sat in rows on the benches, half-changed into riding clothes, listening with shock. I looked at the scene—jockeys in all stages of undress, in underpants, bare-chested, in silks and pulling on nylon tights and boots, and all of them suddenly still, as if in suspended animation, listening with open mouths and eyes turned towards Steve.

Almost automatically I reached for my Nikon, twiddled the controls, and took a couple of photographs: and they were all so accustomed to me doing that sort of thing that no one took any notice.

"It was awful," Steve said. "Bloody disgusting. She'd made some cakes and things, Mum had, for the aunts and everyone, for when we got back from the cremation, and they were all thrown around the place, squashed flat, jam and such, onto the walls, and stamped into the carpet. And there was more mess everywhere, in the kitchen . . . bathroom . . . It looked as if a herd of mad children had rampaged around the whole house making it as filthy as they could. But it wasn't children . . . children wouldn't have stolen all that was taken, the police said."

"Your mother have a load of jewels, did she?" said someone, teasing.

One or two laughed and the first tension was broken, but the sympathy for Steve was genuine enough, and he went on talking about it to anyone who cared to listen; and I did listen, not only because his peg at Sandown was next to mine, which gave me little choice, but also because we always got on well together in a day-to-day superficial way.

"They stripped Dad's darkroom," he said. "Just ripped everything out. And it was senseless . . . like I told the police . . . because they didn't just take things you could sell, like the enlarger and the developing stuff, but all his work, all those pictures taken over all those years, they're all gone. It's such a bloody shame. There's Mum with all that mess, and Dad dead, and now she hasn't even got what he spent his life doing. Just *nothing*. And they took her fur jacket and even the scent Dad gave her for her birthday, that she hadn't opened, and she's just sitting there crying—"

He stopped suddenly and swallowed, as if it was all too much for him too. At twenty-three, although he no longer lived with them, he was still very much his parents' child, attached to them with a difficult loyalty most people admired. George Millace himself might have been widely disliked, but he had never been belittled by his son.

Small-boned, slight in build, Steve had bright dark eyes and ears that stuck out widely, giving him an overall slightly comic look; but in character he was more intense than humorous, and was apt, even without so much cause as on that day, to keep on returning obsessively to things which upset him.

"The police said that burglars do it for spite," Steve said. "Mess up people's houses and steal their photographs. They told Mum it's always happening. They said to be thankful there wasn't urine and shit over everything, which there often was, and she was lucky she didn't have the chairs and settee slashed and all the furniture scratched." He went on compulsively talking to all comers, but I finished changing and went out to ride in the first race, and more or less forgot the Millace burglary for the rest of the afternoon.

It was a day I had been looking forward to, and trying not to, for nearly a month. The day that Daylight was to run in the Sandown Handicap Pattern 'Chase. A big race, a good horse, moderate opposition, and a great chance of winning. Such combinations came my way rarely enough to be prized, but I never liked to believe in them until I was actually on my way down to the post. Daylight, I'd been told, had arrived at the course safe and sound, and for me there was just the first race, a novice hurdle, to come back unscathed from, and then, perhaps, I would win the big Pattern 'Chase and half a dozen people would fall over themselves to offer me the favorite for the Gold Cup.

Two races a day was about my usual mark, and if I ended a season in the top twenty on the jockeys' list, I was happy. For years I'd been able to kid myself that the modesty of my success was due to being taller and heavier than was best for the job. Even with constant semi-starvation I weighed ten stone seven stripped, and was cut off, consequently, from the countless horses running at ten stone ten or less. Most seasons I rode in about two hundred races with forty or so winners, and knew that I was considered "strong," "reliable," "good over fences," and "not first class in a close finish."

Most people think, when they're young, that they're going to the top of their chosen world, and that the climb up is only a formality. Without that faith, I suppose, they might never start. Somewhere on the way they lift their eyes to the summit and know they aren't going to reach it; and happiness then is looking down and enjoying the view they've got, not envying the one they haven't. At around twenty-six I'd come to terms with the view I'd reached, and with knowing I wasn't going any further; and oddly, far from depressing me, the realization had been a relief. I'd never been graspingly ambitious, but only willing to do anything as well as I could. If I couldn't do better, well, I couldn't, and that was that. All the same, I'd no positive objection to having Gold Cup winners thrust upon me, so to speak.

On that afternoon at Sandown I completed the novice hurdle in an uneventful way ("useful but uninspired"), finishing fifth out of eighteen runners. Not too bad. Just the best that I and the horse could do on the day, same as usual.

I changed into Daylight's colors and in due course walked out to the parade ring, feeling nothing but pleasure for the coming race. Daylight's trainer, for whom I rode regularly, was waiting there, and also Daylight's owner.

Daylight's owner waved away my cheerful opener about its being splendid the drizzle had stopped and said without preamble, "You'll lose this one today, Philip."

I smiled. "Not if I can help it."

"Indeed you will," he said sharply. "Lose it. My money's on the other way."

I don't suppose I kept much of the dismay and anger out of my face. He had done this sort of thing before, but not for about three years, and he knew I didn't like it.

Victor Briggs, Daylight's owner, was a sturdily built man in his forties, about whose job and background I knew almost nothing. Unsociable, secretive, he came to the races with a closed unsmiling face, and never talked to me much. He wore always a heavy navy blue overcoat, a black broad-brimmed hat and thick black leather gloves. He had been, in the past, an aggressive gambler, and in riding for him I had had the choice of doing what he said or losing my job with the stable. Harold Osborne, the trainer, had said to me plainly, soon after I'd joined him, that if I wouldn't do what Victor Briggs wanted, I was out.

I had lost races for Victor Briggs that I might have won. It was a fact of life. I needed to eat and to pay off the mortgage on the cottage. For that I needed a good big stable to ride for, and if I had walked out of the one that was giving me a chance, I might easily not have found another. There weren't so very many of them, and apart from Victor Briggs the Osborne set-up was just right. So, like many another rider in a like fix, I had done what I was told, and kept quiet.

Back at the beginning Victor Briggs had offered me a fair-sized cash present for losing. I'd said I didn't want it: I would lose if I had to, but I wouldn't be paid. He said I was a pompous young fool, but after I'd refused his offer a second time he'd kept his bribes in his pocket and his opinion of me to himself.

"Why don't you take it?" Harold Osborne had said. "Don't forget you're passing up the ten per cent you'd get for winning. Mr. Briggs is making it up to you, that's all."

I'd shaken my head, and he hadn't persevered. I thought that probably I was indeed a fool, but somewhere along the line it seemed that Samantha or Chloe or the others had given me this unwelcome, uncomfortable conviction that one should pay for one's sins. And since I'd been free of the dilemma for three years, it was all the more infuriating to be faced with it again.

"I can't lose," I protested. "Daylight's the best of the bunch. Far and away. You know he is."

"Just do it," Victor Briggs said. "And lower your voice, unless you want the stewards to hear you."

I looked at Harold Osborne. He was busy watching the horses plod around the ring and pretending not to listen to what Victor Briggs was saying.

"Harold," I said.

He gave me a brief unemotional glance. "Victor's right. The money's on the other way. You'll cost us a packet if you win, so don't."

"Us?"

He nodded. "Us. That's right. Fall off, if you have to. Come in second, if you like. But not first. Understood?"

I nodded. I understood. Back in the old pincers.

I cantered Daylight down to the start with reality winning out over rebellion, as before. If I hadn't been able to afford to lose the job at twenty-three, still less could I at thirty. I was known as Osborne's jockey. I'd been with him seven years. If he chucked me out, all I'd get would be other stables' odds and ends; ride second string to other jockeys; be on a oneway track to oblivion. He wouldn't say to the press that he'd got rid of me because I wouldn't any longer lose to order. He would tell them (regretfully, of course) that he was looking for someone younger . . . had to do what was best for the owners . . . terribly sad, but an end came to every jockey's career . . . naturally sorry, and all that, but time marches on, don't you know?

God damn it, I thought. I didn't want to lose that race. I hated to be dishonest . . . and the ten per cent I would lose this time was big enough to make me even angrier. Why the bloody hell had Briggs gone back to this caper, after such a long time? I'd thought that he'd stopped because I'd got just far enough as a jockey for him to think it likely I would refuse. A jockey who got high enough on the winners list was safe from that sort of pressure, because if his own stable was silly enough to give him the kick, another would welcome him in. Well, maybe he thought I'd gone past that stage now that I was older, and was back again in the danger area: and he was right.

We circled around while the starter called the roll, and I looked apprehensively at the four horses ranged against Daylight. There wasn't a good one among them. Nothing that on paper could defeat my own powerful gelding, which was why people were at that moment staking four pounds on Daylight to win one.

Four to one on . . .

Far from risking his own money at those odds, Victor Briggs in some subterranean way had taken bets from other people, and would have to pay out if his horse won. And so, it seemed, would Harold also; and however I might feel, I did owe Harold some allegiance.

After seven years of a working relationship that had a firmer base than many a trainer-jockey alliance, I had come to regard him if not with close personal warmth at least with active friendship. He was a man of rages and charms, of black moods and boisterous highs, of tyrannical decisions and generous gifts. His voice could out-shout and outcurse any other on the Berkshire Downs, and stable lads with delicate sensibilities left his employ in droves. On the first day that I rode work for him his blistering opinion of my riding could be heard fortissimo from Wantage to Swindon, and, in his house immediately afterwards, at ten in the morning, he had opened a bottle of champagne, and we had drunk to our forthcoming collaboration.

He had trusted me always and entirely, and had defended me against criticism where many a trainer would not. Every jockey, he had said robustly, had bad patches; and he had employed me steadily through mine. He assumed that I would be, for my part, totally committed to himself and his stable, and for the past three years that had been easy.

The starter called the horses into line, and I wheeled Daylight around to point his nose in the right direction.

No starting stalls. They were never used for jump racing. A gate of elastic tapes instead.

In cold angry misery I decided that the race, from Daylight's point of view, would have to be over as near the start as possible. With thousands of pairs of binoculars trained my way, with television eyes and patrol cameras and perceptive reporters acutely focused, losing would be hard enough anyway, and practically suicidal if I left it until it was clear that Daylight would win. Then, if I just fell off in the last half mile for not much reason, there would be an enquiry and I might lose my license; and it would be no comfort to know that I deserved to.

The starter put his hand on the lever and the tapes flew up, and I kicked Daylight forward into his business. None of the other jockeys wanted to make the running, and we set off in consequence at a slow pace, which compounded my troubles. Daylight, with all the time in the world, wouldn't stumble at any fence. A fluent jumper always, he hardly ever fell. Some horses couldn't be put right on the approach to a fence: Daylight couldn't be put wrong. All he accepted were the smallest indications from his jockey, and he would do the rest himself. I had ridden him many times. Won six races on him. Knew him well.

Cheat the horse. Cheat the public.

Cheat.

Damn it, I thought. *Damn and damn and damn.*

I did it at the third fence, on the decline from the top of the hill, round the sharpish bend, going away from the stands. It was the best from the credibility angle as it was the least visible to the massed watchers, and it had a sharp downhill slope on the approach side: a fence that claimed many a victim during the year.

Daylight, confused by getting the wrong signals from

me, and perhaps feeling some of my turmoil and fury in the telepathic way that horses do, began to waver in the stride before take-off, putting in a small jerky extra stride where none was needed.

God, boy, I thought, I'm bloody sorry, but down you go, if I can make you: and I kicked him at the wrong moment and twitched hard on the bit in his mouth while he was in midair, and shifted my weight forward in front of his shoulder.

He landed awkwardly and stumbled slightly, dipping his head down to recover his balance. It wasn't really enough . . . but it would have to do. I whisked my right foot out of the stirrup and over his back, so that I was entirely on his left side, out of the saddle, clinging onto his neck.

It's almost impossible to stay on, from that position. I clung to him for about three bucking strides and then slid down his chest, irrevocably losing my grip and bouncing onto the grass under his feet. A flurry of thuds from his hooves, and a roll or two, and the noise and the galloping horses were gone.

I sat on the quiet ground and unbuckled my helmet, and felt absolutely wretched.

"Bad luck," they said briefly in the weighing room. "Rotten luck": and got on with the rest of the day. I wondered if any of them guessed, but maybe they didn't. No one nudged or winked or looked sardonic. It was my own embarrassed sense of shame which kept me staring mostly at the floor.

"Cheer up," Steve Millace said, buttoning some orange and blue colors. "It's not the end of the world." He picked up his whip and his helmet. "Always another day."

"Yeah."

He went off to ride, and I changed gloomily back into street clothes. So much, I thought, for the sense of excitement in which I'd arrived. So much for winning, for half a dozen mythical trainers climbing over themselves to secure my services for the Gold Cup. So much for a nice boost to the finances, which were wilting a bit after buying a new car. On all fronts, depression.

I went out to watch the race.

Steve Millace, with more courage than sense, drove his horse at leg-tangling pace into the second last fence and crashed on landing. It was the sort of hard fast fall which cracked bones, and one could see straight away that Steve was in trouble. He struggled up as far as his knees, and then sat on his heels with his head bent forward and his arms wrapped round his body, as if he was hugging himself. Arm, shoulder, ribs . . . something had gone.

His horse, unhurt, got up and galloped away, and I stood watching while two first aid men gingerly helped Steve into an ambulance. A bad day for him, too, I thought, on top of all his family troubles. What on earth made us do it? What ever drove us to persist, disregarding injury and risk and disappointment? What lured us continually to speed, when we could earn as much sitting in an office?

I walked back to the weighing room feeling the bits of me that Daylight had trodden on beginning to stiffen with bruises. I'd be crimson and black the next day, which was nothing but usual. The biffs and bangs of the trade had never bothered me much, and nothing I'd so far broken had made me frightened about the next fall. I normally had, in fact, a great feeling of physical well-being, of living in a strong and supple body, of existing as an efficient coordinated athletic whole. Nothing obtrusive. It was there. It was health.

Disillusion, I thought, would be the killer. If the job no longer seemed worth it, if people like Victor Briggs soured it beyond acceptance, at that point one would give up. But not yet. It was still the life I wanted; still the life I was far from ready to leave.

Steve came into the changing room in boots, breeches,

undervest, clavicle rings, bandage and sling, with his head
inclined stiffly to one side.

"Collarbone," he said crossly. "Bloody nuisance." Discomfort was making his thin face gaunt, digging hollows
in his cheeks and around his eyes, but what he clearly felt
most was annoyance.

His valet helped him to change and dress, touching him
with the gentleness of long practice and pulling off his
boots smoothly so as not to jar the shoulder. A crowd of
other jockeys around us jostled and sang and made jokes,
drank tea and ate fruitcake, slid out of colors and pulled
on trousers, laughed and cursed and hurried. Knocking-
off time, the end of the working week, back again Monday.

"I suppose," Steve said to me, "you couldn't possibly
drive me home?" He sounded tentative, as if not sure our
friendship stretched that far.

"Yes, I should think so," I said.

"To my mother's house? Near Ascot."

"OK."

"I'll get someone to fetch my car tomorrow," he said.
"Goddamn nuisance."

I took a photograph of him and his valet, who was
pulling off the second boot.

"What do you ever do with all them snaps?" the valet
said.

"Put them in a drawer."

He gave a heaven-help-us jerk of the head. "Waste of
time."

Steve glanced at the Nikon. "Dad said once he'd seen
some of your pics. You would put him out of business
one of these days, he said."

"He was laughing at me."

"Yeah. Maybe. I don't know." He inched one arm into
his shirt and let the valet fasten the buttons over the other.
"Ouch," he said, wincing.

George Millace had seen some pictures I'd had in my

car, catching me looking through them as I sat in the parking lot at the end of a sunny spring day, waiting for the friend I'd given a lift to to come out of the racecourse.

"Proper little Cartier Bresson," George had said, faintly smiling. "Let's have a look." He'd put his arm through the open window and grasped the stack, and short of a tug-o'-war I couldn't have prevented him. "Well, well," he said, going through them methodically. "Horses on the Downs, coming out of a mist. Romantic muck." He handed them back. "Keep it up, kid. One of these days you might take a photograph."

He'd gone off across the parking lot with the heavy camera bag hanging from his shoulder, hitching it from time to time to ease its weight: the only photographer I knew with whom I didn't feel at home.

Duncan and Charlie, in the three years I'd lived with them, had patiently taught me all I could learn. No matter that when I was first dumped on them I was only twelve: Charlie had said from the start that as I was there I could sweep the floors and clean up in the darkroom, and I'd been glad to. The rest had come gradually and thoroughly, and I'd finished by regularly doing all of Duncan's printing, and the routine half of Charlie's. "Our lab assistant" Charlie called me. "He mixes our chemicals," he would say. "A wizard, with a hypodermic. Mind now, Philip, only one point four milliliters of benzol alcohol." And I'd suck the tiny amounts accurately into the syringe and add them to the developer, and feel as if I were perhaps of some use in the world after all.

The valet helped Steve into his jacket and gave him his watch and wallet, and we went at Steve's tender pace out to my car.

"I promised to give Mum a hand with clearing up that mess, when I got back. What a bloody hope."

"She's probably got neighbors." I eased him into the modern Ford and went round to the driving seat. Started up in the closing dusk, switched on the lights and drove off in the direction of Ascot.

"I can't get used to the idea of Dad not being there," Steve said.

"What happened?" I asked. "I mean, you said he drove into a tree . . ."

"Yes." He sighed. "He went to sleep. At least, that's what everyone reckons. There weren't any other cars, nothing like that. There was a bend, or something, and he didn't go around it. Just drove straight ahead. He must have had his foot on the accelerator . . . The front of the car was smashed right in." He shivered. "He was on his way home from Doncaster. Mum's always warned him about driving on the highway at night when he's had a long day, but this wasn't the highway. He was much nearer home."

He sounded tired and depressed, which no doubt he was, and in brief sideways glances I could see that for all my care the car's motion was hurting his shoulder.

"He'd stopped for half an hour at a friend's house," Steve said. "And they'd had a couple of whiskies. It was all so stupid. Just going to sleep . . ."

We drove for a long way in silence, he with his problems, and I with mine.

"Only last Saturday," Steve said. "Only a week ago."

Alive one minute, dead the next . . . the same as everybody.

"Turn left here," Steve said.

We turned left and right and left a few times and came finally to a road bordered on one side by a hedge and on the other by neat detached houses in shadowy gardens.

In the middle distance along there things were happening. There were lights and people. An ambulance with its doors open, its blue light flashing on top. A police car. Policemen. People coming and going from one of the houses, hurrying. Every window uncurtained, spilling out light.

"My *God*," Steve said. "That's *their* house. Mum's and Dad's."

I pulled up outside, and he sat unmoving, staring, stricken.

"It's Mum," he said. "It must be. It's Mum."

There was something near the cracking point in his voice. His face was twisted with terrible anxiety, and his eyes in the reflected light looked wide and very young.

"Stay here," I said practically. "I'll go and see."

3

His mum lay on the sofa in the sitting room, quivering and coughing and bleeding. Someone had attacked her pretty nastily, splitting her nose and mouth and eyelid and leaving her with bright raw patches on cheek and jaw. Her clothes were torn here and there, her shoes were off, and her hair stuck out in straggly wisps.

I had seen Steve's mother at the races from time to time: a pleasant well-dressed woman nearing fifty, secure and happy in her life, plainly proud of her husband and son. As the grief-stricken, burgled, beaten-up person on the sofa, she was unrecognizable.

There was a policeman sitting on a stool beside her, and a policewoman, standing, holding a bloodstained cloth. Two ambulance men hovered in the background, with a stretcher propped upright against one wall. A neighborly looking woman stood around looking grave and worried. The room itself was a shambles, with papers and smashed furniture littering the floor. On the wall, the signs of jam and cakes, as Steve had said.

When I walked in, the policeman turned his head. "Are you the doctor?"

"No . . ." I explained who I was.

"Steve." His mother said. Her mouth trembled, and her hands. "Steve's hurt." She could hardly speak, yet the fear for her son came across like a fresh torment, over-shadowing anything she'd yet suffered.

"It's not bad, I promise you," I said hastily. "He's here, outside. It's just his collarbone. I'll get him straight away."

I went outside and told him, and helped him out of the car. He was hunched and stiff, but seemed not to feel it.

"Why?" he said, uselessly, going up the path. "Why did it happen? What for?"

The policeman indoors was asking the same question.

"You were just saying, when your son came home, that there were two of them, with stockings over their faces. Is that right?"

She nodded slightly. "Young," she said. The word came out distorted through her cut, swollen lips. She saw Steve and held her hand out to him, to hold his own hand tight. He himself, at the sight of her, grew still paler and even more gaunt.

"White youths or black?" the policeman said.

"White."

"What were they wearing?"

"Jeans."

"Gloves?"

She closed her eyes and whispered, "Yes."

"Mrs. Millace, please try to answer," the policeman said. "What did they want?"

"Safe," she said, mumbling.

"What?"

"Safe. We haven't got a safe. I told them." A pair of tears rolled down her cheeks. " 'Where's the safe?' they said. They hit me."

"There isn't a safe here," Steve said furiously. "I'd like to kill them."

"Yes, sir," the policeman said. "Just keep quiet, sir, if you wouldn't mind."

"One . . . smashed things," Mrs. Millace said. "The other just hit me."

"Bloody *animals*," Steve said.

"Did they say what they wanted?" the policeman asked.

"Safe."

"Yes, but is that all? Did they say they wanted money? Jewelry? Silver? Gold coins? What exactly did they say they wanted, Mrs. Millace?"

She frowned slightly, as if thinking. Then, forming the words with difficulty, she said, "All they said was, 'Where is the safe?' "

"I suppose you do know," I said to the policeman, "that this house was also burgled yesterday?"

"Yes, I do, sir. I was here yesterday myself." He looked at me assessingly for a few seconds and turned back to Steve's mother.

"Did these two young men in stocking masks say anything about being here yesterday? Try to remember, Mrs. Millace."

"I don't . . . think so."

"Take your time," he said. "Try to remember."

She was silent for a long interval, and two more tears appeared. Poor lady, I thought. Too much pain, too much grief, too much outrage: and a good deal of courage.

At last she said, "They were . . . like bulls. They shouted. They were rough. Rough voices. They . . . shoved me. Pushed. I opened the front door. They shoved in. Pushed me . . . in here. Started . . . smashing things. Making this mess. Shouting, 'Where is the safe? Tell us, where is the safe?' Hit me." She paused. "I don't think . . . they said anything . . . about yesterday."

"I'd like to *kill* them," Steve said.

"Third time," mumbled his mother.

"What was that, Mrs. Millace?" the policeman said.

"Third time burgled. Happened . . . two years ago."

"You can't just let her lie there," Steve said violently.

"Asking all these questions. . . . Haven't you got a doctor?"

"It's all right, Steve dear," the neighborly woman said, moving forward as if to give comfort. "I've rung Dr. Williams. He said he would come at once." Caring and bothered, she was nonetheless enjoying the drama, and I could envisage her looking forward to telling it to all her friends. "I was over here helping your mother earlier, Steve dear," she said, rushing on, "but of course I went home—next door, as you know, dear—to get tea for my family, and then I heard all this shouting and it seemed all wrong, dear, so I was just coming back to see, and calling out to your mother to ask if she was all right, and those two dreadful young men just burst out of the house, dear, just *burst* out, so of course I came in here . . . and well . . . your poor mother . . . so I rang for the police and for the ambulance, and Dr. Williams . . . and everybody." She looked as if she would like at least a pat on the back for all this presence of mind, but Steve was beyond such responses.

The policeman was equally unappreciative. He said to her, "And you still can't remember any more about the car they drove off in?"

Defensively she said, "It was dark outside."

"A lightish colored car, medium sized. Is that all?"

"I don't notice cars much."

No one suggested that this was a car she should have noticed. Everyone thought it.

I cleared my throat and said diffidently to the policeman, "I don't know if it would be of any use, and of course you may want your own man or something, but I've a camera in my car, if you want photographs of all this."

He raised his eyebrows and considered and said yes; so I fetched both cameras and took two sets of pictures, in color and in black and white, with close-ups of Mrs. Millace's damaged face and wide-angle shots of the room.

Steve's mother bore the flashlight without complaint, and none of it took very long.

"Professional, are you, sir?" the policeman said.

I shook my head. "Just had a lot of practice."

He told me where to send the photographs when they were printed, and the doctor arrived.

"Don't go yet," Steve said to me, and I looked at the desperation in his face, and stayed with him through all the ensuing bustle, sitting on the stairs out in the hall.

"I don't know what to do," he said, joining me there. "I can't drive like this, and I'll have to go and see that she's all right. They're taking her to the hospital for the night. I suppose I can get a taxi . . ."

He didn't actually ask it, but the question was there. I stifled a small sigh and offered my services, and he thanked me as if I'd thrown him a lifebelt.

I found myself finally staying the night, because when we got back from the hospital he looked so exhausted that one simply couldn't drive away and leave him. I made us a couple of omelettes as by that time, ten o'clock, we were both starving, neither of us having eaten since breakfast; and after that I picked up some of the mess.

He sat on the edge of the sofa looking white and strained and not mentioning that his fracture was hurting quite a bit. Perhaps he hardly felt it, though one could see the pain in his face. Whenever he spoke, it was of his mother.

"I'll kill them," he said. "Those *bastards*."

More guts than sense, I thought; same as usual. By the sound of things, if nine-stone-seven Steve met up with the two young bulls, it would be those bastards who'd do the killing.

I had started at the far end of the room, picking up a lot of magazines, newspapers and old letters, and also the base and lid of a flat ten-by-eight-inch box which had once held photographic printing paper.

"What shall I do with all this?" I asked Steve.

"Oh, just pile it anywhere," he said vaguely. "Some of it came out of that rack over there by the television."

A wooden-slatted magazine rack, empty, lay on its side on the carpet.

"And that's Dad's rubbish box, that battered old orange thing. He kept it in that rack with the papers. Never threw it away, just left it there, year after year. Funny really." He yawned. "Don't bother too much. Mum's neighbor will do it."

I picked up a small batch of oddments; a transparent piece of film about three inches wide by eight long, several strips of 35-mm color negatives, developed but blank, and an otherwise pleasant picture of Mrs. Millace spoiled by splashes of chemical down the hair and neck.

"Those were in Dad's rubbish box, I think," Steve said, yawning again. "You might as well throw them away."

I put them in the wastepaper basket, and added to them a nearly black black-and-white print, which had been torn in half, and some more color negatives covered in magenta blotches.

"He kept them to remind himself of his worst mistakes," Steve said. "It doesn't seem *possible* that he isn't coming back."

There was another very dark print in a paper folder, showing a shadowy man sitting at a table. "Do you want this?" I asked.

He shook his head. "Dad's junk."

I put some women's magazines and a series on woodwork back in the magazine rack, and piled the letters on the table. The bulk of the mess left on the floor seemed to be broken china ornaments, the remnants of a spindly-legged sewing box, which had been thoroughly smashed, and a small bureau, tipped on its side, with cascades of writing paper falling out of the drawers. None of the damage seemed to have had any purpose beyond a frightening show of power, all of a piece with the pushing, shoving and shouting that Mrs. Millace had described. A rampage designed to confuse and bewilder, and when they got no results from attacking her possessions, they'd started on her face.

I stood the bureau up again, shoveled most of the stuff back into it and collected together a heap of scattered tapestry patterns and dozens of skeins of wool. One began at last to see clear stretches of carpet.

"Bastards," Steve said. "I hate them. I'll kill them."

"Why would they think your mother had a safe?"

"God knows. Perhaps they just go around ripping off new widows, screaming 'safe' at them on the offchance. I mean, if she'd had one, she'd have told them where it was, wouldn't she? After losing Dad like that. And yesterday's burglary, while we were at the funeral. Such dreadful shocks. She'd have told them. I know she would."

I nodded.

"She can't take any more," he said. There were tears in his voice, and his eyes were dark with the effort of trying not to cry. It was he, I thought, who was closest to the edge. His mother would be tucked up with sympathy and sedation.

"Time for bed," I said abruptly. "Come on. I'll help you undress. She'll be better tomorrow."

I woke early after an uneasy night and lay watching the dingy November dawn creep through the window. There was a good deal about life that I didn't want to get up and face: a situation common, no doubt, to the bulk of mankind. Wouldn't it be marvelous, I thought dimly, to be pleased with oneself, to look forward to the day ahead, to not have to think about mean-minded dying grandmothers and one's own depressing dishonesty. Normally fairly happy-go-lucky, a taking-things-as-they-come sort of person, I disliked being backed into uncomfortable corners from which escape meant action.

Things had happened to me all my life. I'd never gone out looking. I had learned whatever had come my way, whatever was there. Like photography, because of Duncan and Charlie. And like riding, because of my mother's dumping me in a racing stable; and if she'd left me with a farmer, I would no doubt be making hay.

Survival for so many years had been a matter of accepting what I was given, of making myself useful, of being quiet and agreeable and no trouble, of repression and introversion and self-control, that I was now, as a man, fundamentally unwilling to make a fuss or fight.

I had taught myself for so long not to want things that weren't offered to me that I now found very little to want. I had made no major decisions. What I had, had simply come.

Harold Osborne had offered me the cottage, along with the job of stable jockey. I'd accepted. The bank had offered a mortgage. I'd accepted. The local garage had suggested a certain car. I'd bought it.

I understood why I was as I was. I knew why I just drifted along, going where the tide took me. I knew why I was passive, but I felt absolutely no desire to change things, to stamp about and insist on being the master of my own fate.

I didn't want to look for my half-sister, and I didn't want to lose my job with Harold. I could simply drift along as usual doing nothing very positive . . . and yet for some obscure reason that instinctive course was seeming increasingly unattractive.

Irritated, I put my clothes on and went downstairs, peering in at Steve on the way and finding him sound asleep.

Someone had perfunctorily swept the kitchen floor since the funeral-day burglary, pushing into a heap a lot of broken crockery and spilled groceries. The evening before I'd discovered the coffee and sugar dumped in the dust, but there was milk along with the eggs in the refrigerator, and I drank some of that. Then, to pass the time, I wandered around, just looking.

The room which had been George Millace's darkroom would have been far and away the most interesting had there been anything there; but the original burglary there had been the most thorough. All that was left was a wide bench down one side, two large deep sinks down the other and rows of empty shelves across the end. Countless grubby outlines and smudges on the walls showed where the loads of equipment had stood, and stains on the floor marked where he'd stored his chemicals.

He had, I knew, done a lot of his own color developing and printing, which most professional photographers did not. The development of color slides and negatives was difficult and exacting, and it was safer, for consistent results, to entrust the process to commercial large-scale labs. Duncan and Charlie had sent all their color developing out; it was only the printing from negatives, much easier, that they had done themselves.

George Millace had been a craftsman of the first order. Pity about his unkind nature.

From the looks of things he had had two enlargers, one big and one smaller, enlargers being machines which held the negatives in what was basically a box up a stick, so that a bright light could shine through the negative onto a baseboard beneath.

The head of the enlarger, holding the light and the negative, could be wound up and down the stick. The higher one wound the head above the baseboard, the larger one saw the picture. The lower the head, the smaller the picture. An enlarger was in fact a projector, and the baseboard was the screen.

Besides the enlargers, George would have had an electric box of tricks for regulating the length of exposures, a mass of developing equipment and a drier for drying the finished prints. He would have had dozens of sheets of various types of photographic paper in different sizes, and light-tight dispensers to store them in. He would have had rows of files holding all his past work in reference order, and safelights and measuring jugs and paper-trimmers and filters.

The whole lot, every scrap, had been stolen.

Like most serious photographers he had kept his unexposed films in the refrigerator. They too had gone, Steve had said, and were presumably at the root of the vandalism in the kitchen.

I went aimlessly into the sitting room and switched on the lights, wondering how soon I could decently wake Steve and say I was going. The half-tidied room looked cold and dreary, a miserable sight for poor Mrs. Millace when she got home. From habit and from having nothing else to do I slowly carried on from where I'd stopped the night before, picking up broken scraps of vases and ornaments and retrieving reels of cotton and bits of sewing from under the chairs.

Half under the sofa itself lay a large black light-proof envelope, an unremarkable object in a photographer's house. I looked inside, but all it seemed to contain was a piece of clear thickish plastic about eight inches square, straight cut on three sides but wavy along the fourth. More rubbish. I put it back in the envelope and threw it in the wastepaper basket.

George Millace's rubbish box lay open and empty on the table. For no reason in particular, and certainly impelled by nothing more than photographic curiosity, I picked up the wastepaper basket and emptied it again on the carpet. Then I put all of George's worst mistakes back in the box where he'd kept them, and returned the broken bits of glass and china to the wastebasket.

Why, I wondered, looking at the spoiled prints and pieces of film, had George ever bothered to keep them? Photographers, like doctors, tended to be quick to bury their mistakes, and didn't usually leave them hanging around in magazine racks as permanent mementos of disaster. I had always been fond of puzzles. I thought it would be quite interesting to find out why such an expert as George should have found these particular things interesting.

Steve came downstairs in his pyjamas looking frail and hugging his injured arm, wanly contemplating the day.

"Good Lord," he said. "You've tidied the lot."

"Might as well."

"Thanks, then." He saw the rubbish box on the table, with all its contents back inside. "He used to keep that lot in the freezer," he said. "Mum told me there was a terrible fuss one day when the freezer broke down and all the peas and stuff unfroze. Dad didn't care a damn about the chickens and things and all the pies she'd made which had spoiled. All he went on and on about, she said, was that some ice-cream had melted all over his rubbish." Steve's tired face lit into a remembering smile. "It must have been quite a scene. She thought it was terribly funny, and when she laughed he got crosser and crosser . . ." He broke off, the smile dying. "I can't believe he isn't coming back."

"Did your father often keep things in the freezer?"

"Oh sure. Masses of stuff. You know what photographers are like. Always having fits about color dyes not being permanent. He was always raving on about his work deteriorating after twenty years. He said the only way to posterity was through the deep freeze, and even that wasn't certain."

"Well . . ." I said. "Did the burglars also empty the freezer?"

"Good Lord." He looked startled. "I don't know. I never thought of that. But why should they want his films?"

"They stole the ones that were in the darkroom."

"But the policeman said that that was just spite. What they really wanted was the equipment, which they could sell."

"Um," I said. "Your father took a lot of pictures which people didn't like."

"Yes, but only as a joke." He was defending George, the same as ever.

"We might look in the freezer," I suggested.

"Yes. All right. It's out at the back, in a sort of shed."

He picked a key out of the pocket of an apron hanging in the kitchen and led the way through the back door into a small covered yard, where there were garbage cans and stacks of logs and a lot of parsley growing in a tub.

"In there," Steve said, giving me the key and nodding to a green-painted door set into a bordering wall; I went in and found a huge chest freezer standing between the motor lawnmover and about six pairs of rubber boots.

I lifted the lid. Inside, filling one end and nestling next to joints of lamb and boxes of beefburgers, was a stack of three large gray metal cashboxes, each one closely wrapped in transparent plastic sheeting. Taped to the top was a terse message:

DO NOT STORE ICE CREAM
NEAR THESE BOXES

I laughed.

Steve looked at the boxes and the message and said, "There you are. Mum said he went berserk when it all melted, but in the end nothing of his was really damaged. The food was all spoiled, but his best transparencies were OK. It was after that that he started storing them in these boxes."

I shut the lid, and we locked the shed and went back into the house.

"You don't really think," Steve said doubtfully, "that the burglars were after Dad's pictures? I mean, they stole all sorts of things. Mum's rings, and his cufflinks, and her fur coat, and everything."

"Yes . . . so they did."

"Do you think I should mention to the police that all that stuff's in the freezer? I'm sure Mum's forgotten it's there. We never gave it a thought."

"You could talk it over with her," I said. "See what she says."

"Yes, that's best." He looked a shade more cheerful. "One good thing, she may have lost all the indexes and the dates and places saying where all the pictures were taken, but she has at least still got some of his best work. It hasn't all gone. Not all of it."

I helped him to get dressed and left soon afterwards, as he said he felt better, and looked it; and I took with me George Millace's box of disasters, which Steve had said to throw in the garbage.

"But you don't mind if I take it?" I said.

"Of course not. I know you like messing about with films, the same as he does . . . same as he did. He liked that old rubbish. Don't know why. Take it, if you want, by all means."

He came out into the drive and watched me stow the box in the trunk, alongside my two camera bags.

"You never go anywhere without a camera, do you?" he said. "Just like Dad."

"I suppose not."

"Dad said he felt naked without one."

"It gets to be part of you." I shut the trunk and locked it from long habit. "It's your shield. Keeps you a step away from the world. Makes you an observer. Gives you an excuse not to feel."

He looked extremely surprised that I should think such things, and so was I surprised, not that I'd thought them, but that I should have said them to him. I smiled to take the serious truth away and leave only an impression of satire, and Steve, photographer's son, looked relieved.

I drove the hour from Ascot to Lambourn at a Sunday morning pace and found a large dark car standing outside my front door.

The cottage was one of a terrace of seven built in the Edwardian era for the not-so-rich and currently inhabited, apart from me, by a schoolteacher, a horsebox driver, a curate, a vet's assistant, sundry wives and children, and two hostels-ful of stable lads. I was the only person living alone. It seemed almost indecent, among such a crowd, to have so much space to myself.

My house was in the center: two rooms upstairs, two down, with a modern kitchen stuck on at the back. A white-painted brick front, nothing fancy, facing straight out onto the road, with no room for a garden. A black door, needing paint. New aluminum window frames replacing the original wood, which had rotted away. Not impressive, but home.

I drove slowly past the visiting car and turned into the muddy drive at the end of the row, continuing around to the back and parking under the corrugated plastic roof of the carport next to the kitchen. As I went I caught a glimpse of a man getting hastily out of the car, and knew he had seen me; for my part I thought only that he had no business to be pursuing me on a Sunday.

I went through the house from the back and opened the front door. Jeremy Folk stood there, tall, thin, physically awkward, using earnest diffidence as a lever, as before.

"Don't solicitors sleep on Sundays?" I said.

"Well, I say, I'm awfully sorry . . ."

"Yeah," I said. "Come on in, then. How long have you been waiting?"

"Nothing to . . . ah . . . worry about."

He stepped through the door with a hint of expectancy and took the immediate disappointment with a blink. I had rearranged the interior of the cottage so that what had once been the front parlor was now divided into an entrance hall and darkroom, and in the hall section there were only a filing cabinet and the window, which looked

out to the street. White walls, white floor tiles; uninformative.

"This way," I said, amused, and led him past the darkroom to what had once been the back kitchen but was
now mostly bathroom and in part a continuation of the
hall. Beyond lay the new kitchen, and to the left, the narrow stairs.

"Which do you want," I said. "Coffee or talk?"

"Er . . . talk."

"Up here, then."

I went up the stairs, and he followed. I used one of the
two original bedrooms as the sitting room, because it was
the largest room in the house and had the best view of
the Downs; the smaller room next to it was where I slept.

The sitting room had white walls, brown carpet, blue
curtains, track lighting, bookshelves, sofa, low table and
floor cushions. My guest looked around with small flick-
ering glances, making assessments.

"Well?" I said neutrally.

"Er . . . that's a nice picture." He walked over to take
a closer look at the only thing hanging on the wall, a view
of pale yellow sunshine falling through some leafless silver birches onto snow. "It's . . . er . . . a print?"

"It's a photograph," I said.

"Oh! Is it really? It looks like a painting." He turned
away and said, "Where would you live if you had a hundred thousand pounds?"

"I told her I didn't want it." I looked at the angular
helpless way he was standing there, dressed that day not
in working charcoal flannel but in a tweed jacket with
decorative leather patches on the elbows. The brain under
the silly ass act couldn't be totally disguised, and I wondered vaguely whether he had developed that surface because he was embarrassed by his own acuteness.

"Sit down," I said, gesturing to the sofa, and he folded
his long legs as if I'd given him a gift. I sat on a beanbag

floor cushion and said, "Why didn't you mention the money when I saw you at Sandown?"

He seemed almost to wriggle. "I just . . . ah . . . thought I'd try you first on blood-stronger-than-water, don't you know?"

"And if that failed, you'd try greed?"

"Sort of."

"So that you would know what you were dealing with?"

He blinked.

"Look," I sighed. "I do understand thoughts of one syllable, so why don't you just . . . drop the act?"

His body relaxed for the first time into approximate naturalness and he gave me a small smile that was mostly in the eyes.

"It gets to be a habit," he said.

"So I gathered."

He cast a fresh look around the room, and I said, "All right, say what you're thinking."

He did so, without squirming and without apology. "You like to be alone. You're emotionally cold. You don't need props. And unless you took that photograph, you've no vanity."

"I took it."

"Tut tut."

"Yes," I said. "So what did you come for?"

"Well, obviously, to persuade you to do what you don't want to."

"To try to find the half-sister I didn't know I had?"

He nodded.

"Why?"

After a very short pause into which I could imagine him packing a lot of pros and cons he said, "Mrs. Nore is insisting on leaving a fortune to someone who can't be found. It is . . . unsatisfactory."

"Why is she insisting?"

"I don't know. She instructs my grandfather. She

doesn't take his advice. He's old and he's fed up with her, and so is my uncle, and they've shoved the whole mess onto me."

"Three detectives couldn't find Amanda."

"They didn't know where to look."

"Nor do I," I said.

He considered me. "You'd know."

"No."

"Do you know who your father is?" he said.

4

I sat with my head turned towards the window, looking out at the bare calm line of the Downs. A measurable silence passed. The Downs would be there forever.

I said, "I don't want to get tangled up in a family I don't feel I belong to. I don't like their threads falling over me like a web. That old woman can't claw me back just because she feels like it, after all these years."

Jeremy Folk didn't answer directly, and when he stood up some of the habitual gaucheness had come back into his movements, though not yet into his voice.

"I brought the reports we received from the three firms of detectives," he said. "I'll leave them with you."

"No, don't."

"It's useless," he said. He looked again around the room. "I see quite plainly that you don't want to be involved. But I'm afraid I'm going to plague you until you are."

"Do your own dirty work."

He smiled. "The dirty work was done about thirty years ago, wasn't it? Before either of us was born. This is just the muck floating back on the tide."

"Thanks a bunch."

He pulled a long bulging envelope out of the inside pocket of his country tweed and put it carefully down on the table. "They're not very long reports. You could just read them, couldn't you?"

He didn't expect an answer, or get one. He just moved vaguely towards the door to indicate that he was ready to leave, and I went downstairs with him and saw him out to his car.

"By the way," he said, pausing awkwardly halfway into the driving seat, "Mrs. Nore really is dying. She has cancer of the spine. Nothing to be done. She'll live maybe six weeks, or maybe six months. They can't tell. So . . . er . . . no time to waste, don't you know?"

I spent the bulk of the day contentedly in the darkroom, developing and printing the black-and-white shots of Mrs. Millace and her troubles. They came out clear and sharp so that one could actually read the papers on the floor, and I wondered casually just where the borderline fell between positive vanity and simple pleasure in a job efficiently done. Perhaps it had been vanity to mount and hang the silver birches . . . but apart from the content the large size of the print had been a technical problem, and it had all come out right . . . and what did a sculptor do, throw a sack over his best statue?

Jeremy Folk's envelope stayed upstairs on the table where he'd put it; unopened, contents unread. I ate some tomatoes and cheese when I grew hungry, and cleared up the darkroom, and at six o'clock locked my doors and walked up the road to see Harold Osborne.

Sunday evenings he expected me for a drink, and each Sunday from six to seven we talked over what had happened in the past week and discussed plans for the week ahead. For all his unpredictable up-and-down moods Harold was a man of method, and he hated anything to interrupt these sessions, which he referred to as our military briefings. His wife during that hour answered the telephone and took messages for him to ring back, and they had once had a blazing row with me because she had burst in to say their dog had been run over and killed.

"You could have told me in twenty minutes," he yelled. "Now how the hell am I going to concentrate on Philip's orders for the Schweppes?"

"But the dog," she wailed.

"Damn the dog." He'd ranted at her for several minutes and then he'd gone out into the road and wept over the body of his mangled friend. Harold, I supposed, was everything I wasn't: moody, emotional, flamboyant, full of rage and love and guile and gusto. Only in our basic belief in getting things right were we alike, and that tacit agreement let us work together in underlying peace. He might scream at me violently, but he didn't expect me to mind, and because I knew him well, I didn't. Other jockeys and trainers and several reporters had said to me often in varying degrees of exasperation or humor, "I don't know how you put up with it," and the answer was always the true one: "Easily."

On that particular Sunday the sacrosanct hour had been interrupted before it could begin, because Harold had a visitor. I walked through his house from the stable entrance and went into the comfortable cluttered sitting room—office, and there in one of the armchairs was Victor Briggs.

"Philip!" Harold said, welcoming and smiling. "Pour yourself a drink. We're just going to run through the videotape of yesterday. Sit down. Are you ready? I'll switch on."

Victor Briggs gave me several nods of approval and a handshake. No gloves, I thought. Cold pale dry hands with nothing aggressive in the grasp. Without the broad-brimmed hat he had thick glossy straight black hair which was receding slightly above the eyebrows to leave a center peak; and without the heavy navy overcoat, a plain dark suit. Indoors he still wore the close-guarded expression as if afraid his thoughts might show, but there was overall a distinct air of satisfaction. Not a smile, just an atmosphere.

I opened a can of Coca-Cola and poured some into a glass.

"Don't you drink?" Victor Briggs asked.

"Champagne," Harold said. "That's what he drinks, don't you, Philip?" He was in great good humor, his voice and presence amplifying the warm russet colors of the room, resonant as brass.

Harold's reddish-brown hair sprang in wiry curls all over his head, as untamable as his nature. He was fifty-two at that time and looked ten years younger, a big burly six feet of active muscle commanded by a strong but ambiguous face, his features more rounded than hawkish.

He switched on the video machine and sat back in his armchair to watch Daylight's debacle in the Sandown Pattern 'Chase, as pleased as if he'd won the Grand National. A good job no stewards were peering in, I thought. There was no mistaking the trainer's joy in his horse's failure.

The recording showed me on Daylight going down to the start, and lining up, and setting off: odds-on favorite at four to one on, said the commentator; only got to jump round to win. Immaculate leaps over the first two fences. Strong and steady up past the stands. Daylight just in the lead, dictating the pace, but all five runners closely bunched. Round the top bend, glued to the rails . . . faster downhill. The approach to the third fence . . . everything looking all right . . . and then the jump in the air and the stumbling landing, and the figure in red and blue silks going over the horse's neck and down under the feet. A groaning roar from the crowd, and the commentator's unemotional voice, "Daylight's down at that fence, and now in the lead is Little Moth . . ."

The rest of the race rolled on into a plodding undistinguished finish, and then came a rerun of Daylight's fall, with afterthought remarks from the commentator. "You can see the horse try to put in an extra stride, throwing

Philip Nore forward. The horse's head ducks on landing, giving his jockey no chance . . . poor Philip Nore clinging on . . . but hopeless . . . horse and jockey both unhurt."

Harold stood up and switched the machine off. "Artistic," he said, beaming down. "I've run through it twenty times. It's impossible to tell."

"No one suspected," Victor Briggs said. "One of the stewards said to me 'what rotten bad luck.'" There was a laugh somewhere inside Briggs, a laugh not quite breaking the surface but quivering in the chest. He picked up a large envelope, which had lain beside his gin and tonic, and held it out to me. "Here's my thank you, Philip."

I said matter-of-factly, "It's kind of you, Mr. Briggs. But nothing's changed. I don't like to be paid for losing. I can't help it."

Victor Briggs put the envelope down again without comment, and it wasn't he who was immediately angry, but Harold.

"Philip," he said loudly, towering above me. "Don't be such a bloody prig. There's a great deal of money in that envelope. Victor's being very generous. Take it and thank him, and shut up."

"I'd . . . rather not."

"I don't care what you'd bloody rather. You're not so squeamish when it comes to committing the crime, are you, it's just the thirty pieces of silver you turn your pious nose up at. You make me sick. And you'll take that bloody money if I have to ram it down your throat."

"Well, you will," I said.

"I will what?"

"Have to ram it down my throat."

Victor Briggs actually laughed, though when I glanced at him his mouth was tight shut as if the sound had escaped without his approval.

"And," I said slowly, "I don't want to do it any more."

"You'll do what you're bloody told," Harold said.

Victor Briggs rose purposefully to his feet, and the two

of them, suddenly silent, stood looking down at me.

It seemed that a long time passed, and then Harold said in a quiet voice which held a great deal more threat than his shouting, "You'll do what you're told, Philip."

I stood up in my turn. My mouth had gone dry, but I made my voice sound as neutral, as calm, as unprovoking as possible.

"Please . . . don't ask me for a repeat of yesterday."

Victor Briggs narrowed his eyes. "Did the horse hurt you? He trod on you . . . you can see it on the video."

I shook my head. "It's not that. It's the losing. You know I hate it. I just . . . don't want you to ask me . . . again."

More silence.

"Look," I said. "There are degrees. Of course I'll give a horse an easy race if he isn't a hundred per cent fit and a hard race would ruin him for next time out. Of course I'll do that, it only makes sense. But no more like Daylight yesterday. I know I used to . . . but yesterday was the last."

Harold said coldly, "You'd better go now, Philip. I'll talk to you in the morning," and I nodded, and left, and there were none of the warm handshakes which had greeted my arrival.

What would they do, I wondered. I walked in the windy dark down the road from Harold's house to mine as I had on hundreds of Sundays, and wondered if it would be for the last time. If he wanted to he could put other jockeys up on his horses from that day onwards. He was under no obligation to give me rides. I was classed as self-employed, because I was paid per race by the owners, and not per week by the trainer; and there were no such things as "unfair dismissal" enquiries for the self-employed.

I suppose it was too much to hope that they would let me get away with it. Yet for three years they had run the Briggs horses honestly, so why not in future? And if they insisted on fraud, couldn't they get some other poor young slob just starting his career, and put the pressure on him when they wanted a race lost? Foolish wishes, all of them. I'd put my job down at their feet like a football and at that moment they were probably kicking it out of the stadium.

It was ironic. I hadn't known I was going to say what I had. It had just forced its own way out, like water through a new spring.

All those races I'd thrown away in the past, not liking it, but doing it . . . Why was it so different now? Why was the revulsion so strong now that I didn't think I *could* do a Daylight again, even if to refuse meant virtually the end of being a jockey?

When had I changed . . . and how could it have happened without my noticing? I didn't know. I just had a sense of having already traveled too far to turn back. Too far down a road where I didn't want to go.

I went upstairs and read the three detectives' reports on Amanda because it was better, on the whole, than thinking about Briggs and Harold.

Two of the reports had come from fairly large firms and one from a one-man outfit, and all three had spent a lot of ingenuity padding out very few results. Justifying their charges, no doubt. Copiously explaining what they had all spent so long not finding out: and all three, not surprisingly, had not found out approximately the same things.

None of them, for a start, could find any trace of her birth having been registered. They all expressed doubt and disbelief over this discovery, but to me it was no surprise at all. I had discovered that I myself was unregistered when I tried to get a passport, and the fuss had gone on for months.

I knew my name, my mother's name, my birthdate, and that I'd been born in London. Officially, however, I didn't exist. "But here I am," I'd protested, and I'd been told, "Ah yes, but you don't have a piece of paper to prove it, do you?" There had been affidavits by the ton and miles of red tape, and I'd missed the race I'd been offered in France by the time I got permission to go there.

Owing to my grandmother's vagueness about when she had received her daughter's letter, the detectives had all scoured Somerset House for records of Amanda Nore, aged between ten and twenty-five, possibly born in Sussex. In spite of the fairly unusual name, they had all completely failed.

I sucked my teeth, thinking that I could do better than that about her age.

She couldn't have been born before I went to live with Duncan and Charlie, because I'd seen my mother fairly often before that, about five or six times a year, and often for a week at a time, and I would have known if she'd had a child. The people she left me with used to talk about her when they thought I wasn't listening, and I gradually understood what I remembered their saying, though sometimes not for years afterwards; but none of them, ever, had hinted that she was pregnant.

That meant that I was at least twelve when Amanda was born; and consequently she couldn't at present be older than eighteen.

At the other end of things she couldn't possibly be as young as ten. My mother, I was sure, had died sometime between Christmas and my eighteenth birthday. She might have been desperate enough at that time to write to her own mother and send her the photograph. Amanda in the photograph had been three . . . so Amanda, if she was still alive, would be at least fifteen.

Sixteen or seventeen, most likely. Born during the three years when I hadn't seen my mother at all, when I'd lived with Duncan and Charlie.

I went back to the reports . . .

All three detectives had been given the last known address of Caroline Nore, Amanda's mother: Pine Woods Lodge, Mindle Bridge, Sussex. All three had trekked there "to make enquiries."

Pine Woods Lodge, they rather plaintively reported, was not as the name might suggest a small private hotel complete with guest register going back umpteen years, forwarding addresses attached. Pine Woods Lodge was an old Georgian mansion gone to ruin and due to be demolished. There were trees growing in what had been the ballroom. Large sections had no roof.

It was owned by a family which had largely died out twenty-five years earlier, leaving distant heirs who had no wish and no money to keep the place up. They had let the house at first to various organizations (list attached, supplied by real estate agents) but more recently it had been inhabited by squatters and vagrants. The dilapidation was now so advanced that even such as they had moved out, and the five acres the house was built on were to come up for auction within three months: but as whoever bought the land was going to have to demolish the mansion, it was not expected to fetch much of a price.

I read through the list of tenants, none of whom had stayed long. A nursing home. A sisterhood of nuns. An artists' commune. A boys' youth club adventure project. A television film company. A musicians' cooperative. Colleagues of Supreme Grace. The Confidential Mail Order Corporation.

One of the detectives, persevering, had investigated the tenants as far as he could, and had added unflattering comments.

Nursing home	——	*Euthanasia for all.*
		Closed by council.
Nuns	——	*Disbanded through bitchiness.*
Artists	——	*Left disgusting murals.*

Boys	——	*Broke everything still whole.*
TV	——	*Needed a ruin to film.*
Musicians	——	*Fused all the electricity.*
Colleagues	——	*Religious nuts.*
Mail order	——	*Perverts' delights.*

There were no dates attached to the tenancies, but presumably if the real estate agents could still furnish the list, they would have kept some other details. If I was right about when my mother had written her desperate letter, I should at least be able to find out which bunch of kooks she had been staying with.

If I wanted to, of course.

Sighing, I read on.

Copies of the photograph of Amanda Nore had been extensively displayed in public places (newsstands' shop windows) in the vicinity of the small town of Mindle Bridge, but no one had come forward to identify either the child or the stable yard or the pony.

Advertisements had been inserted (accounts attached) in various periodicals and one national Sunday newspaper (for six weeks) stating that if Amanda Nore wished to hear something to her advantage she should write to Folk, Langley, Son and Folk, solicitors, of St. Albans, Herts.

One of the detectives, the one who had persisted with the tenants, had also enterprisingly questioned the Pony Club, but to no avail. They had never had a member called Amanda Nore. He had furthermore written to the British Show Jumping Association, with the same result.

A canvass of schools in a wide area around Mindle Bridge had produced no one called Amanda Nore on the registers, past or present.

She had not come into council care in Sussex. She was on no official list of any sort. No doctor or dentist had heard of her. She had not been confirmed, married, buried or cremated within the county.

The reports all came to the same conclusion: that she had been, or was being, brought up elsewhere (possibly under a different name), and was no longer interested in riding.

I shuffled the typed sheets together and returned them to the envelope. They had tried, one had to admit. They had also indicated their willingness to continue to search through each county in the land, if the considerable expenditure should be authorized; but they couldn't in any way guarantee success.

Their collective fee must already have been fearful. The authorization, anyway, seemed not to have been forthcoming. I wondered sardonically if the old woman had thought of me to look for Amanda because it would cost so much less. A promise, a bribe . . . no foal, no fee.

I couldn't understand her late interest in her long-ignored grandchildren. She'd had a son of her own, a boy my mother had called "my hateful little brother." He would have been about ten when I was born, which made him now about forty, presumably with children of his own.

Uncle. Cousins. Half-sister. Grandmother.

I didn't want them. I didn't want to know them or be drawn into their lives. I was in no way whatever going to look for Amanda.

I stood up with decision and went down to the kitchen to do something about cheese and eggs; and to stave off the thought of Harold a bit longer I fetched George Millace's box of trash in from the car and opened it on the kitchen table, taking out the items and looking at them one by one.

On a closer inspection it didn't seem to make much sense that he should have kept these particular odds and ends. They didn't have the appearance of interesting or unique mistakes. Sorting my way through them I concluded with disappointment that it had been a waste of time after all to bring them home.

I picked up the folder which contained the dark print of a shadowy man sitting at a table and thought vaguely that it was odd to have bothered to put such an over-exposed mess into a mount.

Shrugging, I slid the dark print out onto my hand . . . and it was then that I found George's private pot of gold.

5

I t was not, at first sight, very exciting.

Taped onto the back of the print there was an envelope made of the special sort of sulphur-free paper used by careful professionals for the long-term storage of developed film. Inside the envelope, a negative.

It was the negative from which the print had been made, but whereas the print was mostly black and elsewhere very dark grays, the negative itself was clear and sharp with many details and highlights.

I looked at the print and at the negative, side by side.

I had no quickening of the pulse. No suspicions, no theories, merely curiosity. As I also had the means and the time, I went back into the darkroom and made four five-by-four-inch prints, each at a different exposure, from one second to eight seconds.

Not even the longest exposure looked exactly like George's dark print, so I started again with the most suitable exposure, six seconds, and left the photograph in the developer too long, until the sharp outlines first went dark and then mostly disappeared, leaving a gray man sitting at a table against blackness. At that point I lifted the paper from the tray of developer and transferred it to the one containing fixer; and what I had then was another print almost exactly like George's.

Leaving a print too long in the developing fluid had to be one of the commonest mistakes on earth. If George's attention had been distracted and he'd left a print too long in developer, he'd simply have cursed and thrown the ruin away. Why, then had he kept it? And mounted it? And stuck the clear sharp negative onto the back?

It wasn't until I switched on a bright light and looked more closely at the best of the four original exposures I'd made that I understood why; and I stood utterly still in the darkroom, taking in the implications in disbelief.

With something approaching a whistle I finally moved. I switched off the white light, and, when my eyes had accustomed themselves again to the red safelight, I made another print, four times as large, and on a higher contrast grade of paper, to get as clear a result as I could possibly manage. Then I switched on the white light again and fed the finished print through the drier.

What I'd got was a picture of two people talking together who had sworn on oath in a court of law that they had never met.

There wasn't the slightest possibility of a mistake. The shadowy man was now revealed as a customer sitting at a table outside a cafe somewhere in France. He had not been the real focus of the photograph, just an accidental diner with a plate and a glass by his hand. The cafe had a name: Le Lapin d'Argent. There were advertisements for beer and lottery tickets in its half-curtained window, and a waiter in an apron standing in the doorway. A woman some way inside was sitting at a cash desk in front of a mirror, looking out to the street. The detail was sharp throughout, with remarkable depth of focus. George Millace at his usual expert best.

Sitting together at a table outside the cafe window were two men, both of them facing the camera but with their heads turned towards each other, unmistakably deep in conversation. A wine glass stood in front of each of them, half full, with a bottle to one side. There were coffee cups also, and an ashtray with a half-smoked cigar balanced on the edge. All the signs of a lengthy meeting.

Both men had been involved in an affair which had shaken the racing world like a thunderclap eighteen months earlier. Elgin Yaxley, the one on the left of the photograph, had owned five expensive steeplechasers which had been trained in Lambourn. At the end of the 'chasing season all five had been sent to a local farmer for a few weeks' summer break out at grass; and then, out in the fields, they had all been shot dead with a rifle. Terence O'Tree, the man on the right in the photograph, had shot them.

Some smart police work (aided by two young boys out at dawn when their parents thought them safe in bed) had tracked down and identified O'Tree, and brought him to court.

All five horses had been heavily insured. The insurance company, screeching with disbelief, had tried their damnedest to prove that Yaxley himself had hired O'Tree to do the killing, but both men had consistently denied it, and no link between them had been found.

O'Tree, saying he'd shot the horses just because he'd felt like it ("For a bit o' target practice, like, Your Honor, and how was I to know they was valuable racehorses?") had been sent to jail for nine months with a recommendation that he should see a psychiatrist.

Elgin Yaxley, indignantly proclaiming his virtue and threatening to sue the insurance company for defamation of character if they didn't instantly pay up, had wrung out of them the whole amount and had then faded out of the racing scene.

The insurance company, I thought, would surely have paid George Millace a great deal for his photograph, if they had known it existed. Probably ten per cent of what they would not have had to pay Yaxley. I couldn't remember the exact sums, but I knew the total insured value of the five horses had been close to a hundred and fifty thousand pounds. It had been, in fact, the very size of the pay-out which had infuriated the insurers into suspecting fraud.

So why hadn't George asked for a reward . . . and why had he so carefully hidden the negative . . . and why had his house been burgled three times? For all that I'd never liked George Millace, it was the obvious answer to those questions that I disliked even more.

In the morning I walked up to the stables and rode out at early exercise as usual. Harold behaved in his normal blustery fashion, raising his voice over the scouring note of the November wind. The lads scowled and sulked as the vocal lash landed, and one or two, I reckoned, would be gone by the week's end. When lads left any stable nowadays they tended simply not to turn up one morning. They would sidle off to some other stable and the first news their old masters would have would be requests for references from the new. Notice, for many of the modern breed of lads, was something they never gave. Notice led to arguments and aggravation, and who wanted that, man, when ducking out was so much easier? The lad population washed in and out of British stables like a swirling endless river, with long-stayers being an exception rather than the rule.

"Breakfast," Harold bellowed at me at one point. "Be there."

I nodded. I usually went home for breakfast even if I was riding out second lot, which I did only on nonracing days, and not always even then. Breakfast, in Harold's wife's view, consisted of a huge fryup accompanied by mountains of toast served on the big kitchen table with generosity and warmth. It always smelled and looked delicious, and I always fell.

"Another sausage, Philip?" Harold's wife said, lavishly

shoveling straight from the pan. "And some hot fried potatoes?"

"You're destroying him, woman," Harold said, reaching for the butter.

Harold's wife smiled at me in her special way. She thought I was too thin; and she thought I needed a wife. She told me so, often. I disagreed with her on both counts, but I dare say she was right.

"Last night," Harold said. "We didn't discuss the week's plans."

"No."

"There's Pamphlet at Kempton on Wednesday," he said. "In the two-mile hurdle; and Tishoo and Sharpener on Thursday . . ."

He talked about the races for some time, munching vigorously all the while, so that I got my riding instructions out of the side of his mouth accompanied by crumbs.

"Understood?" he said finally.

"Yes."

It appeared that after all I had not been given the instant sack, and for that I was relieved and grateful, but it was clear all the same that the precipice wasn't all that far away.

Harold glanced across the big kitchen to where his wife was stacking things in the dishwasher and said, "Victor doesn't like your attitude."

I didn't answer.

Harold said, "The first thing one demands from a jockey is loyalty."

That was rubbish. The first thing one demanded from a jockey was value for money.

"My Fuehrer, right or wrong?" I said.

"Owners won't stand for jockeys' passing moral judgments on them."

"Owners shouldn't defraud the public, then."

"Have you finished eating?" he demanded.

I sighed regretfully. "Yes."

"Then come into my office."

He led the way into the russet-colored room, which was filled with chill bluish Monday morning light and had no fire in the grate.

"Shut the door," he said.

I shut it.

"You'll have to choose, Philip," he said. He stood by the fireplace with one foot on the hearth, a big man in riding clothes, smelling of horses and fresh air and fried eggs.

I waited noncommittally.

"Victor will eventually want another race lost. Not at once, I grant you, because it would be too obvious. But in the end, yes. He says if you really mean you won't do it, we'll have to get someone else."

"For those races only?"

"Don't be stupid. You're not stupid. You're too bloody smart for your own good."

I shook my head. "Why does he want to start this caper again? He's won a lot of prize money playing it straight these last three years."

Harold shrugged. "I don't know. What does it matter? He told me on Saturday when we got to Sandown that he'd laid his horse and that I was on to a big share of the profit. We've all done it before . . . why not again? Just what has got into you, Philip, that you're swooning over a little fiddle like a bloody virgin?"

I didn't know the answer. He swept on anyway before I'd thought of a reply. "Well, you just work it out, boy. Whose are the best horses in the yard? Victor's. Who buys good new horses to replace the old? Victor. Who pays his training bills on the nose? Victor. Who owns more horses in this yard than anyone else? Victor. And which owner can I least afford to lose, particularly as he has been with me for more than ten years and has provided me with a large proportion of the winners I've trained in the past, and is likely to provide most of those I train in the future?

Just who, do you think, my business most depends on?"

I stared at him. I supposed that I hadn't realized until then that he was in perhaps the same position as myself. Do what Victor wanted, or else.

"I don't want to lose you, Philip," he said. "You're a prickly bastard, but we've got on all right all these years. You won't go on forever, though. You've been racing . . . what . . . ten years?"

I nodded.

"Three or four more, then. At the most, five. Pretty soon you won't bounce back from those falls the way you do now. And at any time a bad one might put you out of action for good. So look at it straight, Philip. Who do I need most in the long term, you or Victor?"

In a sort of melancholy we walked into the yard, where Harold shouted, but halfheartedly, at a couple of dawdling lads.

"Let me know," he said, turning towards me.

"All right."

"I want you to stay."

I was surprised, but also pleased.

"Thanks," I said.

He gave me a clumsy buffet on the shoulder, the nearest he'd ever come to the slightest show of affection. More than all the threatening and screaming on earth it made me want to agree to do what he asked; a reaction, I acknowledged flickeringly, as old as the hills. It was often kindness that finally broke the prisoner's spirit, not torture. One's defenses were always defiantly angled outward to withstand aggression; it was kindness which crept around behind and stabbed you in the back, so that your will evaporated into tears and gratitude. Defenses against kindness were much harder to build. And not the defenses I would ever have thought I needed against Harold.

I sought instinctively to change the subject, and came

up with the nearest thought to hand, which was George Millace and his photograph.

"Um," I said, as we stood a shade awkwardly, "do you remember those five horses of Elgin Yaxley's, that were shot?"

"What?" He looked bewildered. "What's that got to do with Victor?"

"Nothing at all," I said. "I was just thinking about them, yesterday."

Irritation immediately canceled out the passing moment of emotion, which was probably a relief to us both.

"For God's sake," he said sharply. "I'm serious. Your career's at stake. You can do what you damn well like. You can bloody well go to hell. It's up to you."

I nodded.

He turned away abruptly and took two purposeful steps. Then he stopped, looked back, and said, "If you're so bloody interested in Elgin Yaxley's horses, why don't you ask Kenny?" He pointed to one of the lads, who was filling two buckets by the tap. "He looked after them."

He turned his back again and firmly strode away, outrage and anger thumping down with every foot.

I walked irresolutely over to Kenny, not sure what questions I wanted to ask, or even if I wanted to ask questions at all.

Kenny was one of those people whose defenses were the other way around: impervious to kindness, open to fright. Kenny was a near-delinquent who had been treated with so much understanding by social workers that he could shrug off pleasant approaches with contempt.

He watched me come with an expression willfully blank to the point of insolence, his habitual expression. Skin reddened by the wind; eyes slightly watering; spots.

"Mr. Osborne said you used to work for Bart Underfield," I said.

"So what?"

The water splashed over the top of the first bucket. He

bent to remove it, and kicked the second one forward under the tap.

"And looked after some of Elgin Yaxley's horses?"

"So what?"

"So were you sorry when they were shot?"

He shrugged. "Suppose so."

"What did Mr. Underfield say about it?"

"Huh?" His gaze rested squarely on my face. "He didn't say nothing."

"Wasn't he angry?"

"Not as I noticed."

"He must have been," I said.

Kenny shrugged again.

"At the very least," I said, "he was five horses short, and no trainer with his size stable can afford that."

"He didn't say nothing." The second bucket was nearly full, and Kenny turned off the tap. "He didn't seem to care much about losing them. Something pissed him off a bit later, though."

"What did?"

Kenny looked uninterested and picked up the buckets. "Don't know. He was right grumpy. Some of the owners got fed up and left."

"So did you," I said.

"Yeah." He started walking across the yard with water sloshing gently at each step. I went with him, warily keeping a dry distance. "What's the point of staying when a place is going down the drain?"

"Were Yaxley's horses in good shape when they went off to the farm?" I asked.

"Sure." He looked slightly puzzled. "Why are you asking?"

"No real reason. Someone mentioned those horses . . . and Mr. Osborne said you looked after them. I was just interested."

"Oh." He nodded. "They had the vet in court, you know, to say the horses were fine the day before they died.

He went to the farm to give one of them some antitetanus jabs, and he said he looked them all over, and they were OK."

"Did you go to the trial?"

"No. Read it in the *Sporting Life*." He reached the row of boxes and put the buckets down outside one of the doors. "That all, then?"

"Yes. Thanks, Kenny."

"Tell you something . . ." He looked almost surprised at his own sudden helpfulness.

"What?"

"That Mr. Yaxley," he said. "You'd've thought he'd been pleased getting all that cash, even if he had lost his horses, but he came into Underfield's yard one day in a right proper rage. Come to think of it, it was after that that Underfield went sour. And Yaxley, of course, quit racing and we never saw no more of him. Not while I was there, we didn't."

I walked thoughtfully home, and when I got there the telephone was ringing.

"Jeremy Folk," a familiar voice said.

"Oh, not again," I protested.

"Did you read those reports?"

"Yes, I did. And I'm not going looking for her."

"Be a good fellow," he said.

"No." I paused. "To get you off my back, I'll help you a bit. But you must do the looking."

"Well . . ." He sighed. "What sort of help?"

I told him of my conclusions about Amanda's age, and also suggested he should get the dates of the various tenancies of Pine Woods Lodge from the real estate agents.

"My mother was probably there thirteen years ago," I said. "And now it's all yours."

"But I *say* . . ." he almost wailed. "You simply can't stop there."

"I simply can."

"I'll get back to you."

"Just leave me alone," I said.

I drove into Swindon to take the color film to the processors, and on the way thought about the life and times of Bart Underfield.

I knew him in the way one got to know everyone in racing if one lived long enough in Lambourn. We met occasionally in the village shops and in other people's houses, as well as at the races. We exchanged "Good mornings" and "Hard lucks" and a variety of vague nods. I had never ridden for him because he had never asked me; and he'd never asked me, I thought, because he didn't like me.

He was a small busy man full of importance, given to telling people confidentially what other more successful trainers had done wrong. "Of course Walwyn shouldn't have run such-and-such at Ascot," he would say. "The distance was all wrong, one could see it a mile off." Strangers thought him very knowledgeable. Lambourn thought him an ass.

No one had suggested, however, that he was such an ass as to deliver his five best horses to the slaughter. Everyone had undoubtedly felt sorry for him, particularly as Elgin Yaxley had not spent the insurance money on buying new and equal animals, but had merely departed altogether, leaving Bart a great deal worse off.

Those horses, I reflected, had undoubtedly been good, and must always have earned more than their keep, and could have been sold for high prices. They had been insured above their market value, certainly, but not by impossible margins if one took into account the prizes they couldn't win if they were dead. It was the fact that there seemed to be little profit in killing them that had finally baffled the suspicious insurers into paying up.

That . . . and no trace of a link between Elgin Yaxley and Terence O'Tree.

In Swindon the processors, who knew me well, said I was lucky, they were just going to feed a batch through, and if I cared to hang about I could have my negatives back in a couple of hours. I did some shopping and in due course picked up the developed films, and went home.

In the afternoon I printed the colored versions of Mrs. Millace, and sent them off with the black-and-white lot to the police; and in the evening I tried—and failed—to stop thinking in uncomfortable circles about Amanda and Victor Briggs and George Millace.

By far the worst thoughts concerned Victor Briggs and Harold's ultimatum. The jockey life suited me fine in every way, physically, mentally, financially. I'd put off for years the thought that one day I would have to do something else: the "one day" had always been in the mists of the future, not staring me brutally in the face.

The only thing I knew anything about besides horses was photography, but there were thousands of photographers all over the place . . . Everyone took photographs, every family had a camera, the whole Western world was awash in photographers . . . and to make a living at it one had to be exceptionally good.

One also had to work exceptionally hard. The photographers I knew on the racecourse were always running about: scurrying from the start to the last fence and from there up to the unsaddling enclosure before the winner got there, and then down the course again for the next race, and six times, at least, every afternoon, five or six days a week. Some of their pictures they rushed off to news agencies who might offer them to newspapers, and some they sent to magazines, and some they flogged to the owners of the horses, and some to sponsors handing over cups.

If you were a racing photographer the pictures didn't come to you, you had to go out looking. And when you'd got them, the customers didn't flock to your door, you had to go out selling. It was all a lot different from Duncan and Charlie, who had mostly done still-life things like pots and pans and clocks and garden furniture for advertisements.

There were very few full-time successful racing photographers. Fewer than ten, probably. Of those perhaps four were outstanding; and one of those four had been George Millace.

If I tried to join their ranks, the others wouldn't hinder me, but they wouldn't help me either. I'd be out there on my own, stand or fall.

I wouldn't mind the running about, I thought; it was the selling part that daunted. Even if I considered my pictures good enough, I couldn't push.

And what else?

Setting up as a trainer was out. I hadn't the capital, and training racehorses was no sort of life for someone who liked stretches of silent time and being alone. Trainers talked to people from dawn to bedtime and lived in a whirl.

What I wanted, and instinctively knew that I would always need, was to continue to be self-employed. A regular wage packet looked like chains. An illogical feeling, but overwhelming. Whatever I did, I would have to do it on my own.

The habit of never making decisions would have to be broken. I could drift, I saw, into jobs which had none of the terrific satisfactions of being a jockey. I had been lucky so far, but if I wanted to find contentment in the next chapter I would have for once to be positive.

Damn Victor Briggs, I thought violently.

Inciting jockeys to throw races was a warning-off defense, but even if I could manage to get Victor Briggs warned-off, the person who would most suffer would be Harold. And I'd lose my job anyway, as Harold would hardly keep me on after that, even if we didn't both lose our licenses altogether because of the races I'd thrown in the past. I couldn't prove Victor Brigg's villainy without having to admit Harold's and my own.

Cheat or retire. A stark choice . . . absolutely comfort-less.

Nothing changed much on the Tuesday, but when I went to Kempton on Wednesday to ride Pamphlet, the weighing room was electric with two pieces of gossip.

Ivor den Relgan had been made a member of the Jockey Club, and Steve Millace's mother's house had burned down.

6

"Ivor den Relgan?" I heard the name on every side, repeated in varying tones of astonishment and disbelief. "A member of the Jockey Club! Incredible!"

The Jockey Club, that exclusive and gentlemanly body, had apparently that morning voted into its fastidious ranks someone they had been holding at arm's length for years, a rich self-important man from no one knew where, who had spread his money about in racing and done a certain amount of good in a way that affronted the recipients.

He was supposed to be of Dutch extraction. Extraction, that is, from some unspecified ex-Dutch colony. He spoke with an accent that sounded like a mixture of South African, Australian and American, a conglomerate midglobe amalgam of vowels and consonants which could have been attractive but came out as patronizing. He, the voice seemed to say, was a great deal more sophisticated than the stuffy British upper crust. He sought not favors from the entrenched powers, but admiration. It was they, he implied, who would prosper if they took his advice. He offered it to them free, frequently, in letters to the *Sporting Life*.

Until that morning the Jockey Club had indeed ob-

servably taken his advice on several occasions while
steadfastly refusing to acknowledge he had given it. I
wondered fleetingly what had brought them to such a turn-
around; what had caused them suddenly to embrace the
anathema.

Steve Millace was in the changing room, waiting by
my peg.

The strain in him that was visible from the doorway
was at close quarters overpowering. White-faced, shaking,
he stood with his arm in a black webbing sling and looked
at me from sunken desperate eyes.

"Have you heard?" he said.

I nodded.

"It happened on Monday night. Well, yesterday morning, I suppose . . . about three o'clock. By the time anyone
noticed, the whole place had gone."

"Your mother wasn't there?"

"They'd kept her in the hospital. She's still there. It's
too much for her. I mean . . ." He was trembling. "Too
much."

I made some sincerely sympathetic noises.

"Tell me what to do," he said; and I thought, he's
elected me as some sort of elder brother, an unofficial
advice bureau.

"Didn't you say something about aunts?" I asked. "At
the funeral?"

He shook his head impatiently. "They're Dad's sisters.
Older sisters. They've never liked Mum."

"All the same . . ."

"They're *cats*," he said, exploding. "I rang them . . .
they said what a shame." He mimicked their voices ven-
omously. " 'Tell poor dear Marie she can get quite a nice
little bungalow near the seaside with the insurance
money.' They make me sick."

I began taking off my street clothes to change into
colors, aware that to Steve the day's work was irrelevant.

"Philip," he said imploringly. "You saw her. All

bashed about . . . and without Dad . . . and now the whole house . . . Please . . . *please* . . . help me."

"All right," I said resignedly. What else could one say? "When I've finished riding, we'll work something out."

He sat down on the bench as if his legs wouldn't hold him and just stayed there staring into space while I finished changing and went to weigh out.

Harold was by the scales as usual, waiting to take my saddle when I'd been weighed. Since Monday he'd made no reference to the life-altering decision he'd handed me, and perhaps he took my silence not for spirit-tearing indecision but tacit acceptance of a return to things past. At any rate it was with a totally normal manner that he said, as I put the saddle over his arm, "Did you hear who's been elected to the Jockey Club?"

"Yeah."

"They'll take Genghis Khan next."

He walked out to put the saddle on Pamphlet, and in due course I joined him in the parade ring, where the horse walked nonchalantly around and his pop star owner bit his nails with concentration.

Harold had gleaned some more news. "I hear that it was the Great White Chief who insisted on den Relgan joining the club."

"Lord White?" I was surprised.

"Old Driven Snow himself."

Pamphlet's youngish owner flicked his fingers and said, "Hey, man, how's about a little sweet music on this baby?"

"A tenner each way," Harold suggested, having learned the pop star's language. The pop star was using the horse for publicity and would only let it run when its race would be televised: and he was, as usual, wholly aware of the positions of the cameras, so that if they should chance to point his way he would not be carelessly obscured behind Harold or me. I admired his expertise in this respect, and indeed his whole performance, because offstage, so to speak, he was apt to relapse into middle-class suburban. The jazzed-up working-class image was all a fake.

He had come to the races that day with dark-blue hair. The onset of a mild apoplexy could be observed in the parade ring all about us, but Harold behaved as if he hadn't noticed, on the basis that owners who paid their bills could be as eccentric as they liked.

"Philip darling," said the pop star, "bring this baby back for Daddy."

He must have learned it out of old movies, I thought. Surely not even pop musicians talked like that anymore. He reverted to biting his nails and I got up on Pamphlet and rode out to see what I could do about the tenner each way.

I was not popularly supposed to be much good over hurdles, but maybe Pamphlet had winning on his mind that day as much as I did. He soared around the whole thing with bursting joie-de-vivre, even to the extent of passing the favorite on the run-in, and we came back to bear hugs from the blue hair (for the benefit of television) and an offer to me of a spare ride in the fifth race, from a worried-looking small-time trainer. Stable jockey hurt . . . would I mind? I wouldn't mind, I'd be delighted. Fine, the valet has the colors, see you in the parade ring. Great.

Steve was still brooding by my peg.

"Was the shed burned?" I asked.

"What?"

"The shed. The deep freeze. Your Dad's photos."

"Oh, well, yes it was . . . but Dad's stuff wasn't in there."

I stripped off the pop star's orange and pink colors and went in search of the calmer green and brown of the spare ride.

"Where was it, then?" I said, returning.

"I told Mum what you said about people maybe not liking Dad's pictures of them, and she reckoned that you thought all the burglaries were really aimed at the photos, not at her fur and all that, and that if so she didn't want to leave those transparencies where they could still be stolen, so on Monday she got me to move them next door, to her neighbor's. And that's where they are now, in a sort of outhouse."

I buttoned the green-and-brown shirt, thinking it over.

"Do you want me to visit her in the hospital?" I said.

Almost on my direct route home. No great shakes. He fell on it, though, with embarrassing fervor. He had come to the races, he said, with the pub-keeper from the Sussex village where he lived in digs near the stable he rode for, and if I would visit his mother he could go home with the pub-keeper, because otherwise he had no transport, because of his collarbone. I hadn't exactly meant I would see Mrs. Millace alone, but on reflection I didn't mind.

Having shifted his burden Steve cheered up a bit and asked if I would telephone him when I got home.

"Yes," I said absently. "Did your father often go to France?"

"France?"

"Ever heard of it?" I said.

"Oh . . ." He was in no mood to be teased. "Of course he did. Longchamps, Auteuil, St. Cloud. Everywhere."

"And around the world?" I said, packing lead into my weightcloth.

"Huh?" He was decidedly puzzled. "What do you mean?"

"What did he spend his money on?"

"Lenses, mostly. Telephotos as long as your arm. Any new equipment."

I took my saddle and weightcloth over to the trial scales and added another flat pound of lead. Steve got up and followed me.

"What do you mean, what did he spend his money on?"

I said, "Nothing. Nothing at all. Just wondered what he liked doing, away from the races."

"He just took pictures. All the time, everywhere. He wasn't interested in anything else."

In time I went out to ride the green-and-brown horse and it was one of those days, which happened so seldom, when absolutely everything went right. In unqualified euphoria I dismounted once again in the winners' enclosure, and thought that I couldn't possibly give up the life; I couldn't *possibly*. Not when winning put you higher than heroin.

My mother had likely died of heroin.

Steve's mother lay alone in a glass-walled side ward, isolated but indecently exposed to the curious glances of any stranger walking past. There were curtains, which might have shielded her from public gaze, but they were not pulled across. I hated the system which denied privacy to people in the hospital: who on earth, if they were ill or injured, wanted their indignities gawped at?

Marie Millace lay on her back with two flat pillows under her head and a sheet and a thin blue blanket covering her. Her eyes were shut. Her brown hair, greasy and in disarray, straggled on the pillow. Her face was dreadful.

The raw patches of Saturday night were now covered by extensive dark scabs. The cut eyelid, stitched, was monstrously swollen and black. The nose was crimson under some shaping plaster-of-paris, which had been stuck onto forehead and cheeks with white sticky tape. Her mouth, open and also swollen, looked purple. All the rest showed deep signs of bruising: crimson, gray, black and yellow. Fresh, the injuries had looked merely nasty: it was in the healing process that their true extent showed.

I'd seen people in that state before, and worse than that, damaged by horses' galloping hooves; but this, done out of malice to an inoffensive lady in her own home, was differently disturbing. I felt not sympathy but anger: Steve's "I'll kill the bastards" anger.

She heard me come in, and opened her less battered

eye a fraction as I approached. What I could see of her expression looked merely blank, as if I was the last person she would have expected.

"Steve asked me to come," I said. "He couldn't get here because of his shoulder. He can't drive . . . not for a day or two."

The eye closed.

I fetched a chair from against the wall and put it by the bed, to sit beside her. The eye opened again; and then her hand, which had been lying on the blanket, slowly stretched out towards me. I took it, and she gripped me hard, holding on fiercely, seeking, it seemed, support and comfort and reassurance. The spirit of need ebbed after a while, and she let go of my hand and put her own weakly back on the blanket.

"Did Steve tell you," she said, "about the house?"

"Yes, he did. I'm so sorry." It sounded feeble. Anything sounded feeble in the face of such knocks as she'd taken.

"Have you seen it?" she said.

"No. Steve told me about it at the races. At Kempton, this afternoon."

Her speech was slurred and difficult to understand; she moved her tongue as if it were stiff inside the swollen lips.

"My nose is broken," she said, fluttering her fingers on the blanket.

"Yes," I said. "I broke mine once. They put a plaster on me, too, just like yours. You'll be as good as new in a week."

Her silent response couldn't be interpreted as anything but dissent.

"You'll be surprised," I said.

There was the sort of pause that occurs at hospital bedsides. Perhaps it was there that the ward system scored, I thought: when you'd run out of platitudes you could always discuss the gruesome symptoms in the next bed.

"George said you took photographs, like him," she said.

"Not like him," I said. "George was the best."

No dissent at all, this time. Discernibly the intention of a smile.

"Steve told me you'd had George's boxes of transparencies moved out before the fire," I said. "That was lucky."

Her smile, however, disappeared, and was slowly replaced by distress.

"The police came today," she said. A sort of shudder shook her, and her breathing grew more troubled. She could get no air through her nose so the change was audible and rasped in her throat.

"They came here?" I asked.

"Yes. They said . . . Oh God . . ." Her chest heaved and she coughed.

I put my hand flatly over hers on the blanket and said urgently, "Don't get upset. You'll make everything hurt worse. Just take three slow deep breaths. Four or five, if you need them. Don't talk until you can make it cold."

She lay silent for a while until the heavy breathing slackened. I watched the tightened muscles relax under the blanket, and eventually she said, "You're much older than Steve."

"Eight years," I agreed, letting go of her hand.

"No. Much . . . much older." There was a pause. "Could you give me some water?"

There was a glass on the locker beside her bed. Water in the glass, angled tube for drinking. I steered the tube to her mouth, and she sucked up a couple of inches.

"Thanks." Another pause, then she tried again, this time much more calmly. "The police said . . . The police said it was arson."

"Did they?"

"You're not . . . surprised?"

"After two burglaries, no."

"Paraffin," she said. "Five-gallon drum. Police found it in the hall."

"Was it your paraffin?"

"No."

Another pause.

"The police asked . . . if George had any enemies." She moved her head restlessly. "I said of course not . . . and they asked . . . if he had anything someone would want . . . enough . . . enough . . . oh . . ."

"Mrs. Millace," I said matter-of-factly. "Did they ask if George had any photographs worth burglary and burning?"

"George wouldn't . . ." she said intensely.

George had, I thought.

"Look," I said slowly, "you might not want me to . . . you might not trust me . . . but if you like I could look through those transparencies for you, and I could tell you if I thought there were any which could possibly come into the category we're talking about."

After a while she said only, "Tonight?"

"Yes, certainly. Then if they're OK you can tell the police they exist . . . if you want to."

"George isn't a blackmailer," she said. Coming from the swollen mouth the words sounded extraordinary, distorted but passionately meant. She was not saying, "I don't want to believe George would blackmail anyone," but "George didn't." Yet she hadn't been sure enough to give the transparencies to the police. Emotionally sure. Rationally unsure. In a nonsensical way, that made sense.

She hadn't much left except that instinctive faith. It was beyond me entirely to tell her it was misplaced.

I collected the three metal boxes from the neighbor, who had been told, it appeared, that they contained just odds and ends the burglars had missed, and I was given in exchange a conducted tour of the burned mess next door.

Even in the dark one could see that there was nothing

to salvage. Five gallons of paraffin had made no mistake. The house was a shell, roofless, windowless, acrid and creaking; and it was to this savage destruction that Marie would have to return.

I drove home with George's life's work and spent the rest of the evening and half of the night projecting his slides onto the flat white wall of my sitting room.

His talent had been stupendous. Seeing his pictures there together, one after the other, and not scattered in books and newspapers and magazines across a canvas of years, I was struck continually by the speed of his vision. He had caught life over and over and over again at the moment when a painter would have composed it: nothing left out, nothing disruptive let in. An absolute master.

The best of his racing pictures were there, some in color, some in black and white, but there were also several stunning series on unexpected subjects like card players and alcoholics and giraffes and sculptors in action and hot Sundays in New York. These series stretched back almost to George's youth, the date and place being written on each mount in tiny fine-nibbed letters.

There were dozens of portraits of people: some posed in a studio, mostly not. Again and again he had caught the fleeting expression which exposed the soul, and even if he had originally taken twenty shots to keep but one, the ones he had kept were collectively breathtaking.

Pictures of France. Paris, St. Tropez, cycle racing, fish docks. No pictures of people sitting outside cafes, talking to who they shouldn't.

When I'd got to the end of the third box I sat for a while thinking of what George hadn't photographed, or hadn't in any case kept.

No wars. No riots. No horrors. No mangled bodies or starving children or executions or cars bombed apart by terrorists.

What had yelled from my wall for hours had been a satirical baring of the essence under the external; and perhaps George had felt the external satire of violence left him nothing to say.

I was rather deeply aware that I was never going to see the world in quite the same way again: that George's piercing view of things would intrude when I least expected it and nudge me in the ribs. But George had had no compassion. The pictures were brilliant. Objective, exciting, imaginative and revealing; but none of them kind.

None of them either, in any way that I could see, could have been used as a basis for blackmail.

I telephoned to Marie Millace in the morning, and told her so. The relief in her voice when she answered betrayed the existence of her doubts, and she heard it herself and immediately began a cover-up.

"I mean," she said, "of course, I knew George wouldn't . . ."

"Of course," I said. "What shall I do with the pictures?"

"Oh dear, I don't know. No one will try to steal them now though, will they?" The mumbling voice was even less distinct over the wire. "What do you think?"

"Well," I said. "You can't exactly advertise that although George's pictures still exist no one needs to feel threatened. So I do think they may still be at risk."

"But that means . . . that means . . ."

"I'm terribly sorry. I know it means that I agree with the police. That George did have something which someone desperately wanted destroyed. But please don't worry. Please don't. Whatever it was has probably gone with the house . . . and it's all over." And God forgive me, I thought.

"Oh dear . . . George didn't . . . I know he didn't . . ."

I could hear the distress rising again in the noise of her breathing.

"Listen," I said quickly. "About those transparencies. Are you listening?"

"Yes."

"I think the best thing for now would be to put them into cold storage somewhere. Then when you feel better, you could get an agent to put on an exhibition of George's work. The collection is marvelous, it really is. An exhibition would celebrate his talent, and make you a bit of money . . . and also reassure anyone who might be worrying that there was nothing to . . . er . . . worry about."

There was a silence, but I knew she was still there, because of the breathing.

"George wouldn't use an agent," she said at last. "How could I find one?"

"I know one or two. I could give you their names."

"Oh . . ." She sounded weak and there was another long pause. Then she said, "I know . . . I'm asking such a lot . . . but could you . . . put those transparencies into storage? I'd ask Steve . . . but you seem to know . . . what to do."

I said that I would, and when we disconnected I wrapped the three boxes in their plastic sheets and took them along to the local butcher, who already kept a box of my own in his walk-in freezer room. He cheerfully agreed to the extra lodgers, suggested a reasonable rental, and gave me a receipt.

Back home I looked at the negative and the print of Elgir Yaxley talking to Terence O'Tree, and wondered what on earth I should do with them.

If George had extorted from Elgin Yaxley all the profits from the murdered horses—and it looked as if he must have done, because of Bart Underfield's gloominess and Yaxley's own disappearance from racing—then it had to be Elgin Yaxley who was now desperate to find the photograph before anyone else did.

If Elgin Yaxley had arranged the burglaries, the beating-up and the burning, should retribution not follow? If I gave the photograph to the police, with explanations, Elgin Yaxley would be in line for prosecution for most crimes on the statutes, not least perjury and defrauding an insurance company of a hundred and fifty thousand.

If I gave the photograph to the police, I was telling the world that George Millace had been a blackmailer.

Which would Marie Millace prefer, I thought: never to know who had attacked her, or to know for sure that George had been a villain . . . and to have everyone else know it too.

There was no doubt about the answer.

I had no qualms about legal justice. I put the negative back where I'd found it, in its envelope stuck onto the back of the dark print in its paper mount. I put the mount back into the box of rubbish which still lay on the kitchen dresser, and I put the clear big print I'd make into a folder in the filing cabinet in the hall.

No one knew I had them. No one would come looking. No one would burgle or burn my house, or beat me up. Nothing at all would happen from now on.

I locked my doors and went to the races to ride Tishoo and Sharpener and to agonize over that other thorny problem, Victor Briggs.

7

Ivor den Relgan was again the big news, and what was more, he was there.

I saw him immediately when I arrived, as he was standing just outside the weighing room door talking to two reporters. I was a face among many to him, but to me, as to everyone else whose business was racing, he was as recognizable as a poppy in corn.

He wore, as he often did, an expensively soft camel-colored coat, buttoned and belted, and he stood bare-headed with graying hair neatly brushed, a stocky slightly pugnacious-looking man with an air of expecting people to notice his presence. A lot of people considered it a plus to be in his favor, but for some reason I found his self-confidence repellent, and his strong gravitational pull was something I instinctively resisted.

I would have been more than happy never to have come into his focus, but as I was passing one of the reporters shot out a hand and fastened it on my arm.

"Philip," he said, "you can tell us. You're always on the business end of a camera."

"Tell you what?" I said, hovering in midstride, and intending to walk on.

"How do you photograph a wild horse?"

"Point and click," I said pleasantly.

"No, Philip," he said, exasperated. "You know Mr. den Relgan, don't you?"

I inclined my head slightly and said, "By sight."

"Mr. den Relgan, this is Philip Nore. Jockey, of course." The reporter was unaccustomedly obsequious: I'd noticed den Relgan often had that effect. "Mr. den Relgan wants photographs of all his horses, but one of them rears up all the time when he sees a camera. How would you get him to stand still?"

"I know one photographer," I said, "who got a wild horse to stand still by playing a tape of a hunt in full cry. The horse just stood and listened. The pictures were great."

Den Relgan smiled superciliously as if he didn't want to hear good ideas that weren't his own, and I nodded with about as much fervor and went on into the weighing room thinking that the Jockey Club must have been mad. The existing members of the Jockey Club were for the most part forward-looking people who put good will and energy into running a huge industry fairly. That they were also self-electing meant in practice that they were almost all aristocrats or upper class, but the ideal of service bred into them worked pretty well for the good of racing. The old autocratic change-resistant bunch had died out, and there were fewer bitter jokes nowadays about boneheads at the top. All the more surprising that they should have beckoned to a semi-phony like den Relgan.

Harold was inside the weighing room talking to Lord White, which gave me a frisson like seeing a traffic warden standing next to one's wrongly parked car; but it appeared that Lord White, powerful steward of the Jockey Club, was not enquiring into the outcome of the Sandown Pattern 'Chase, nor into any other committed sins. He was telling Harold that there was a special trophy for Sharpener's race, and, should he happen to win it, both Harold and I, as well as the owner, would be required to put in an appearance and receive our gifts.

"It wasn't advertised as a sponsored race," Harold said, surprised.

"No . . . but Mr. den Relgan has generously made this gesture. And incidentally it will be his daughter who does the actual presentations." He looked directly at me. "Nore, isn't it?"

"Yes, sir."

"You heard all that? Good. Fine." He nodded, turned, and left us, crossing to speak to another trainer with a runner in the same race.

"How many trophies does it take," Harold said under his breath, "to buy your way into the Jockey Club?" And in a normal voice he added, "Victor's here."

I said anxiously, "But Sharpener will do his best."

Harold looked amused. "Yes, he will. This time. Win that pot if you can. It would really give Victor a buzz, taking Ivor den Relgan's cup. They can't stand each other."

"I didn't know they knew—"

"Everyone knows everyone," Harold said, shrugging. "I think they belong to the same gaming club." He lost interest and went out of the weighing room, and I stood for a few aimless moments watching Lord White make his way towards yet another trainer to pass on the instructions.

Lord White, in his fifties, was a well-built goodlooking man with thick light-gray hair progressively turning the color of his name. He had disconcertingly bright blue eyes and a manner that disarmed anyone advancing on him with a grievance; and it was he, although not senior steward, who was the true leader of the Jockey Club, elected not by votes but by the natural force born in him.

An upright man, widely respected, whose nickname Driven Snow (spoken only behind his back) had been coined, I thought, only partly through admiration and mostly to poke fun at the presence of so much noticeable virtue.

I went off to the changing room and on into the business of the day, and was guiltily relieved to find Steve Millace had not made the journey. No beseeching eyes and general helplessness to inveigle me into yet another round of fetching and carrying and visiting the sick. I changed into Tishoo's colors and thought only about the race, which was for novices over hurdles.

In the event there were no great problems but no repeat either of the previous day's joys. Tishoo galloped willingly enough into fourth place at the finish, which pleased his woman owner, and I carried my saddle to the scales to be weighed in, and so back to my changing-room peg to put on Victor Brigg's colors for Sharpener. Just another day's work. Each day unique in itself, but in essence the same. On two thousand days, or thereabouts, I had gone into changing rooms and put on colors and passed the scales and ridden the races. Two thousand days of hope and effort and sweat and just and unjust rewards. More than a job: part of my fabric.

I put on a jacket over Victor Briggs' colors, because there were two other races to be run before Sharpener's, and went outside for a while to see what was happening in general; and what was happening in particular was Lady White with a scowl on her thin aristocratic face.

Lady White didn't know me especially, but I, along with most other jump jockeys, had shaken her hand as she stood elegantly at Lord White's side at two parties they had given to the racing world. They had been large everyone-invited affairs three or four years apart, held at Cheltenham racecourse during the March meeting; and they had been Lord White's own idea, paid for by him, and given, one understood, because of his belief that everyone in jump racing belonged at heart to a brotherhood of friends, and should meet as such to enjoy themselves. Old

Driven Snow at his priceless best, and like everyone else
I'd gone to the parties and enjoyed them.

Lady White was hugging her mink around her and almost glaring from under a wide-brimmed brown hat. Her
intensity was such that I followed her gaze and found it
fixed on her paragon of a husband, who was himself talking to a girl.

Lord White was not simply talking to the girl but rev-
eling in it, radiating flirtatious fun from his sparkling eyes
to his gesturing fingertips. I looked sardonically back from
this picture telling the old old story and found Lady
White's attention still balefully fixed on it, and I thought
in amusement, "Oh dear," as one does. The pure white
lord, that evening, would be in for an unaristocratic ticking off.

Ivor den Relgan was still holding court in a clutch of
journalists, among whom were two racing writers and
three gossip columnists from the larger daily papers. Ivor
den Relgan was definitely a gossip man's man.

Bart Underfield was loudly telling an elderly married
couple that Osborne should know better than to run Sharpener in a three-mile 'chase when any fool knew that the
horse couldn't go further than two. The elderly couple
nodded, impressed.

I gradually became aware that a man standing near me
was also, like Lady White, intently watching Lord White
and the girl. The man near me was physically unremarkable; an average man no longer young, not quite middleaged, with dark thinning hair and black-framed glasses.
He was wearing gray trousers, olive-green jacket, suede,
not tweed, well-cut. When he realized that I was looking
at him, he gave me a quick annoyed glance and moved
away; and I thought no more about him for another hour.

Victor Briggs, when I joined him in the parade ring
before Sharpener's race, was heavily pleasant and made
no reference to the issue hanging between us. Harold had
boosted himself into a state of confidence and was stand-

ing with his long legs apart, his hat tipped back on his head, and his binoculars swinging rhythmically from one hand.

"A formality," he was saying. "Sharpener's never been better, eh, Philip? Gave you a good feel on the Downs, didn't he? Worked like a train." His robust voice floated easily over several nearby owner-trainer-jockey groups who were all suffering from their own prerace tensions and could have done without Harold's.

"Jumping out of his skin," Harold said, booming. "Never been better. He'll run the legs off 'em, today, eh, Victor?"

The only good thing one could say about Harold's bursts of overconfidence was that if in the event they proved to be misplaced he would not relapse into acrimony and gloom. Failures were apt to be expansively forgiven with "it was the weight that beat him, of course" and were seldom held to be the jockey's fault, even when they were.

Sharpener himself reacted to Harold's optimism in a thoroughly positive way, and encouraged also perhaps by my confidence left over from the two winners the day before, ran a faultless race with energy and courage, so that for the third time at that meeting my mount returned to applause.

Harold was metaphorically by this time two feet off the ground, and even Victor allowed his mouth a small smile.

Ivor den Relgan manfully shaped up to the fact that his fancy trophy had been won by a man he disliked, and Lord White fluttered around the girl he'd been talking to, clearing a passage for her through the throng.

When I'd weighed in and handed my saddle to my valet, and combed my hair and gone out to the prizegiving, the scene had sorted itself out into a square table with a blue cloth bearing one large silver object and two smaller ones surrounded by Lord White, the girl, Ivor den Relgan, Victor and Harold.

Lord White said through a hand microphone to the small watching crowd that Miss Dana den Relgan would present the trophies so kindly given by her father; and it cannot have been only in my mind that the cynical speculation arose. Was it the Dad that Lord White wanted in the Jockey Club, or Dad's daughter? Perish the thought. Lord White with a girlfriend? Impossible.

At close quarters it was clear that he was attracted beyond sober good sense. He touched her continually under the guise of arranging everyone suitably for the presentations, and he was vivacious where normally staid. It all remained just within the acceptable limits of roguishly avuncular behavior, but discreet it was not.

Dana den Relgan was enough, I supposed, to excite any man she cared to respond to; and to Lord White she was responding with sweetness. Slender and graceful and not very tall, she had a lot of blonde-flecked hair curling casually onto her shoulders. There was also a curving mouth, wide spread eyes, excellent skin, and a quality of being smarter than her looks would suggest. Her manner was observably more restrained than Lord White's, as if she didn't dislike his attentions but thought them too obvious, and she presented the trophies to Victor and Harold and myself without much conversation.

To me she said merely, "Well done," and gave me the small silver object (which turned out to be a saddle-shaped paper-weight) with the bright surface smile of someone who isn't really looking at you and is going to forget you again within five minutes. Her voice, from what I heard of it, held the same modified American accent as her father's, but in her it lacked the patronizing quality and was, to me at least, attractive. A pretty girl but not mine. Life was full of them.

While Victor and Harold and I compared trophies, the average-looking man in spectacles reappeared, walking quietly up to Dana den Relgan's shoulder and speaking softly into her ear. She turned away from the presentation table and began slowly to move off with him, smiling a little, and listening to what he was saying.

This apparently harmless proceeding had the most extraordinary effect upon den Relgan, who stopped looking fatuously pleased with himself in one five-hundredth of a second and flung himself into action. He almost ran after his daughter, gripped the inoffensive-looking man by the shoulder and threw him away from her with such force that he staggered and went down on one knee.

"I've told you to keep away from her," den Relgan said, looking as if kicking a man when he was down was something he had no reservations about; and Lord White muttered, "I say," and, "Oh dear," and looked embarrassed.

"Who is that man?" I asked of no one in particular, and it was Victor Briggs, surprisingly, who answered.

"Film director. Fellow called Lance Kinship."

"And why the fuss?"

Victor Briggs knew the answer, but it took a fair amount of internal calculation before he decided to part with it. "Cocaine," he said finally. "White powder, for sniffing straight up the nose. Very fashionable. All these stupid little girls . . . their noses will collapse when the bone dissolves, and then where will they be?"

Both Harold and I looked at him with astonishment; it was the longest speech I'd ever heard him make, and certainly the only one containing any private opinion.

"Lance Kinship supplies it," he said. "He gets asked to parties for what he takes along."

Lance Kinship was up on his feet and brushing dirt off his trousers; setting his glasses firmly on his nose and looking murderous.

"If I want to talk to Dana, I'll talk to her," he said.

"Not while I'm there, you won't."

Den Relgan's Jockey Club manners were in tatters and

the bedrock under the camouflage was plainly on view. A
bully, I thought; a bad enemy, even if his cause was just.

Lance Kinship seemed unintimidated. "Little girls
don't always have their daddies with them," he said nastily; and den Relgan hit him; a hard sharp efficient crunch
on the nose.

Noses bleed easily, and there was a good deal of gore.
Lance Kinship tried to wipe it away with his hands and
succeeded only in smearing it all over his face. It poured
down on his mouth and chin, and fell in big splashing
drops on his olive suede jacket.

Lord White, hating the whole thing, stretched out an
arm towards Kinship and held out a huge white handkerchief as if with tongs. Kinship grabbed it without thanks
and soaked it scarlet as he tried to staunch the flow.

"First aid room, don't you think?" Lord White said,
looking around. "Er . . . Nore," he said, his gaze alighting.
"You know where the first aid room is, don't you? Take
this gentleman there, would you? Awfully good of
you . . ." He waved me towards the errand, but when I put
a hand out towards the olive-green sleeve, to guide Kinship in the direction of cold compresses and succor, he
jerked away from me.

"Bleed, then," I said.

Unfriendly eyes behind the black frames glared out at
me, but he was too busy mopping to speak.

"I'll show you," I said. "Follow if you want."

I set off past the parade ring towards the green-painted
hut where the motherly ladies would be waiting to patch
up the damaged, and not only did Kinship follow, but den
Relgan also. I heard his voice as clearly as Kinship did,
and there was no doubt about the message.

"If you come near Dana again, I'll break your neck."

Kinship again didn't answer.

Den Relgan said, "Did you hear, you vicious little
shit?"

We had gone far enough for there to be plenty of people blocking us from the view of the group outside the weighing room. I heard a scuffle behind me and looked over my shoulder in time to see Kinship aim a hard karate kick at den Relgan's crotch and land deftly on target. Kinship turned back to me and gave me another unfriendly stare over the reddening handkerchief, which he had held uninterruptedly to his nose.

Den Relgan was making choking noises and clutching himself. The whole fracas was hardly what one expected as the outcome of a decorous racecourse presentation on a Thursday afternoon.

"In there," I said to Kinship, jerking my head, and he gave me a final reptilian glance as the first aid room opened its doors. Den Relgan said "aaah . . ." and walked around in a small circle half doubled over, one hand pressed hard under the lower front of his camel-hair coat.

A pity George Millace had gone to his fathers, I thought. He of all people would have relished the ding-dong, and he, unlike everyone else, would have been there with his lens sharply focused, pointing the right way and taking inexorable notes at three-point-five frames per second. Den Relgan could thank George's couple of scotches and a tree in the wrong place that he wouldn't find his tangle with Kinship illustrating in the daily papers the edifying news of his elevation to the Jockey Club.

Harold and Victor Briggs were still where I'd left them, but Lord White and Dana den Relgan had gone.

"His lordship took her off to calm her nerves," Harold said dryly. "The old goat's practically dancing around her, silly fool."

"She's pretty," I said.

"Wars have been fought for pretty girls," said Victor Briggs.

I looked at him with renewed astonishment and received in return the usual stonewall closed-in expression. Victor might have unexpected hidden depths, but that was just what they still were, hidden.

* * *

When I left the weighing room to set off for home I was apologetically intercepted by the tall loitering figure of Jeremy Folk.

"I don't believe it," I said.

"I did . . . er . . . warn you."

"So you did."

"Could I . . . um . . . have a word with you?"

"What do you want?"

"Ah yes . . . well . . ."

"The answer's no," I said.

"But you don't know what I'm going to ask."

"I can see that it's something I don't want to do."

"Um," he said. "Your grandmother asks you to visit her."

"Absolutely not," I said.

There was a pause. People around us were going home, calling goodnights. It was four o'clock. Goodnights started early in the racing world.

"I went to see her," Jeremy said. "I told her you wouldn't look for your sister for money. I told her she would have to give you something else."

I was puzzled. "Give me what?"

Jeremy looked vaguely around from his great height and said, "You could find her, couldn't you, if you really tried?"

"I don't think so."

"But you might."

I didn't answer, and his attention came gently back to my face.

"Your grandmother agreed," he said, "that she had a flaming row with Caroline . . . your mother . . . and chucked her out when she was pregnant."

"My mother," I said, "was seventeen."

"Um. That's right." He smiled. "Funny, isn't it, to think of one's mother being so *young*."

Poor defenseless little butterfly . . . "Yes," I said.

"Your grandmother says . . . has agreed . . . that if you
will look for Amanda she will tell you why she threw
Caroline out. And also she will tell you who your father
is."

"My God!"

I took two compulsive steps away from him, and
stopped, and turned, and stared at him.

"Is that what you said to her?" I demanded. "Tell him
who his father is, and he'll do what you want?"

"You don't know who your father is," he said reason-
ably. "But you'd want to know, wouldn't you?"

"No," I said.

"I don't believe you."

We practically glared at each other.

"You have to want to know," he said. "It's human nature."

I swallowed. "Did she tell you who he is?"

He shook his head. "No. She didn't. She's apparently
never told anyone. No one at all. If you don't go and find
out, you'll never know."

"You're a real bastard, Jeremy," I said.

He wriggled his body with an embarrassment he didn't
actually feel. The light in his eyes, which would have
done a checkmating chessplayer justice, was a far more
accurate indicator of how he operated.

I said bitterly, "I thought solicitors were supposed to
sit behind desks and pontificate, not go tearing about ma-
nipulating old ladies."

"This particular old lady is a . . . a challenge."

I had an idea he had changed his sentence in midstride,
but I said only, "Why doesn't she leave her money to her
son?"

"I don't know. She won't give reasons. She told my
grandfather simply that she wanted to cancel her old will,
which left everything to her son, and make a new one in
favor of Amanda. The son will contest it, of course.

We've told her that, but it makes no difference. She's . . . er . . . stubborn."

"Have you met her son?"

"No," he said. "Have you?"

I shook my head. Jeremy took another long vague look around the racecourse and said, "Why don't we get cracking on this together? We'd turn Amanda up in no time, wouldn't we? Then you could go back into your shell and forget the whole thing, if you want."

"You couldn't forget . . . who your father was."

His gaze sharpened instantly. "Are you on, then?"

He would persevere, I thought, with or without my help. He would bother me whenever he wanted, catch me at the races any day he cared to read the programs in the newspapers, and never let up, because he wanted, as he'd told me at the beginning, to prove to his grandfather and uncle that when he set his mind to sorting something out, it got sorted.

As for me . . . the mists around my birth were there for the parting. The cataclysm which had echoed like a storm receding over the horizon through my earliest memories could at last be explained and understood. I could learn what the shouting had been about behind the white-painted door, while I waited in the hall in my new clothes.

I might in the event detest the man who'd fathered me. I might be horrified. I might wish I hadn't been told anything about him. But Jeremy was right. Given the chance . . . one had to know.

"Well?" he said.

"All right."

"Find her together?"

"Yes."

He was visibly pleased. "That's great."

I wasn't so sure; but it was settled.

"Can you go this evening?" he said. "I'll telephone and tell her you're coming." He plunged lankily towards the public telephone box and disappeared inside with his eyes switched anxiously my way, watching all through his call to make sure I didn't go back on my decision and scram.

The call, however, gave him no joy.

"Blast," he said, rejoining me. "I spoke to a nurse. Mrs. Nore had a bad day and they've given her an injection. She's asleep. No visitors. Ring tomorrow."

I felt a distinct sense of relief, which he noticed.

"It's all very well for you," I said. "But how would you like to be on the verge of finding out that you owe your existence to a quickie in the bushes with the milkman?"

"Is that what you think?"

"Something like that. It has to be, doesn't it?"

"All the same . . ." he said doubtfully.

"All the same," I agreed resignedly, "one wants to know."

I set off towards the parking lot thinking that Jeremy's errand was concluded, but it appeared not. He came in my wake, but slowly, so that I looked back and waited.

"About Mrs. Nore's son," he said. "Her son James."

"What about him?"

"I just thought you might visit him. Find out why he's been disinherited."

"You just thought . . ."

"As we're working together," he said hastily.

"You could go yourself," I suggested.

"Er, no," he said. "As Mrs. Nore's solicitor, I'd be asking questions I shouldn't."

"And I can just see this James bird answering mine."

He pulled a card out of his charcoal pocket. "I brought his address," he said, holding it out. "And you've promised to help."

"A pact is a pact," I said, and took the card. "But you're still a bastard.

8

James Nore lived in London, and since I was more than halfway there I drove straight from the races to the house on Camden Hill. I hoped all the way there that he would be out, but when I'd found the street and the number and pressed the right bell, the door was opened by a man of about forty who agreed that James Nore was his name.

He was astounded, as well he might be, to find an unknown nephew standing unannounced on his mat, but with only a slight hesitation he invited me in, leading the way into a sitting room crammed with Victorian bric-a-brac and vibrant with color.

"I thought Caroline had aborted you," he said baldly. "Mother said the child had been got rid of."

He was nothing like my memories of his sister. He was plump, soft-muscled and small-mouthed, and had a mournful droop to his eyes. None of her giggly lightness or grace of movement or hectic speed could ever have lived in his flaccid body. I felt ill at ease with him on sight, disliking my errand more by the minute.

He listened with his small lips pouted while I explained

about looking for Amanda, and he showed more and more annoyance.

"The old bag's been saying for months that she's going to cut me off," he said furiously. "Ever since she came here." He glanced around the room, but nothing there seemed to me likely to alienate a mother. "Everything was all right as long as I went to Northamptonshire now and then. Then she came *here*. Uninvited. The old bag."

"She's ill now," I said.

"Of course she is." He flung out his arms in an exaggerated gesture. "I suggest visiting. She says no. Won't see me. Pigheaded old crone."

A brass clock on the mantelshelf sweetly chimed the half hour, and I took note that everything there was of fine quality and carefully dusted. James Nore's bric-a-brac wasn't just junk but antiques.

"I'd be a fool to help you find this wretched second by-blow of Caroline's, wouldn't I?" he said. "If no one can find her, the whole estate reverts to me anyway, will or no will. But I'd have to wait years for it. Years and years. Mother's just being spiteful."

"Why?" I said mildly.

"She loved Noel Coward," he said resentfully, meaning, by the sound of it, if she loved Noel Coward she should have loved *him*.

"The abstract," I said, enlightened, "isn't always the same as the particular."

"I didn't want her to come here. It would have saved all this fuss if she hadn't." He shrugged. "Are you going now? There's no point in your staying."

He began to walk towards the door, but before he reached it, it was opened by a man wearing a plastic cooking apron and limply carrying a wooden spoon. He was much younger than James, naturally camp, and unmistakable.

"Oh, hello dear," he said, seeing me. "Are you staying for supper?"

"He's just going," James said sharply. "He's not . . . er . . ."

They both stood back to leave me room to pass, and as I went out into the hall I said to the man in the apron, "Did you meet Mrs. Nore when she came here?"

"Sure did, dear," he said ruefully, and then caught sight of James shaking his head vigorously at him and meaning shut up. I smiled halfheartedly at a point in the air near their heads, and went to the front door.

"I wish you bad luck," James said. "That beastly Caroline, spawning all over the place. I never did like her."

"Do you remember her?"

"Always laughing at me and tripping me up. I was glad when she went."

I nodded, and opened the door.

"Wait," he said suddenly.

He came towards me along the hall, and I could see he had had an idea that pleased him.

"Mother would never leave *you* anything, of course," he began.

"Why not?" I said.

He frowned. "There was a terrible drama, wasn't there, when Caroline got pregnant? Frightful scenes. Lots of screaming. I remember it . . . but no one would ever explain. All I do know is that everything changed because of you. Caroline went and Mother turned into a bitter old bag and I had beastly miserable years in that big house with her, before I left. She hated you . . . the thought of you. Do you know what she called you? 'Caroline's disgusting fetus,' that's what. Caroline's disgusting fetus."

He peered at me expectantly, but in truth I felt nothing. The old woman's hatred hadn't troubled me for years.

"I'll give you some of the money, though," he said, "if you can prove that Amanda is dead."

On Saturday morning Jeremy Folk telephoned.

"Will you be at home tomorrow?" he said.

"Yes, but . . ."

"Good. I'll be over." He put down his receiver without giving me a chance to say I didn't want him. It was an advance, I supposed, that he'd announced his visit and not simply turned up.

Also on Saturday I ran into Bart Underfield in the post office and in place of our usual unenthusiastic "good mornings" I asked him a question.

"Where is Elgin Yaxley these days, Bart?"

"Hong Kong," he said.

"For a holiday?" I said.

"Of course not. He lives there."

"But he's over here now, isn't he?"

"No, he isn't. He'd've told me."

"But he must be," I said insistently.

Bart said irritably, "Why must he be? He isn't. He's working for a bloodstock agency and they don't give him much time off. And what's it to do with you?"

"I just thought . . . I saw him."

"You couldn't have. When?"

"Oh . . . last week. A week ago yesterday."

"Well, you're wrong," Bart said triumphantly. "That was the day of George Millace's funeral, and Elgin sent me a cable . . ." He hesitated and his eyes flickered, but he went on. "And the cable came from Hong Kong."

"A cable of regrets, was it?"

"George Millace," Bart said with venom, "was a shit."

"You didn't go to the funeral yourself, then?"

"Are you crazy? I'd have spat on his coffin."

"Catch you bending with his camera, did he Bart?"

He narrowed his eyes and didn't answer.

"Oh well," I said, shrugging, "I must say a good many people will be relieved now he's gone."

"More like down on their knees giving thanks."

"Do you ever hear anything nowadays about that chap who shot Elgin's horses? What's his name . . . Terence O'Tree?"

"He's still in jail," Bart said.

"But," I said, counting with my fingers, "March, April, May . . . he should be out by now."

"He lost his remission," Bart said. "He hit a warder."

"How do you know?" I asked curiously.

"I . . . er . . . heard." He had suddenly had too much of this conversation, and began backing away.

"And did you hear also that George Millace's house had burned down?" I said.

He nodded. "Of course. Heard it at the races."

"And that it was arson?"

He stopped in midstride. "Arson?" he said, looking surprised. "Why would anyone want . . . ? Oh!" He abruptly at that point understood why; and I thought that he couldn't possibly have achieved that revelationary expression by art.

He hadn't known.

Elgin Yaxley was in Hong Kong and Terence O'Tree was in jail, and neither they nor Bart Underfield had burgled or beaten or burned. ·

The easy explanations were all wrong.

I had jumped, I thought penitently, to conclusions.

It was only because I'd disliked George Millace that I'd been so ready to believe ill of him. He had taken that incriminating photograph, but there was really nothing to prove that he'd used it, except that Elgin Yaxley had taken a paid job in Hong Kong instead of plowing his insurance money back into racehorses. Still any man had a right to do that. It didn't make him a villain.

Yet he had been a villain. He had sworn he'd never met Terence O'Tree, and he had. And it had to have been before the trial in February at least, since O'Tree had been in jail ever since. Not during the winter months just before the trial either, because it had been siting-in-the-street weather; and there had been . . . I had unconsciously noticed and now remembered . . . there had been a newspaper lying on the table in front of the Frenchman, on which one might possibly see a date.

I walked slowly and thoughtfully home, and projected my big new print hugely onto the sitting room wall through an epidiascope.

The Frenchman's newspaper lay too flat on the table. Neither the date nor any useful headlines could be seen.

Regretfully I studied the rest of the picture for anything at all which might date it; in the background, beside Madame at her cash desk inside the cafe, there was a calendar hanging on a hook. The letters and numbers on it could be discerned by the general shape even if not with pin-sharp clarity, and they announced that it was *Avril* of the previous year.

Elgin Yaxley's horses had been sent out to grass late that same month, and they had been shot on the fourth of May.

I switched off the projector and drove to Windsor races puzzling over the inconsistencies and feeling that I had gone around a corner in a maze confidently expecting to have reached the center only to find myself in a dead end surrounded by ten-foot hedges.

It was a moderate day's racing at Windsor, all the star names having gone to the more important meeting at Cheltenham, and because of the weak opposition one of Harold's slowest old 'chasers finally had his day. Half of the rest of the equally old runners obligingly fell, and my geriatric pal with his head down in exhaustion loped in first after three and a half miles of slog.

He stood with his chest heaving in the unsaddling enclosure as I, scarcely less tired, lugged at the girth buckles and pulled off my saddle, but the surprised delight of his faithful elderly lady owner made it all well worth the effort.

"I knew he'd do it one day," she said enthusiastically. "I knew he would. Isn't he a great old boy?"

"Great," I agreed.

"It's his last season, you know. I'll have to retire him."
She patted his neck. "We're all getting on a bit, old boy,
aren't we? Can't go on forever, more's the pity. Everything ends, doesn't it, old boy? But today it's been great."

I went in and sat on the scales and her words came
with me; everything ends, but today it's been great. Ten
years had been great, but everything ends.

My mind still rebelled against the thought of retire-
ment, particularly one dictated by Victor Briggs; but
somewhere the frail seedling of acceptance was stretching
its first leaf in the dark. Life changes, everything ends. I
myself was changing. I didn't want it, but it was happening. My long contented float was slowly drifting to shore.

Outside the weighing room one wouldn't have guessed
it. I had uncharacteristically won four races that week. I
was the jockey in form. I had brought a no-hoper home.
I was offered five rides for the following week by trainers
other than Harold. The success-breeds-success syndrome
was coming up trumps. Everything on a high note, with
smiles all around. Seven days away from Daylight, and
seven leagues in mood.

I enjoyed the congratulations and thrust away the
doubt, and if anyone had asked me in that moment about
retiring I'd've said, "Oh yes . . . in five years' time."

They didn't ask me. They didn't expect me to retire.
"Retire" was a word in my mind, not in theirs.

Jeremy Folk arrived the following morning, as he'd said
he would, angling his storklike figure apologetically
through my front door and following me along to the
kitchen.

"Champagne?" I said, picking a bottle out of the refrigerator.

"It's . . . er . . . only ten o'clock," he said.

"Four winners," I said, "need celebrating. Would you
rather have coffee?"

"Er . . . actually . . . no."

He took his first sip all the same as if the wickedness of it would overwhelm him, and I thought that for all his wily ways he was a conformist at heart.

He had made an effort to be casual in his clothes: wool checked shirt, woolly tie, neat pale-blue sweater. Whatever he thought of my unbuttoned collar, unbuttoned cuffs and unshaven jaw, he didn't say. He let his gaze do its usual inventorial travel and as usual return to my face when he'd shaped his question.

"Did you see ... ah ... James Nore?"

"Yes, I did."

I gestured to him to sit on the leather-covered corner bench around the kitchen table, and joined him, with the bottle in reach.

"He's cohabiting happily on Camden Hill."

"Oh," Jeremy said. "Ah."

I smiled. "Mrs. Nore visited his house unexpectedly one day. She hadn't been there before. She met James' friend, and she realized, I suppose for the first time, that her son was one hundred per cent homosexual."

"Oh," Jeremy said, understanding much.

I nodded. "No descendants."

"So she thought of Amanda." He sighed and drank some pale gold fizz. "Are you sure he's homosexual. I mean ... did he say so?"

"As good as. But anyway, I'm used to homosexuals. I lived with two of them for a while. You get to know, somehow."

He looked slightly shocked and covered it with a relapse into the silly-ass act.

"Did you? I mean ... are you ... ? Er ... I mean ... living alone ... ? I shouldn't ask. Sorry."

"If I take someone to bed, she's female," I said mildly. "I just don't like permanence."

He buried his nose and his embarrassment in his glass, and I thought of Duncan and Charlie who had hugged and kissed and loved each other all around me for three years.

Charlie had been older than Duncan; a mature man in his
forties, solid and industrious and kind. Charlie, to me, had
been father, uncle, guardian, all in one. Duncan had been
chatty and quarrelsome and very good company, and neither of them had tried to teach me their way.

Duncan had slowly grown less chatty, more quarrelsome and less good company, and one day he fell in love
with someone else and walked out. Charlie's grief had
been white-faced and desperately deep. He had put his
arm around my shoulders and hugged me, and wept; and
I'd wept for Charlie's unhappiness.

My mother had arrived within a week, blowing in like
a whirlwind. Huge eyes, hollow cheeks, fluffy silk
scarves.

"But you must see, Charlie darling," she said, "that I
can't leave Philip with you now that Duncan's gone. Look
at him. Look at him, darling, he's hardly ugly, the way
he's grown up. Darling Charlie, you must see that he can't
stay here. Not anymore." She'd looked across at me,
bright and more brittle than I remembered, and less beautiful. "Go and pack, Philip darling. We're going down to
the country."

Charlie had come into the little boxlike room he and
Duncan had built for me in one corner of the studio, and
I'd told him I didn't want to leave him.

"Your mother's right, boy," he said. "It's time you
were off. We must do what she says."

He'd helped me pack and given me one of his cameras
as a goodbye present, and from the old life I'd been flung
straight into the new in the space of a day. That evening
I learned how to muck out a horsebox, and the next morning I started to ride.

After a week I'd written to Charlie to say I was missing
him, and he replied encouragingly that I'd soon get over
it; and get over it I did, while Charlie himself pined mis-
erably for Duncan and swallowed two hundred sleeping
pills. Charlie made a will a week before the pills leaving

all his possessions to me, including all his other cameras and darkroom equipment. He also left a letter saying he was sorry and wishing me luck.

"Look after your mother," he wrote. "I think she's sick. Keep on taking photographs, you already have the eye. You'll be all right, boy. So long now. Charlie."

I drank some champagne and said to Jeremy, "Did you get the list of the Pine Woods Lodge tenancies from the real estate agents?"

"Oh gosh, yes," he said, relieved to be back on firm ground. "I've got it here somewhere." He patted several pockets but stuck two fingers unerringly into the one where he'd stored the slip of paper he wanted; and I wondered how much energy he wasted each day in camouflage movements.

"Here we are . . ." He spread the sheet of paper out, and pointed. "If your mother was there thirteen years ago, the people she was with would have been the boy scouts, the television company, or the musicians. But the television people didn't live there, the agents say. They just worked there during the day. The musicians did live there, though. They were . . . er . . . experimental musicians, whatever that means."

"More soul than success."

He gave me a quick bright glance. "A man in the real estate agents' says he remembers they ruined the electric wiring and were supposed to be high all the time on drugs. Does any of that sound . . . er . . . like your mother?"

I pondered.

"Boy scouts don't sound like her a bit," I said. "We can leave them out. Drugs sounds like her, but musicians don't. Especially unsuccessful musicians. She never left me with anyone unsuccessful . . . or anyone musical, come to that." I thought some more. "I suppose if she was really drug-dependent by that time, she mightn't have cared. But she liked comfort." I paused again. "I think I'd try the television company first. They could at least tell us what program they were making then, and who worked on it. They're bound to have kept the credits somewhere."

Jeremy's face showed a jumble of emotions varying, I thought, from incredulity to bewilderment.

"Er . . ." he said, "I mean . . ."

"Look," I interrupted. "Just ask the questions. If I don't like them I won't answer."

"You're so frantically direct," he complained. "All right, then. What do you mean about your mother leaving you with people, and what do you mean about your mother and drugs?"

I outlined the dumping procedure and what I owed to the Deborahs, Samanthas and Chloes. Jeremy's shattered expression alone would have told me that this was not every child's experience of life.

"Drugs," I said, "are more difficult. I didn't understand about the drugs until I grew up, and I only saw her once after I was twelve . . . the day she took me away from the homosexuals and put me in the racing stable. But certainly she was taking drugs for as long as I remember. She kept me with her for a week, sometimes, and there would be a smell, an acrid distinctive smell. I smelled it again years later . . . I must have been past twenty . . . and it was marijuana. Cannabis. I smoked it when I was little. One of my mother's friends gave it to me when she was out, and she was furious. She did try, you know, in her way, to see I grew up properly. Another time a man she was with gave me some acid. She was absolutely livid."

"Acid," Jeremy said. "Do you mean LSD?"

"Yeah. I could see all the blood running through my arteries and veins, just as if the skin was transparent. I could see the bones, like X-rays. It's extraordinary. You realize the limitations of our everyday senses. I could hear sounds as if they were three-dimensional. A clock ticking. Amazing. My mother came into the room and found me wanting to fly out of the window. I could see the blood going around in her, too." I remembered it all vividly, though I'd been about five. "I didn't know why she was so angry. The man was laughing, and she slapped him." I paused. "She did keep me away from drugs. She died from heroin, I think, but she kept me free of even the sight of it."

"Why do you think she died of heroin?"

I poured refills of champagne.

"Something the racing people said. Margaret and Bill. Soon after I got there I went into the sitting room one day when they were arguing. I didn't realize at first that it was about me, but they stopped abruptly when they saw me, so then I did. Bill had been saying, 'His place is with his mother,' and Margaret interrupted, 'She's a heroin . . .' and then she saw me and stopped. It's ironic, but I was so pleased they should think my mother a heroine. I felt warmly towards them." I smiled lopsidedly. "It wasn't for years that I realized what Margaret had really been going to say was, 'She's a heroin addict.' I asked her later and she told me that she and Bill had known that my mother was taking heroin, but they didn't know, any more than I did, where to find her. They guessed, as I did, that she'd died, and of course, long before I did, they guessed why. They didn't tell me, to save me pain. Kind people. Very kind."

Jeremy shook his head. "I'm so sorry," he said.

"Don't be. It was all long ago. I never grieved for my mother. I think perhaps now that I should have done, but I didn't."

I had grieved for Charlie, though. For a short intense time when I was fifteen, and vaguely, sporadically, ever since. I used Charlie's legacy almost every day, literally in the case of photographic equipment and figuratively in the knowledge he'd given me. Any photograph I took was thanks to Charlie.

"I'll try the television people," Jeremy said.

"OK."

"And you'll see your grandmother?"

I said without enthusiasm, "I suppose so."

Jeremy half smiled. "Where else can we look? For Amanda, I mean. If your mother dumped you all over the place like that, she must have done the same for Amanda. Haven't you thought of that?"

"Yes. I have."

"Well, then?"

I was silent. All those people. All so long in the past. Chloe, Deborah, Samantha . . . all shadows without faces. I wouldn't know any of them if they walked into the room.

"What are you thinking?" Jeremy demanded.

"No one I was left with had a pony. I would have remembered a pony. I was never left where Amanda was in the photograph."

"Oh, I see."

"And I don't think," I said, "that the same friends would be pressed into looking after a second child. I very rarely went back to the same place myself. My mother at least spread the load."

Jeremy sighed. "It's all so irregular."

I said slowly, unwillingly, "I might find one place I stayed. Perhaps I could try. But even then . . . there might be different people in the house after all this time, and anyway they're unlikely to know anything about Amanda . . ."

Jeremy pounced on it. "It's a chance."

"Very distant."

"Well worth trying."

I drank some champagne and looked thoughtfully across the kitchen to where George Millace's box of rubbish lay on the dresser; and a hovering intention suddenly crystallized. Well worth trying. Why not?

"I've lost you," Jeremy said.

"Yes." I looked at him. "You're welcome to stay, but I want to spend the day on a different sort of puzzle. Nothing to do with Amanda. A sort of treasure hunt . . .

but there may be no treasure. I just want to find out."

"I don't . . ." he said vaguely, and I got up and fetched the box and put it on the table.

"Tell me what you think of that lot," I said.

He opened the box and poked through the contents, lifting things out and putting them back. From expectancy his face changed to disappointment, and he said, "They're just . . . nothing."

"Mm." I stretched over and picked out the piece of clear-looking film which was about two and a half inches across by seven inches long. "Look at that against the light."

He took the piece of film and held it up. "It's got smudges on it," he said. "Very faint. You can hardly see them."

"They're pictures," I said. "Three pictures on one-twenty roll film."

"Well . . . you can't see them."

"No," I agreed. "But if I'm careful . . . and lucky . . . we might."

He was puzzled. "How?"

"With intensifying chemicals."

"But what's the point? Why bother?"

I sucked my teeth. "I found something of great interest in that box. All those things were kept by a great photographer who was also an odd sort of man. I just think that maybe some more of those bits aren't the rubbish they look."

"But . . . which ones?"

"That's the question. Which ones . . . if any."

Jeremy took a gulp of champagne. "Let's stick to Amanda."

"You stick to Amanda. I'm better at photographs."

He watched with interest, however, while I rummaged in one of the cupboards in the darkroom.

"This all looks frightfully workmanlike," he said, doing the eye-travel around the enlargers and print processor. "I'd no idea you did this sort of thing."

I explained briefly about Charlie and finally found what I was looking for, a tucked-away bottle that I'd acquired on an American holiday three years earlier. It said Negative Intensifier on the label, followed by instructions. Most helpful. Many manufacturers printed their instructions on separate flimsy sheets of paper, which got wet or lost. I carried the bottle across to the sink, where there was a water filter fixed under the tap.

"What's that?" Jeremy asked, pointing at its round bulbous shape.

"You have to use ultra-clean soft water for photographic processing. And no iron pipes, otherwise you get a lot of little black dots on the prints."

"It's all mad," he said.

"It's precise."

In a plastic measure I mixed water and intensifier into the strength of solution that the instructions said, and poured it into the developing tray.

"I've never done this before," I said to Jeremy. "It may not work. Do you want to watch, or would you rather stay with the bubbly in the kitchen?"

"I'm . . . ah . . . absolutely riveted, as a matter of fact. What exactly are you going to do?"

"I'm going to contact-print this clear strip of film with the ultra-faint smudges onto some ordinary black-and-white paper and see what it looks like. And then I'm going to put the negative into this intensifying liquid, and after that I'm going to make another black-and-white print to see if there's any difference. And after that . . . well, we'll have to see."

He watched while I worked in dim red light, peering into the developing tray with his nose right down to the liquid.

"Can't see anything happening," he said.

"It's a bit trial-and-error," I agreed. I tried printing the clear film four times at different exposures, but all we got on the prints was a fairly uniform black, or a uniform gray, or a uniform white.

"There's nothing there," Jeremy said. "It's useless."

"Wait until we try the intensifier."

With more hope than expectation I slid the clear film into the intensifying liquid and sloshed it about for a good deal longer than the required minimum time. Then I washed it and looked at it against the light: and the ultra-faint smudges were still ultra-faint.

"No good?" Jeremy asked, disappointed.

"I don't know. I don't really know what should happen. And maybe that intensifier is too old. Some photographic chemicals lose their power with age. Shelf life, and so on."

I printed the negative again at the same variety of exposures as before, and as before we got a uniform black and a uniform dark gray, but this time on the light gray print there were patchy marks, and on the nearly white print, swirly shapes.

"Huh," Jeremy said. "Well, that's that."

We retreated to the kitchen for thought and another drink.

"Too bad," he said. "Never mind, it was impossible to start with."

I sipped the champagne and popped its bubbles round my teeth.

"I think," I said reflectively, "that we might get further if I print that negative not onto paper, but onto another film."

"Print it onto a film? Do you mean the stuff you load into cameras? I didn't know it was possible."

"Oh yes. You can print onto anything which has a photographic emulsion. And you can coat practically anything with photographic emulsion. I mean, it doesn't have to be paper, though that's the way everyone thinks of it, because of seeing snapshots in family albums, and all that. But you could coat canvas with emulsion, and print on

that. Or glass. Or wood. On the back of your hand, I dare
say, if you'd like to stand around in darkness for a while."

"Good gracious."

"Black and white, of course," I said. "Not color."

I popped a few more bubbles.

"Let's have another go, then," I said.

"You really do love this sort of thing, don't you?" Jeremy said.

"Love it? Do you mean photography . . . or puzzles?"

"Both."

"Well . . . I suppose so."

I got up and went back to the darkroom, and he again
followed to watch. In the dim red light I took a new roll
of high contrast Kodak 2556 film, pulling it off its spool
into a long strip and cutting it into five pieces. Onto each
separate piece I printed the almost-clear negative, exposing it under the white light of the enlarger for various
exposure times: one second, the shortest, up to ten seconds, the longest. After exposure each piece went into the
tray of developer, with Jeremy sloshing the liquid about.

The results, after taking each piece of film out of the
developer at what looked like the best moment and trans-
ferring it to the fixing tray, and finally washing it, were
five new positives. From those positives I repeated the
whole process, ending with negatives. Seen in bright light,
all of the new negatives were much denser than the one
I'd started with. On two of them there was a decipherable
image . . . and the smudges had come alive.

"What are you smiling at?" Jeremy demanded.

"Take a look," I said.

He held the negative strip I gave him up to the light
and said, "I can see that you've got much clearer smudges.
But they're still smudges, all the same."

"No they're not. They're three pictures of a girl and a
man."

"How can you tell?"

"You get used to reading negatives, after a while."

"And you look smug," Jeremy complained.

"To be honest," I said, "I'm dead pleased with myself. Let's finish the champagne and then do the next bit."

"What next bit?" he said, as we again drank in the kitchen.

"Positive prints from the new negatives. Black-and-white pictures. All revealed."

"What's so funny?"

"The girl's nude, more or less."

He nearly spilled his drink. "Are you sure?"

"You can see her breasts." I laughed at him. "They're the clearest part of the negatives, actually."

"What . . . I mean . . . about her face?"

"We'll see better soon. Are you hungry?"

"Good heavens. It's one o'clock."

We ate ham and tomatoes and brown toast, and finished the champagne, and then returned to the darkroom.

Printing onto paper from such faint negatives was still a critical business as again one had first to judge the exposure right and then stop the developing print at exactly the best instant and switch it to the fixer, or all that came out was a flat light or a dark gray sheet with no depth and no highlights. It took me several tries with each of the two best new strips to get truly visible results, but I finished with three pictures which were moderately clear, and more than clear enough to reveal what George had photographed. I looked at them with the bright lights on, and with a magnifying glass; and there was no chance of a mistake.

"What's the matter?" Jeremy said. "They're wonderful. Unbelievable. Why aren't you blowing your trumpets and patting yourself on the back?"

I put the finished articles into the print drier, and silently cleared up the developing trays.

"What is it?" Jeremy asked. "What's the matter?"

"They're bloody dynamite," I said.

9

I took Jeremy and the new pictures upstairs and switched on the epidiascope, which hummed slightly in its idiosyncratic way as it warmed up.

"What's that?" Jeremy said, looking at the machine.

"You must have seen one," I said, surprised. "It's pretty old, I know. I inherited it from Charlie. But all the same, they must still be around. You put things in here on this baseboard and their image is projected large and bright onto a screen—or in my case, a wall. You can project anything. Pages of books, illustrations, photographs, letters, dead leaves. All done by mirrors."

The photograph of Elgin Yaxley and Terence O'Tree still lay in position, and at the flick of a switch came into sharp focus as before, calendar and dates and all. I drew the curtains against the fading afternoon light and let the picture shine bright in the dark room. After a minute I unclamped it and took it out, and put in instead the best strip I'd made downstairs, adjusting the lens, and enlarging each third separately, showing each of the three pictures on its own.

Even in their unavoidably imperfect state, even in shades of white to dark gray, they pulsated off the wall.

The first one showed the top half of a girl as far down as the waist, and also the head and shoulders of a man. They were facing each other, the girl's head higher than the man's. Neither of them wore clothes. The man had his hands under the girl's breasts, lifting them up, with his mouth against the nipple furthest away from the camera.

"Good heavens," Jeremy said faintly.

"Mm," I said. "Do you want to see the others?"

"They didn't look so bad in snapshot size."

I projected the second picture, which was of much the same pose, except that the camera had been at a different angle, showing less of the girl's front and nearly all of the man's face.

"It's just pornography," Jeremy said.

"No, it isn't."

I unclamped the second picture and showed the third, which was different entirely. Events had moved on. The girl, whose own face this time was clearly visible, seemed to be lying on her back. The picture now stretched down to her knees, which were apart. Over her lay the man, his head turned to one side, showing his profile. His hand cupped the one visible breast, and there wasn't much doubt about the activity they were engaged in.

There was nothing to indicate where the pictures had been taken. No distinguishable background. The faint smudges on the transparent film had turned into people, but behind them there was nothing but gray.

I switched off the epidiascope and put on the room lights.

"Why do you say it isn't pornography?" Jeremy said. "What else is it?"

"I've met them," I said. "I know who they are."

He stared.

"As you're a lawyer," I said. "You can tell me. What do you do if you find out after a man's death that he may have been a blackmailer while he was alive?"

"Are you serious?"

"Absolutely."

"Well . . . ah . . . he can't be prosecuted, exactly."

"So one does nothing?"

He frowned. "Are you . . . um . . . going to tell me what you're on about?"

"Yes, I think so."

I told him about George Millace. About the burglaries, the attack on Marie Millace and the burning of their house. I told him about Elgin Yaxley and Terence O'Tree and the five murdered horses; and I told him about the lovers.

"George very carefully kept those oddments in that box," I said. "I've deciphered two of them. What if some of the others are riddles too? What if they all are?"

"And all . . . the basis for blackmail?"

"Heaven knows."

"Heaven knows . . . and you want to find out."

I slowly nodded. "It's not so much the blackmail angle, but the photographic puzzles. If George made them, I'd like to solve them. Just to see if I can. You were quite right. I do enjoy that sort of thing."

Jeremy stared at the floor. He shivered as if he were cold. He said abruptly, "I think you should destroy the whole lot."

"That's instinct, not reason."

"You have the same instinct. You said . . . dynamite."

"Well . . . someone burgled and burned George Millace's house. When I found the first picture I thought it must have been Elgin Yaxley who'd done it, but he was in Hong Kong, and it doesn't seem likely . . . And now one would think the lovers did it . . . but it might not be them either."

Jeremy stood up and moved restlessly around the room in angular uncoordinated jerks.

"I don't like the feel of it," he said. "It could be dangerous."

"To me?"

"Of course to you."

"No one knows what I've got," I said. "Except, of course, you."

His movements grew even more disturbed, his elbows bending and flapping almost as if he were imitating a bird. Agitation, I thought: real agitation, not camouflage.

"I suppose . . ." he said. "Um . . . ah . . ."

"Ask the question."

He shot me a glance. "Oh yes . . . well . . . was there any doubt . . . about the way George Millace died?"

"Dear . . . God," I said. I felt as if he'd punched the air out of my lungs. "I don't think so."

"What happened exactly?"

"He was driving home from Doncaster, and he went to sleep and ran into a tree."

"Is that all? Precisely all?"

"Um . . ." I thought back. "His son said his father stopped at a friend's house for a drink. Then he drove on towards home. Then he hit a tree."

Jeremy jerked around a little more and said, "How did anyone know he had stopped at a friend's house? And how does anyone know he went to sleep?"

"These are true lawyer's questions," I said. "I don't know the answer to the first, and as to the second, of course nobody knows; it's just what everyone supposes. Going to sleep in the dark towards the end of a long drive isn't all that uncommon. Deadly. Tragic. But always happening."

"Did they do an autopsy?" he said.

"I don't know. Do they usually?"

He shrugged. "Sometimes. They'd have tested his blood for the alcohol level. They might have checked for heart attack or stroke, if he wasn't too badly damaged. If there were no suspicious circumstances, that would be all."

"His son would have told me—have told everyone on

the racecourse—if there had been any odd questions asked. I'm sure there weren't any."

"Those burglaries must have made the police think a bit, though," he said frowning.

I said weakly, "The first serious burglary occurred actually during the funeral."

"Cremation?"

I nodded. "Cremation." I pondered. "The police might have wondered . . . in fact they did hint very broadly to Marie Millace, and upset her considerably . . . about George possessing photographs other people might not want found. But they don't *know* he had them."

"Like we do."

"As you say."

"Give it up," he said abruptly. "Burn those pictures. Stick to looking for Amanda."

"You're a lawyer. I'm surprised you want to suppress incriminating evidence."

"You can damn well stop laughing," he said. "You could end up with George Millace. Splat on a tree."

Jeremy left at six, and I walked along to Harold's for the military briefing. He had six runners planned for me during the week, and with those and the five spare rides I'd been offered at Windsor I looked like having an exceptionally busy time.

"Don't come crashing down on one of those hyenas you've accepted," Harold said. "What you take them for when you've got all my horses to ride I don't know."

"Money," I said.

"Huh."

He never liked me taking outside rides, although as I was self-employed he couldn't stop me. He never admitted that some of the biggest races I'd won had been for other stables. In those cases, he would point out if pressed, I had been riding second string horses, which had confounded the trainer's assessments and won when they weren't expected to.

"Next Saturday at Ascot I'm running two of Victor's," he said. "Chainmail . . . and Daylight."

I glanced at him quickly, but he didn't meet my eyes.

"He didn't have a proper race at Sandown, of course," he said. "He's still at his peak."

"He'll have a harder job at Ascot. Much stronger opponents."

He nodded, and after a pause he said casually, "Chainmail might be the best bet. Depends what's left in at the four-day stage, of course. And there's the overnights . . . we'll see better what the prospects are on Friday."

There was a silence.

"Prospects for winning?" I said at last. "Or for losing?"

"Philip . . ."

"I'm not going to," I said.

"But . . ."

"You tell me, Harold," I said. "Tell me early Saturday morning, if you've any feeling for me at all. I'll get an acute stomachache. Vomiting. Diarrhea. Won't be able to go racing."

"But there's Daylight."

I compressed my mouth and stifled the tremble of anger.

"We had four winners last week," I said tightly. "Isn't that enough for you?"

"But Victor . . ."

I said, "I'll ride my bloody guts out for Victor as long as we're trying to win. You tell him that. Tell him just that." I stood up, unable to sit calmly. "And don't you forget, Harold, that Chainmail's still only four, and pretty wayward, for all that he's fast. He pulls like a train and tries to duck out of the huddles, and he's not above sinking his teeth into any horse that bumps him. He's the devil of a hard ride, but he's brave and I like him . . . and I'm not going to help you ruin him. And you *will* damn well

ruin him if you muck him about. You'll turn him sour.
You'll make him a real rogue. Apart from dishonest, it's
stupid."

"Have you finished?"

"I guess so."

"Then I agree with you about Chainmail. I'll say it all
to Victor. But in the end it's Victor's horse."

I stood without speaking. Anything I said, I thought,
could prove too decisive. While I was still riding for the
stable, there was hope.

"Do you want a drink?" Harold said; and I said yes,
Coke; and the fraught moment passed. We talked normally about the chances and plans for the other three
runners, and only when I was leaving did Harold make
any reference to the awaiting chasm.

"If necessary," he said heavily, "I'll give you time to
get sick."

At Fontwell races the next day I rode one horse for Harold, which fell three from home, and two for other people,
resulting in a second place and a third, and faint congrat-
ulatory noises but no avalanches of further work. An average sort of day; better than some. The fall had been
slow and easy: a bruise but no damage.

No hot gossip in the weighing room.

No unseemly fighting between newly elected Jockey
Club members and cocaine-pushing film directors. No elderly lords drooling over delectable dollies. Not even any
worried broken-collarboned jockeys agonizing over battered mothers.

No heavy-blue-overcoated owners putting pressure on
their going-straight jockeys.

A quiet day at the office.

Tuesday, with no racing engagements, I rode out both lots
with Harold's string and schooled some of the horses over
training jumps. It was a raw damp morning, the sort to

endure, not enjoy, and even Harold seemed to take no pleasure in the work. The mood of the Downs, I thought, walking my mount back through Lambourn, infected the whole village. On days like this the inhabitants scarcely said good morning.

From twelve o'clock onwards the day was my own.

Eating some muesli I contemplated George Millace's box of riddles, but felt too restless for another long spell in the darkroom. I thought of my promised visit to my grandmother, and hastily sought a good reason for postponing it. Finally I decided to placate the accusing image of Jeremy Folk by seeing if I could find one of the houses where my mother had left me in my childhood. A nice vague expedition with no expectation of success. A drift-around day; undemanding.

I set off accordingly to London and cruised up and down a whole lot of little streets between Chiswick and Hammersmith. All of them looked familiar to me in a way: rows of tidy terraces and mostly three stories and a basement, bow-fronted townhouses for middle-income people, misleadingly narrow frontages stretching far back to small enclosed gardens. I had lived in several houses like that at some time or another, and I couldn't remember even the name of a road.

The years, too, had brought a host of changes. Whole streets had obviously disappeared with the building of bigger roads. Little remaining blocks of houses stood in lonely islands, marooned. Cinemas had closed. Asian shops had moved in. The buses looked the same.

Bus routes.

The buses triggered the memory. The house I was looking for had been three or four from the end of the road, and just around the corner there had been a bus stop. I had been on the buses often, catching them at that stop.

Going to where?

Going to the river, for walks.

The knowledge drifted quietly back across twenty-plus

years. We'd gone down to the river in the afternoons, to look at the houseboats and the seagulls and the mud when the tide was out; and we'd looked across the gardens at Kew.

I drove down to the Kew Bridge and started from there, following buses.

A slow business, because I stopped when the bus did. Unproductive also, because none of the stops anywhere seemed to be near the corners of roads. I gave it up after an hour and simply cruised around, resigned to not finding anything I recognized. Probably I'd got even the district wrong. Probably I should be looking in Hampstead, where I knew I'd been also.

It was a pub that finally oriented me. The Willing Horse. An old pub. Dark brown paint. Frosted glass in the windows with tracery patterns around the edges. I parked the car around the corner and walked back to the chocolate doors, and simply stood there, waiting.

After a while I seemed to know which way to go. Turn left, walk three hundred yards, cross the road, first turning on the right.

I turned into a street of bow-fronted terrace houses, three stories high, narrow and neat and typical. Cars lined both sides of the street, with many front gardens converted to parking places. There were a few bare-branched trees growing from earthpatches near the edge of the pavement, and hedges and shrubs by the houses. Three steps up to a small flat area outside each front door.

I crossed that road and walked slowly up it, but the impetus had gone. Nothing told me whether I was in the right place, or which house to try. I walked more slowly, indecisively, wondering what to do next.

Four houses from the end I went up the short footpath, and up the steps, and rang the doorbell.

A woman with a cigarette opened the door.

"Excuse me," I said. "Does Samantha live here?"

"Who?"

"Samantha?"

"No." She looked me up and down with the utmost suspicion, and closed the door.

I tried six more houses. Two no answers, one "clear off," one "no dear, I'm Popsy, like to come in?" one "we don't want no brushes," and one "is that a cat?"

At the eighth an old lady told me I was up to no good, she'd watched me go from house to house, and if I didn't stop it she would call the police.

"I'm looking for someone called Samantha," I said. "She used to live here."

"I'm watching you," she said. "If you try to climb in through any windows, I'll call the police."

I walked away from her grim little face and she came right out into the street to watch me.

It wasn't much good, I thought. I wouldn't find Samantha. She might be out, she might have moved, she might never have lived in that street in the first place. Under the old woman's baleful gaze I tried another house where no one answered, and another where a girl of about twenty opened the door.

"Excuse me," I said, "Does anyone called Samantha live there?" I'd said it so often it now sounded ridiculous. This is the last one, I thought. I may as well give it up and go home.

"Who?"

"Samantha?"

"Samantha what? Samantha who?"

"I'm afraid I don't know."

She pursed her lips, not quite liking it.

"Wait a moment," she said. "I'll go and see." She shut the door and went away. I walked down the steps to the front garden where a small red car stood on some tarmac. Hovered, waiting to see if the girl returned, aware of the old woman beadily watching from along the road.

The door behind me opened as I turned. There were two people there, the girl and an older woman. When I

took a step towards them the woman made a sharp movement of the arm, to keep me away. Raising her voice she
said, "What do you want?"

"Well . . . I'm looking for someone called Samantha."

"So I hear. What for?"

"Are you," I said slowly, "Samantha?"

She looked me up and down with the suspicion I was
by now used to. A comfortably sized lady, gray-brown
wavy hair to her shoulders.

"What do you want?" she said again, unsmiling.

I said, "Would the name Nore mean anything to you?
Philip Nore, or Caroline Nore?"

To the girl the names meant nothing, but in the woman
there was a fast sharpening of attention.

"What exactly do you want?" she demanded.

"I'm . . . Philip Nore."

The guarded expression turned to incredulity. Not exactly to pleasure, but certainly to acknowledgment.

"You'd better come in," she said. "I'm Samantha Bergen."

I went up the steps and through the front door, and
didn't have, as I'd half expected, the feeling of coming
home.

"Downstairs," she said, leading the way and looking
over her shoulder, and I followed her through the hall and
down the stairs, which in all those London houses led to
the kitchen and to the door out to the garden. The girl
followed after me, looking mystified and still wary.

"Sorry not to have been more welcoming," Samantha
said, "but you know what it is these days. So many burglaries. You have to be careful. And strange young men
coming to the door asking for Samantha . . ."

"Yes," I said.

She went through a doorway into a large room, which
looked more like a country kitchen than most kitchens in
the country. A row of pine-covered cupboards on the
right. A big table, with chairs. A red-tiled floor. French

windows to the garden. A big basket-chair hanging on a chain from the ceiling. Beams. Bits of gleaming copper.

Without thinking I walked across the red floor and sat in the hanging basket chair, tucking my feet under me, out of sight.

Samantha Bergen stood there looking astounded.

"You are!" she said. "You are Philip. Little Philip. He always used to sit there like that, with his feet up. I'd forgotten. But seeing you do it . . . good gracious heavens."

"I'm sorry," I said, half stammering and standing up again, steadying the swinging chair. "I just . . . did it."

"My dear man," she said. "It's all right. It's extraordinary to see you, that's all." She turned to the girl but said still to me, "This is my daughter, Clare. She wasn't born when you stayed here." And to her daughter she said, "I looked after a friend's child now and then. Heavens . . . it must be twenty-two years since the last time. I don't suppose I ever told you."

The girl shook her head but looked less mystified and a good deal more friendly. They were both of them attractive in an unforced sort of way, both of them wearing jeans and sloppy jerseys and unpainted Tuesday afternoon faces. The girl was slimmer and had darker and shorter hair, but they both had large gray eyes, straight noses, and unaggressive chins. Both were self-assured; and both undefinably intelligent.

The work I had interrupted lay spread out on the table. Galley proofs and drawings and photographs, the makings of a book. When I glanced at it, Clare said, "Mother's cook book," and Samantha said, "Clare is a publishers' assistant," and they invited me to sit down again.

We sat around the table, and I told them about looking for Amanda, and the off-chance which had brought me to their door.

Samantha regretfully shook her head. "An off-chance is all it was," she said. "I never saw Caroline after she took you away the last time. I didn't even know she had a daughter. She never brought her here."

"Tell me about her," I said. "What was she like?"

"Caroline? So pretty you wanted to hug her. Full of light and fun. She could get anyone to do anything. But . . ." she stopped.

"But what?" I said. "And please do be frank. She's been dead for twelve years, and you won't hurt my feelings."

"Well . . . she took drugs." Samantha looked at me anxiously, and seemed relieved when I nodded. "Cocaine. LSD. Marijuana. Almost anything. She tried the lot. She told me she didn't want you around when she and her friends were all high. She begged me to look after you for a few days . . . it always turned into a few weeks . . . and you were such a quiet little mouse . . . you were quite good company, actually. I never minded, when she brought you."

"How often?" I said slowly.

"How often did she bring you? Oh . . . half a dozen times. You were about four the first time . . . and about eight at the end, I suppose. I told her I couldn't take you again, as Clare was imminent."

"I've always been grateful to you," I said.

"Have you?" She seemed pleased. "I wouldn't have thought you'd remember . . . but I suppose you must have done, as you're here."

"Did you know anyone called Chloe or Deborah or Miranda?" I said.

"Deborah Baederbeck? Went to live in Brussels?"

"I don't know."

Samantha shook her head dubiously. "She wouldn't know anything about your Amanda. She must have been in Brussels for . . . oh . . . twenty-five years."

Clare made some tea and I asked Samantha if my mother had ever told her anything about my father.

"No, nothing," she said positively. "An absolutely taboo subject, I gathered. She was supposed to have an abortion, and didn't. Left it too late. Just like Caroline, absolutely irresponsible." She made a comical face. "I suppose you wouldn't be here if she'd done what she promised her old dragon of a mother."

"She made up for it by not registering my birth."

"Oh God." She chuckled with appreciation. "I must say that's typical Caroline. We went to the same school. I'd known her for years. We'd not long left when she got landed with you."

"Did she take drugs then? At school?"

"Heavens, no." She frowned, thinking. "Afterwards. We all did. I don't mean she and I together. But our generation . . . we all tried it, I should think, some time or other, when we were young. Pot mostly."

Clare looked surprised, as if mothers didn't do that sort of thing.

I said, "Did you know the friends she got high with?"

Samantha shook her head. "Never met any of them. Caroline called them friends in the plural, but I always thought of it as one friend, a man."

"No," I said. "Sometimes there were more. People lying on floor cushions half asleep, with the room full of haze. All enormously peaceful."

They were the people with words like "skins" and "grass" and "joints," which never seemed to mean what my childish brain expected; and it was one of them who had given me a cigarette and urged me to suck in the smoke. Suck it into your lungs, he'd said, and then hold your breath while you count ten. I'd coughed all the smoke out before I counted two, and he'd laughed and told me to try again. Three or four small drags, I'd had.

The result, which I'd dreamed of occasionally afterwards rather than actively remembered, was a great feeling of tranquility. Relaxed limbs, quiet breathing, slight lightness of head. My mother had come home and slapped me, which put an end to all that. The friend who'd initiated me never reappeared. I hadn't met hash again until I was twenty, when I'd been given a present of some greeny-yellow Lebanese resin to sprinkle onto tobacco.

I'd smoked some, and given some away, and never bothered again. The results, to me, weren't worth the trouble and expense. They would have been, a doctor friend had told me, if I'd had asthma. Marijuana was terrific for asthmatics, he'd said, sadly. Pity they couldn't smoke it on the National Health.

We drank the tea Clare had made, and Samantha asked what I did in the way of a job.

"I'm a jockey."

They were incredulous. "You're too tall," Samantha said, and Clare said, "People just aren't jockeys."

"People are," I said. "I am. And jockeys don't have to be small. Six-footers have been known."

"Extraordinary thing to be," Clare said. "Pretty pointless, isn't it?"

"Clare!" Samantha said, protesting.

"If you mean," I said equably, "that being a jockey contributes nothing useful to society, I'm not so sure."

"Proceed," Clare said.

"Recreation gives health. I provide recreation."

"And betting?" she demanded. "Is that healthy?"

"Sublimation of risk-taking. Stake your money, not your life. If everyone actually set out to climb Everest, just think of the rescue parties."

She started to smile and converted it into a chewing motion with her lips. "But you yourself . . . take the risks."

"I don't bet."

"Clare will tie you in knots," her mother said. "Don't listen to her."

Clare however shook her head. "I would think your little Philip is as easy to tie in knots as a stream of water."

Samantha gave her a surprised glance and asked me where I lived.

"In Lambourn. It's a village in Berkshire. Out on the Downs."

Clare frowned and looked at me with sharpened concentration.

"Lambourn . . . isn't that the village where there are a lot of racing stables, rather like Newmarket?"

"That's right."

"Hm." She thought for a minute. "I think I'll just ring up my boss. He's doing a book on British villages and village life. He was saying this morning the book's still a bit thin—asked me if I had any ideas. He has a writer chap doing it. Going to villages, staying a week and writing a chapter. He's just done one on a village that produces its own operas. Look, do you mind if I give him a call?"

"Of course not."

She was on her feet and going across to a telephone extension on the kitchen worktop before I'd even answered. Samantha gave her a fond motherly look, and I thought how odd it was to find Samantha in her late forties, when I'd always imagined her perpetually young. From under the unrecognizable exterior, though, the warmth, the directness, the steady values and the basic goodness came across to me as something long known; and I was reassured to find that those half-buried impressions had been right.

"Clare will bully you into things," she said. "She bullied me into doing this cook book. She's got more energy than a power station. She told me when she was about six that she was going to be a publisher and she's well on her way. She's already second-in-command to the man she's talking to. She'll be running the whole firm before they know where they are." She sighed with pleased resignation, vividly illuminating the trials and prides of mothering a prodigy.

The prodigy herself, who looked normal enough, finished talking on the telephone and came back to the table nodding.

"He's interested. He says we'll both go down and look the place over, and then if it's OK he'll send the writer, and a photographer."

I said diffidently, "I've taken pictures of Lambourn . . . If you'd like to . . ."

She interrupted with a shake of her head. "We'd need professional work. Sorry and all that. But my boss says if you don't mind we'll call at your apartment or whatever, if you'd be willing to help us with directions and general information."

"Yes . . . I'd be willing."

"That's great." She gave me a sudden smile that was more like a pat on the back than a declaration of friendship. She knows she's bright, I thought. She's used to being brighter than most. She's not as good as Jeremy Folk at concealing that she knows it.

"Can we come on Friday?" she said.

10

Lance Kinship was wandering around at the head of a retinue of cameramen, sound recordists and general dogbodies when I arrived at Newbury racecourse on the following day, Wednesday. We heard in the changing room that he was taking stock shots for a film with the blessing of the management and that jockeys were asked to cooperate. Not, it was said, to the point of grinning into the camera lens at every opportunity, but just to not treading on the crew if one found them underfoot.

I slung my Nikon around my neck inside my raincoat and unobtrusively took a few pictures of the men taking pictures.

Technically speaking, cameras were not welcome at race meetings except in the hands of recognized photographers, but most racecourses didn't fidget unduly about the general public taking snaps anywhere except in the members' enclosure. And because I'd been doing it for so long, most racecourse managers looked tolerantly upon my own efforts. Only at Royal Ascot was the crackdown on amateurs complete: the one meeting where people had to park their cameras at the entrance, like gunslingers riding into a bullet-free town.

Lance Kinship looked as if he had tried hard not to seem like a film director. In place of his olive suede jacket, now presumably having its bloodstains removed at the cleaners, he wore a brownish tweed suit topped by a brown trilby set at a conservative angle and accompanied by checked shirt, quiet tie, and raceglasses. He looked, I thought, as if he'd cast himself as an uppercrust extra in his own film.

He was telling his crew what to do with indecisive gestures. It was only in the tenseness with which they listened to him, their eyes sliding his way every time he spoke, that one saw any authority. I took a couple of shots of that reaction; the eyes all looking towards him from averted heads. I reckoned that when printed those pictures might quite clearly show men obeying someone they didn't like.

At one point, around by the saddling boxes, where the crew were filming the trainers fitting on the saddles before the first race, Lance Kinship turned his head in the instant I pressed the button, and stared straight into my lens.

He strode across to me looking annoyed.

"What are you doing?" he said, though it must have been obvious.

"I was just interested," I said inoffensively.

He looked at my boots, my white breeches and the red and yellow shirt which I wore under the raincoat.

"A jockey," he said, as if to himself. He peered through his black-framed spectacles at my camera. "A Nikon." He raised his eyes to my face and frowned with half-recognition.

"How's the nose?" I said politely.

He grunted, finally placing me.

"Don't get into the film," he said. "You're not typical. I don't want Nikon-toting jocks lousing up the footage. Right?"

"I'll be careful," I said.

He seemed on the point of telling me to go away altogether, but he glanced from side to side and took note that a few racegoers were listening, and decided against it. With a brief disapproving nod he went back to his crew, and presently they moved off and began taking pictures of the saddled horses walking into the parade ring.

The chief cameraman carried his big movie camera on his shoulder and mostly operated it from there. An assistant walked one step behind, carrying a tripod. One sound recorder carried the charcoal sausage-shaped boom and a second fiddled endlessly with knobs on an electric box. A young man with frizzy hair operated a clapper board, and a girl took copious notes. They trailed around all afternoon getting in everyone's way and apologizing like mad so that no one much minded.

They were down at the start when I lined up on a scatty novice 'chaser for Harold, and thankfully absent from the eighth fence, where the novice 'chaser put his forefeet into the open ditch on the take-off side and crossed the birch almost upside down. Somewhere during this wild somersault I fell out of the saddle, but by the mercy of heaven when the half-ton of horse crashed to the ground I was not underneath it.

He lay prostrate for a few moments, winded and panting, giving me plenty of time to grasp hold of the reins and save his lad the frustrating job of catching him loose. Some horses I loved and some I didn't. This was a clumsy stubborn delinquent with a hard mouth, just starting what was likely to be a long career of bad jumping. I'd schooled him at home several times and knew him too well. If he met a fence right, he was safe enough, but if he met it wrong he ignored signals to change his stride; and every horse met a fence wrong now and then, however skillful his rider. I reckoned every time he completed a race, I'd be lucky.

Resignedly I waited until he was on his feet and prancing about a bit, then remounted him and trotted him back to the stands, and made encouraging remarks to the downcast owner and honest ones to Harold.

"Tell him to cut his losses and buy a better horse."

"He can't afford it."

"He's wasting the training fees."

"I dare say," Harold said. "But we're not telling him, are we?"

I grinned at him. "No, I guess not."

I took my saddle into the weighing room and Harold went off to join the owner in a consolatory drink. Harold needed the training fees. I needed the riding fees. The owner was buying a dream and kidding himself. It happened every day, all the time, in racing. It was only occasionally that the dream came superbly, soul-fillingly true, and when that happened you saw points of light like stars in the owner's eyes. Thank God for the owners, I thought. Without them racing wouldn't exist.

When I was changing back into street clothes someone came and told me there was a man outside asking for the jockey with the camera. I went to see, and found Lance Kinship trudging up and down and looking impatient.

"Oh there you are," he said, as if I'd seriously kept him waiting. "What's your name?"

"Philip Nore."

"Well, Phil, what do you say? You took some photographs today. If they're any good I'll buy them from you. How's that?"

"Well . . ." I was nonplussed. "Yes, if you like."

"Good. Where's your camera? Get it then, get it. The crew is over by the winning post. Take some photographs of them shooting the finish of the next race. Right? Right?"

"Yes," I said dazedly.

"Come on then. Come on."

I fetched the camera from the changing room and found him still waiting for me but definitely in a hurry. I would have to get over there and assess the best angles, he explained, and I'd only have one chance because the crew would be moving out to the parking lot presently to film the racegoers going home.

He had apparently tried to get the regular racing photographer to do the present job, but they had said they were too busy.

"I remembered you. Worth trying, I thought. With that camera, you at least have to be able to focus. Right?"

We were walking fast. He broke now and then into a sort of trotting stride, and his breathing gradually grew shorter. His mental energy however was unflagging.

"We need these pics for publicity. Right?"

"I see," I said.

His words and manner were so much at variance with his appearance that the whole expedition seemed to me powerfully unreal. Urgent film producers (who might or might not provide cocaine for sniffing at parties) were surely not accustomed to look the country gentleman, nor tweeded country gentlemen to speak with slovenly vowels and glottalstop consonants. The "right?" he was so fond of was pronounced without its final "t."

I would have thought, if he wanted publicity pictures, that he would have brought a photographer of his own; and I asked him.

"Sure," he said. "I had one lined up. Then he died. Didn't get around to it again. Then today, saw you. Reminded me. Asked the news photographers. No dice. Thought of you, right? Asked them about you. They said you were good, you could do it. You may be lousy. If your pics are no good, I don't buy, right?"

He panted across the course to the winning post on the far side, and I asked him which photographer had died.

"Fellow called Millace. Know him?"

"I knew him," I said.

"He said he'd do it. Died in a car crash. Here we are. You get on with it. Take what you want. Got color film in there, have you?"

I nodded and he nodded, and he turned away to give instructions to the crew. They again listened to him with the slightly averted heads, and I wandered away. Lance

Kinship was not immediately likeable, but I again had a strong feeling that his crew felt positive discontent. He wouldn't buy photographs showing that response, I thought dryly, so I waited until the crew were not looking at him, and shot them absorbed in their work.

Lance Kinship's breathing returned to normal and he himself merged again into the racing background as if he'd been born there. An actor at heart, I thought; but unlike an actor he was dressing a part in real life, which seemed odd.

"What film are you making?" I asked.

"Stock shots," he said uninformatively. "Background."

I left it, and walked around the crew looking for useful angles for pictures. The horses came out onto the course and cantered down to the start, and the frizzy-haired boy with the clapper board, who happened to be close to me, said with sudden and unexpected fierceness, "You'd think he was God Almighty. You'd think this was an epic, the way he frigs about. We're making commercials. Half a second on screen, flash off. Huh!"

I half smiled. "What's the product?"

"Some sort of brandy."

Lance Kinship came towards me and told me it was important that he should be included in my photographs, and that I should take them from where he would be prominently in shot.

The frizzy-haired boy surreptitiously raised his eyebrows into comical peaks, and I assured Lance Kinship with a trembling straight face that I would do my absolute best.

I did by good luck get one or two reasonable pictures, but no doubt George Millace and his inner eye and his motor-drive camera would have outstripped me by miles. Lance Kinship gave me a card with his address and told me again that he would buy the pictures if he liked them, right?

He didn't say for how much, and I didn't like to ask.

I would never be a salesman.

Taking photographs for a living, I thought ruefully, would find me starving within a week.

Reaching home I switched on the lights and drew the curtains, and sat by the kitchen table going again through George Millace's rubbish box, thinking of his talents and his cruel mind, and wondering just how much profit he had made from his deadly photographs.

It was true that if he'd left any more pictures in that box I wanted to decipher them. The urge to solve the puzzles was overpowering. But if I learned any more secrets, what would I do with them . . . and what ought I to do with those I already had?

In a fairly typical manner I decided to do pretty well nothing. To let events take their course. To see what happened.

Meanwhile there were those tantalizing bits that looked so pointless . . .

I lifted out the black plastic light-proof envelope, which was of about the same size as the box and lying at the bottom of it, under everything else. I looked again at its contents, as I had in Steve Millace's house, and saw again the page-sized piece of clear plastic, and also, what hadn't registered before, two sheets of paper of about the same size.

I looked at them briefly and closed them again into their light-proof holder, because it had suddenly occurred to me that George might not have stored them like that unless it was necessary. That plastic and that paper might bear latent images . . . which I might already have destroyed by exposing them to light.

The piece of plastic and the sheets of paper didn't actually look to me like photographic materials at all. They looked like a piece of plastic and two sheets of typing paper. If they bore latent images, I didn't know how to develop them. If they didn't, why had George kept them in a light-proof envelope?

I sat staring vaguely at the silent black plastic and thinking about developers. To bring out the image on any particular type of film or any type of paper one had to use the right type of developer, the matched mixture of chemicals made for the task. All of which meant that unless I knew the make and type of the plastic and of the two sheets of paper I couldn't get any further.

A little pensively I pushed the black envelope aside and took up the strips of blank negatives, which at least didn't have the built-in difficulty of being still sensitive to light. They had already been developed. They just looked as if they had held no latent images to bring out.

They were thirty-five-millimeter color film negatives, and there were a lot of them, some simply blank and others blank with uneven magenta blotches here and there. The negatives were in strips, mostly of six. I laid them all out end to end and made the first interesting discovery.

All the plain blank negatives had come from one film, and those with magenta blotches from another. The frame numbers along the top of each strip ran consecutively from one to thirty-six in each case. Two films of thirty-six exposures each.

I knew what make of film they were, because each manufacturer placed the frame numbers differently, but I didn't suppose that that was important. What might be important, however, was the very nature of color negatives.

While slide films—transparencies—appeared to the eye in their true lifelike colors, negative film appeared in the reciprocal colors: and to get back to the true colors one had of course to make a print from the negative.

The primary colors of light were blue, green and red. The reciprocal colors, in which they appeared on a negative, were yellow, magenta and cyan. Negatives therefore would have looked like mixtures of yellow, deep pink (magenta) and greeny-blue (cyan), except that to get good whites and highlights all manufacturers gave their negatives an overall pale orange cast. Color negatives therefore always looked a pale clear orange at the edges. The overall orange color also had the effect of masking the yellow sections so that they didn't show to the eye as yellow bits of negative, but as orange.

George Millace's negatives looked a pale clear transparent orange throughout. Just suppose, I thought, that under the orange there was an image in yellow, which at the moment didn't show.

If I printed those negatives, the yellow would become blue.

An invisible yellow negative image could turn into a totally visible printed image in blue.

Worth trying, I thought. I went into the darkroom and mixed the developing chemicals, and set up the color print processor. It meant waiting half an hour for the built-in thermostatic heaters to raise the various chemical baths to the correct temperatures, but after that the prints were conveyed automatically inside the closed processor from one bath to another on rollers, each sheet of photographic paper taking seven minutes to travel from entry to exit.

I found out almost at once, by making contact prints, that under the orange masking there was indeed blue: but not blue images. Just blue.

There were so many variables in color printing that searching for an image on blank negatives was like walking blindfold through a forest, and although in the end I printed every negative separately and tried every way I knew, I was only partially successful.

I ended, in fact, with thirty-six solid blue oblongs, enlarged to four inches by five and printed four to a sheet, and thirty-six more with greenish blotches here and there.

The only thing one could say, I thought, as I let them wash thoroughly in running water, was that George wouldn't have taken seventy-two pictures of a blue oblong for nothing.

I dried some of the prints and looked at them closely,

and it did seem to me that there were faint darker marks on some of them. Nothing one could plainly see, but something.

When it dawned on me far too late what George had done I was too tired to start all over again. I cleaned up the processor and everything else, and went to bed.

Jeremy Folk telephoned early the next morning and asked if I'd been to see my grandmother.

Give me time, I said, and he said I'd had time, and did I remember I had promised?

"Well . . . I'll go," I said. "Saturday, after Ascot."

"What have you been doing?" he asked plaintively. "You could have gone any day this week. Don't forget she really is dying."

"I've been working," I said. "And printing."

"From that box?" he said suspiciously.

"Uh huh."

"Don't do it," he said, and then, "What have you got?"

"Blue prints. Blue pictures."

"What?"

"Blue as in blue. Pure deep blue. Forty-seven B."

"*What* did you say? Are you sober?"

"I am awake and yawning," I said. "So listen. George Millace screwed a deep blue filter onto his camera and pointed it at a black-and-white picture, and he photographed the black-and-white picture through the blue filter onto color negative film. Forty-seven B is the most intense blue filter you can buy, and I bet that's what he used."

"You're talking Chinese."

"I'm talking Millace. Crafty double Millace. Second cousin to double Dutch."

"You really are drunk."

"Don't be silly. As soon as I work out how to unscramble the blue, and do it, the next riveting Millace installment will fall into our hands."

"I seriously think you should burn the lot."

"Not a chance."

"You think of it as a game. It isn't a game."

"No."

"For God's sake be careful."

I said I would. One says things like that so easily.

I went to Wincanton races in Wiltshire and rode twice for Harold and three times for other people. The day was dry with a sharp wind that brought tears to the eyes, tears which the standard of racing did nothing to dispel, since all the good horses had cried off and gone to Newbury or Ascot instead, leaving chances for the blundering majority. I fumbled and booted my way around five times in safety, and in the novice 'chase, owing to most of the field having fallen over each other at the first open ditch, found myself finishing in front, all alone.

My mount's thin little trainer greeted my return with a huge grin, tear-filled eyes and blue dripping nose.

"By gum, lad, well done. By gum, it's bloody cold. Get thee in and weighed. Don't stand about. By gum, then, that was a bit of all right, wasn't it, all them others falling?"

"You'd schooled yours a treat," I said, pulling off the saddle. "He jumped great."

His mouth nearly split its sides with pleasure. "By gum, lad, he'd jump Aintree, the way he went today. Get thee in. Get thee in."

I went in and weighed, and changed and weighed out, and raced, and returned, and changed and weighed . . .

There had been a time, when it was all new, that my heart had pumped madly every time I walked from the changing room to the parade ring, every time I cantered to the start. After ten years my heart pumped above normal only for the big ones, the Grand National and so on, and then only if my horse had a reasonable chance. The once-fiendish excitement had turned to routine.

Bad weather, long journeys, disappointments and injuries had at first been shrugged off as "part of the job." After ten years I saw that they *were* the job. The peaks, the winners, those were the bonuses.

The tools of my trade were a liking for speed and a liking for horses, and the power to combine those two feelings. Also strong bones, an ability to bounce, and a tendency to mend quickly when I didn't.

None of those tools, except probably the liking for horses, would be of the slightest use to me as a photographer.

I walked irritably out to my car at the end of the afternoon. I didn't want to be a photographer. I wanted to remain a jockey. I wanted to stay where I was, in the known; not to step irrevocably into the future. I wanted things to go on as they were, and not to change.

Early the following morning Clare Bergen appeared on my doorstep accompanied by a dark young man whose fingertips in a handshake almost tingled with energy. Publishers, I had vaguely supposed, were portly father figures. Another out-of-date illusion gone bust.

Clare herself had come in a bright woolly hat, bright scarf, afghan sheepskin jacket, yellow ski pants and huge fleece-lined boots. Ah well, I thought, she would only frighten half of the horses. The nervous half.

I drove them up onto the Downs in the Land Rover borrowed from Harold for the occasion, and we watched a few strings work. Then I drove them round the village, pointing out which trainers lived where. Then I took them back to the cottage for coffee and cogitation.

The publisher said he would like to poke round a little on foot, and walked off. Clare drank her second steaming cup and said how on earth did we bear it with a wind like that sawing everyone in half.

"It always seems to be windy here," I agreed, thinking about it.

"All those naked hills."

"Good for horses."

"I don't think I've ever actually touched a horse." She looked faintly surprised. "Most of the people I know despise horse people."

"Everyone likes to feel superior," I said, uninsulted. "Particularly when they aren't."

"Ouch," she said. "That's a damned fast riposte."

I smiled. "You'd be surprised the sort of hate that gets aimed at horses. Anything from sneers to hysteria."

"And you don't mind?"

"What those people feel is their problem, not mine."

She looked at me straightly with the wide gray eyes.

"What hurts you?" she said.

"People saying I jumped overboard when I went down with the ship."

"Er . . . what?"

"People saying I fell off when it was the horse which fell, and took me with it."

"And there's a distinction?"

"Most important."

"You're having me on," she said.

"A bit." I took her empty cup and put it in the dishwasher. "So what hurts you?"

She blinked, but after a pause she answered. "Being thought to be a fool."

"That," I said, "is a piercingly truthful reply."

She looked away from me as if embarrassed, and said she liked the cottage and the kitchen and could she borrow the bathroom. She emerged from there shortly minus the woolly hat and plus some fresh lipstick and asked if the rest of the house was on a par.

"You want to see it?" I said.

"Love to."

I showed her the sitting room, the bedroom, and finally the darkroom. "And that's all," I said.

She turned slowly from the darkroom to where I stood behind her in the hall.

"You said you took photographs."

"Yes, I do."

"But I thought you meant . . ." She frowned. "Mother said I was short with you when you offered . . . but I'd no idea . . ."

"It doesn't matter," I said. "It's quite all right."

"Well . . . can I see them?"

"If you like. They're in that filing cabinet over there."

I pulled open one of the drawers and sorted through the folders. "Here you are, Lambourn village."

"What are all those others?" she said.

"Just pictures."

"What of?"

"Fifteen years."

She looked at me sharply as if I wasn't making sense, so I added, "Since I owned my own camera."

"Oh." She looked along the tags on the folders, reading aloud, "America, France, Children, Harold's Place, Jockey's Life . . . What's Jockey's Life?"

"Just everyday living, if you're a jockey."

"Can I look?"

"Sure."

She eased the well-filled folder out of the drawer and peeped inside. Then she carried it away towards the kitchen and I followed with the pictures of Lambourn.

She laid the folder she carried on the kitchen table and opened it, and went through the bulky contents picture by picture, steadily and frowning. No comments.

"Can I see Lambourn?" she said.

I gave her Lambourn, and she looked through those also in silence.

"I know they're not marvelous," I said mildly. "You don't have to rack your brains for something kind to say."

She looked up at me fiercely. "You're lying. You know damned well they're good."

She closed the Lambourn file and drummed her fingers

on it. "I can't see why we can't use these," she said. "But it's not my decision, of course."

She fished into her large brown handbag and came up with cigarettes and a lighter. She put a cigarette to her mouth and lit it, and I noticed with surprise that her fingers were trembling. What on earth, I wondered, could have made her nervous? Something had disturbed her deeply, because all the glittery extrovert surface had vanished, and what I saw was a dark-haired young woman concentrating acutely on the thoughts in her head.

She took several deep inhaling breaths of smoke, and looked unseeingly at her fingers, which went on trembling.

"What's the matter?" I said at last.

"Nothing." She gave me a quick glance and looked away, and said, "I've been looking for something like you."

"Something?" I echoed, puzzled.

"Mm." She tapped off some ash. "Mother told you, didn't she, that I wanted to be a publisher?"

"Yes, she did."

"Most people smile, because I'm still young. But I've worked in publishing for five years . . . and I know what I'm doing."

"I don't doubt it."

"No . . . but I need . . . I want . . . I need to make a book that will establish my own personal reputation in publishing. I need to be known as the person who produced such-and-such a book. A very successful book. Then my future will be assured. Do you understand?"

"Yes."

"So I've been looking for that book for a year or two now. Looking and despairing, because what I want is exceptional. And now . . ." She took a deep breath. "Now I've found it."

"But," I said, puzzled, "Lambourn's not news, and anyway I thought it was your boss's book . . ."

"Not that, you fool," she said. "This." She put her hand on the Jockey's Life folder. "The pictures in here. They don't need a text. They tell the story on their own." She drew on the cigarette. "Arranged in the right order . . . presented as a way of living . . . as an autobiography, a social comment, an insight into human nature . . . as well as how an industry works . . . it'll make a spectacular change from flowers and fish."

"The flowers sold about two million copies, didn't they?"

"You don't believe me, do you?" she demanded. "You simply don't see . . ." She broke off and frowned. "You haven't had any of these photographs published before, have you? In papers or magazines, or anywhere?"

I shook my head. "Nowhere. I've never tried."

"You're amazing. You have this talent, and you don't use it."

"But . . . everyone takes photographs."

"Sure they do. But not everyone takes a long series of photographs which illustrate a whole way of life." She tapped off the ash. "It's all there, isn't it? The hard work, the dedication, the bad weather, the humdrum, the triumphs, the pain . . . I've only looked through these pictures once, and in no sort of order and I know what your life's like. I know it *intimately*. Because that's how you've photographed it. I know your life from inside. I see what you've seen. I see the enthusiasm in those owners. I see their variety. I see what you owe to the stable lads. I see the worry of trainers, it's everywhere. I see the laughter in jockeys, and the stoicism. I see what you've felt. I see what you've understood about people. I see people in a way I hadn't before, because of what you've seen."

"I didn't know," I said slowly, "that these pictures were quite so revealing."

"Look at this last one," she said, pulling it out. "This picture of a man in an overall pulling the boot off this boy with the broken shoulder . . . you don't need any words to say the man is doing it as gently as he can, or that it hurts . . . you can see it all, in every line of their bodies and faces." She replaced the picture in the folder and said seriously, "It's going to take me some time to set things up the way I want. Will you give me your assurance that you won't go straight off and sell these pictures to someone else?"

"Of course," I said.

"And don't mention any of this to my boss when he comes back. I want this to be my book, not his."

I half smiled. "All right."

"You may have no ambition," she said sharply. "But I have."

"Yes."

"And my ambition won't do you any harm either," she said. "If the book's a seller . . . and it will be . . . you'll get royalties." She paused. "You can have an advance, anyway, as soon as the contracts are signed."

"Contracts . . ."

"Contracts, naturally," she said. "And keep these pictures safe, will you? I'll come back for them soon, on my own."

She thrust the folder into my hands and I replaced it in the filing cabinet, so that when her energetic young boss returned it was only the views of Lambourn that he saw. He said without too much excitement that they would do well enough, and shortly afterwards he and Clare bore them away.

When they'd gone I thought that Clare's certainty about her book would evaporate. She would remember that most of the people she knew despised horse people. She would work out that a book of pictures taken by a jockey about his life would have a very limited appeal, and she would write apologetically, or briskly, and say that after all, on reflection . . .

I shrugged. I had no expectations. When the letter came, that would be that.

11

I went into Swindon to collect the films I'd left there for processing on my way to Wincanton the previous morning, and spent the rest of that Friday printing the shots of Lance Kinship and his crew.

Apart from those showing clearly the crew's unease in his company, which I didn't intend in any case to show him, I thought that quite likely he might approve. I'd been fortunate in the way the crew had arranged themselves into natural patterns, and there was Kinship himself looking frantically upper-class in his racing tweeds directing them with a conductor's gestures, and in one sequence the horses behind them were all coming head on satisfactorily towards the winning post.

There were also several close-ups of Kinship with the crew in blurred focus behind him, and a couple of slightly surrealistic views which I'd taken from directly behind the cameraman, in which the camera itself looked large with Kinship's sharply focused figure standing in a stray shaft of sunlight in the middle field. The total effect, looking through them all, was a record of a substantial operator in command of his job, and that, I presumed, was what he'd wanted. No matter that the product had been two seconds in a commercial, the production itself looked an epic.

In the evening I captioned the dried prints with typed strips of thin paper taped onto the backs, and feeling faintly foolish added the words *Copyright Philip Nore*, in the way I'd seen Charlie do, all those long years ago. Charlie seemed almost to be leaning over my shoulder, reminding me to keep control of my work.

Work.

The very word filled me with disquiet. It was the first time I'd actively thought of my photographs in those terms.

No, I thought, I'm a jockey.

When I woke early on Saturday morning, I waited for Harold to telephone and tell me to get sick, and it wouldn't have been much trouble as I already felt sick with waiting.

He called at a quarter to ten.

"Are you well?" he said.

"Christ."

"You'd better be," he said. "Victor rang just now. I didn't wait to hear what he meant to say. I told him straight away that Chainmail's future depended on his being handled right in all his races."

"What happened?"

"Victor said an easy race wouldn't hurt him, so I told him what you said. Word for word. And I told him you'd said you would ride your bloody guts out for him as long as we're trying to win." Harold's voice boomed down the wire with cheerfulness. "And do you know what Victor said? He said tell the pious bastard that that's just what I'll expect."

"Do you mean . . . ?"

"I mean," Harold bellowed, "he's changed his mind. You can win on Chainmail if you can. In fact you'd better."

"But Chainmail isn't . . ."

"Damn it, do you want to ride the horse or don't you?"

"I do."

"Right, then. See you at Ascot." He slammed the receiver down, informing me that he didn't think I'd been properly grateful for his efforts with Victor; but if he had promised Victor that Chainmail would win—and it seemed only too likely that he had—I would be in a worse fix than ever.

At Ascot I sought out Harold's head traveling lad, who had as usual come with the horses, and asked how Chainmail was feeling that day.

"Bucking and kicking fit to murder."

"And Daylight?"

"Placid as an old cow."

"Where have the lads put their money?"

He gave me a sharp sideways look. "A bit on both of them. Why, shouldn't they?"

"Sure," I said casually. "They should. But you know how it is . . . sometimes the lads know more about a horse's chances than the trainer does."

He grinned. "I'll say. But today . . ." He shrugged. "A bit on both. Not the week's wages, mind. Just some beer money, like."

"Thanks." I nodded and went off to the weighing room with at least no added anxieties. The lads wouldn't be staking even beer money without what they considered to be a good reason. The legs, stomachs and spirits of both horses could be held to be normal. One didn't ask more.

I saw Victor Briggs standing in a group of one on the area of grass outside the weighing-room door. Always the same clothes: the broad-brimmed hat, the thick navy overcoat, the black leather gloves. Always the same expression: the wiped-clean slate. He saw me, and no doubt he also saw the falter in my stride as I wondered whether I could possibly walk right past him without speaking.

I couldn't.

"Good morning, Mr. Briggs."

"Morning." His voice was curt, but no more. He didn't seem to want me to stop for conversation, so after a slight hesitation I went on towards the weighing room. As I passed him he said grittily, "I'll see your guts."

I stopped and turned my head. His face was still expressionless. His eyes looked cold and hard. I stopped myself from swallowing, and said merely, "All right," and went on again, wishing I'd never made that stupidly flamboyant promise.

Inside the changing room someone was telling a funny story about two statues, and Steve Millace was flexing his mending arm and complaining that the doctor wouldn't pass him fit to ride, and someone else was voicing the first rumor of a major racing upheaval. I took off my street clothes and listened to all three at once.

"So these two naked statues, the man and the woman, they had been standing looking at each other in this park for a hundred years . . ."

"I told him I'd got all the movement back. It's not fair . . ."

"Is it true the Jockey Club is forming a new committee . . ."

"So an angel comes to visit them, and says that as they've stood there patiently through such ages of summers and winters, they will be rewarded by half an hour of human life to do what they have been wanting to do most . . ."

"Look, I can swing my arm around in a circle. What do you think?"

"A committee for appointing paid stewards, or something."

"So these two statues come to life, and look at each other and laugh a bit, and say 'Shall we?' and 'Yes, let's,' and then they nip off behind some bushes, and there's a lot of rustling . . ."

"I could hold any horse. I told him so, but the sod wouldn't listen."

". . . like paying the senior steward a salary."

"After a quarter of an hour they come out from behind the bushes all hot and flustered and happy, and the angel says they've only used half the time, why don't they start all over again . . ."

"How long do collarbones usually take, anyway?"

"I heard Lord White has agreed to the scheme . . ."

"So the statues giggle a bit and the man statue says to the girl statue, 'OK, let's do it again, only this time we'll do it the other way round. I'll hold down the effing pigeon, and you shit on it."

Amid the burst of laughter I heard the man discussing the racing upheaval say, ". . . and Ivor den Relgan is to be chairman."

I turned to him. "What did you say?"

"I don't know if it's true . . . one of the gossip writers told me Ivor den Relgan's been appointed to set up a committee to appoint paid stewards."

I frowned. "That gives den Relgan an awful lot of power all of a sudden, doesn't it?"

He shrugged. "Don't know."

He might not, but others did. During the afternoon one could almost see the onward march of the rumor as uneasy surprise spread from one Jockey Club face to the next. The only group seeming unaffected by the general reaction were the ill-assorted bunch of people attracting the glances of everyone else: Lord White, Lady White, Ivor den Relgan, Dana den Relgan.

They stood outside the weighing room in weak November sunshine, the women both dressed in mink. Lady White, always thin, looked gaunt and plain and unhappy. Dana den Relgan glowed with health, laughed with bright teeth, twinkled her eyes at Lord White, and cast patronizing glances at his Lady.

Lord White basked in the light of Dana's smile, shedding years like snakeskins. Ivor den Relgan smirked at the world in general and smoked a cigar with proprietorial gestures, as if Ascot racecourse were his own. He wore again the belted camel overcoat and the swept-back grayish hair, and commanded attention as his natural right.

Harold appeared at my elbow, following my gaze.

"Ghenghis Khan," he said, "is setting out to rule the world."

"This committee?"

"Wouldn't you say," Harold asked acidly, "that asking someone like den Relgan to chair a committee of his own choosing is a paint job?"

"Cosmetic . . . or camouflage?"

"Both. What they're really doing is saying to den Relgan 'OK, you choose anyone you like as stewards, and we'll pay them.' It's incredible."

"Yes, it is."

"Old Driven Snow," Harold said, "is so besotted with that girl that he'll give her father *anything*."

"Was it all Lord White's idea?"

Harold grimaced wolfishly. "Be your age, Philip. Just who has been trying for years to muscle into the Jockey Club? And just who has a knockout of a daughter who is now old enough to play up to old Driven Snow? Ivor den Relgan has at last got his lever into the door to power in racing, and once he's inside the citadel and making decisions the old guard will have a hopeless job trying to get him out."

"You really care," I said wonderingly.

"Of course I do. This is a great sport, and at the moment, free. Who the hell wants the top management of racing to be carved up and manipulated and sold and *tainted* like some other sports we could mention. The health of racing is guaranteed by having unpaid aristocrats working for the love of it. Sure, they make stupid fuckups occasionally, but we get them put right. If den Relgan appoints paid stewards, for whom do you think those stewards will be working? For us? For racing? Or for the interests of Ivor den Relgan?"

I listened to his passion and his conviction and felt the tremor of his extreme dismay.

"Surely," I said, "the Jockey Club won't let it happen."

"It is happening. The ones at the top are all so used to being led by Lord White that they've agreed to his proposal for this committee without thinking it through. They take it for granted he's virtuous and well-meaning and dead honest. And so he is. But he's also infatuated. And that's damn bloody dangerous."

We watched the group of four. Lord White made continual small gestures which involved laying his hand on Dana's arm, or across her shoulders, or against her cheek. Her father watched with an indulgent smile and a noticeable air of satisfaction; and poor Lady White seemed to shrink even further into her mink. When she eventually walked away, not one of the others seemed to notice her go.

"Someone," Harold said grimly, "has got to do something to stop all this. And before it goes too far."

He saw Victor Briggs standing as usual alone in the distance and strode off to join him, and I watched Lord White and Dana flirt together like two joyful hummingbirds, and thought that today she was responding to him with much less discretion than she had at Kempton.

I turned away, troubled, and found Lance Kinship coming slowly towards me, his gaze flicking rapidly from me to the den Relgans and back again. It struck me that he wanted to talk to me without den Relgan noticing he was there, and with an inward smile I went to meet him.

"I've got your pictures in the car," I said. "I brought them in case you were here."

"Have you? Good, good. I want to talk to that girl." He flicked another quick glance. "Can you get near her? Give her a message? Without that man hearing. Without either of them hearing. Can you?"

"I might try," I said.

"Right. Good. You tell her, then, that I'll meet her after the third race in one of the private boxes." He told me the number. "You tell her to come up there. Right?"

"I'll try," I said again.

"Good. I'll watch you. From over there." He pointed. "When you've given her the message, you come and tell me. Right?"

I nodded, and with another quick peek at Dana he scuttled away. His clothes that day were much as they had been at Newbury, except that he'd ruined the overall true-blue impression with some pale green socks. A pathetic man, I thought. Making himself out to be what he wasn't. Neither a significant film producer nor bred in the purple. They asked him to parties, Victor Briggs had said, because of what he brings. A sad ineffectual man buying his way into the big time with little packets of white powder.

I looked from him to den Relgan, who was using Dana, instead, for much the same purpose. Nothing sad or pathetic, though, about Ivor den Relgan. A bully boy on the march, power hungry and complacent, a trampler of little men.

I went up to him, and in an ingratiating voice, which after years of buttering up owners I could regrettably do quite convincingly, thanked him again for the gifts he had scattered at Kempton.

"The silver saddle . . . thought I must tell you," I said. "Great to have around, just to look at."

"So glad," he said, his gaze passing over me without interest. "My daughter selected it."

"Splendid taste," Lord White said fondly, and I said directly to Dana, "Thank you very much."

"So glad," she murmured also with an almost identical lack of interest.

"Please do tell me," I said, "whether it is unique, or whether it is one of many."

I moved a step or two so that to answer she had to turn away from the two men, and almost before she had finished replying that it was the only one she'd seen, but she couldn't be certain . . . I said to her quietly, "Lance Kinship is here, wanting to see you."

"Oh." She glanced quickly to the two men, returned Lord White's automatic smile with a dazzling one of her own, and softly said to me, "Where?"

"After the third race in a private box." I gave her the number.

"So glad you liked the saddle," she said clearly, turning back towards Lord White. "Isn't it fun," she said to him, "to give pleasure?"

"My dear girl," he said roguishly, "you give pleasure just by being yourself."

Enough to bring angels to tears, I thought.

I wandered away and by a roundabout route arrived at Lance Kinship's side. "She got the message," I said, and he said, "Good," and we arranged for me to give him his pictures outside the weighing room during the running of the last race.

Daylight's race was third on the card, and Chainmail's fourth. When I went out for the third I was stopped on my way from weighing room to parade ring by a pleasant-mannered woman who I realized with delayed shock was Marie Millace.

Marie Millace with scarcely a trace showing of the devastation of her face. Mrs. Millace on her feet, dressed in brown, pale and ill-looking, but healed.

"You said there wouldn't be a mark," she said, "and there isn't."

"You look great."

"Can I talk to you?"

I looked to where all the other jockeys I'd started out with were already filing into the parade ring. "Well . . . how about later? How about . . . um . . . after the fourth race? After I've changed. Somewhere warm."

She mentioned a particular bar, and we agreed on it, and I went on to the ring where Harold and Victor Briggs waited. Neither of them said anything to me, nor I to them. Everything of importance had already been said and for the unimportant there was no appetite. Harold gave me a leg up onto Daylight, and I nodded to him and Victor and got a grade-one blank Briggs stare in return.

There was no certainty that day that Daylight would win. With much stronger opponents, he wasn't even favorite, let alone odds-on.

I cantered down to the starting gate thinking about courage, which was not normally a word I found much in my mind. The process of getting a horse to go fast over jumps seemed to me merely natural, and something I very much liked doing. One knew theoretically that there would be falls and injuries, but the risk of them seldom affected the way I rode. I had no constant preoccupation with my own safety.

On the other hand I'd never been reckless, as some were, as Steve Millace was, and perhaps my aim had been a little too much to bring myself and the horse back together, and not enough to throw my heart over the fence and let the horse catch up if he could.

It was the latter style of riding that Victor Briggs would expect on that day. My own fault, I thought. And moreover I'd have to do it twice.

On Daylight it turned out to be fairly easy, as his jumping style held good enough though I could sense his surprise at the change of mental gears in his rider. The telepathic quality of horses, that remarkable extra sense, picked up instantaneously the strength of my intention, and although I knew horses did tune in in that way, it freshly amazed me. One got used to a certain response from horses, because it was to oneself they were responding. When one's own cast of mind changed radically, so did the horse's response.

Daylight and I therefore turned in what was for us a

thoroughly uncharacteristic performance, leaving more to luck than judgment. He was accustomed to measure his distance from a fence and alter his stride accordingly; but infected by my urgency he began not to do that but simply to take off when he was vaguely within striking distance of getting over. We hit the tops of three fences hard, which was unheard of for him, and when we came to the last and met it right we raced over it as if it had been but a shadow on the ground.

Hard as we tried, we didn't win the race. Although we persevered to the end, a stronger, faster, fitter—whatever—horse beat us into second place by three lengths.

In the unsaddling enclosure I unbuckled the girths while Daylight panted and rocketed around in a highly excitable state, which was a world away from his "placid cow" image; and Victor Briggs watched without giving a thought surface life.

"Sorry," I said to Harold, as he walked in with me to the scales.

He grunted, and said merely, "I'll wait for your saddle."

I nodded, went into the changing room for a change of lead weights in the weight cloth and returned to the scales to check out for Chainmail.

"Don't kill yourself," Harold said, taking my saddle. "It won't prove anything except that you're a bloody fool."

I smiled at him. "People die crossing the road."

"What you're doing is no accident."

He walked off with the saddle and I noticed that he had not in fact instructed me to return to a more sober style of his second runner. Perhaps he too, I reflected, wanted Victor to run his horses straight, and if this was the only way to achieve that, well . . . so be it.

With Chainmail things were different to the extent that the four-year-old hurdler was unstable to begin with, and what I was doing to him was much like urging a juvenile delinquent to go mugging. The rage within him, which made him fight against the jockey and duck out at the jumps and bite other horses, needed to be controlled by a calm mind and steady handling: or so I'd always thought.

On that day he didn't get it. He got a rider prepared to overlook every aggressive act except that of ducking out, and when he tried that at the third hurdle he got such a fierce slash from my whip that I could almost feel him thinking resentfully, "Hey, that's not like you," and it wasn't.

He fought and scrambled and surged and flew. I went with him to his ultimate speed, to total disregard of good sense. I did without any reservation ride my bloody guts out for Victor Briggs.

It wasn't enough. Chainmail finished third in a field of fourteen. Undisgraced. Better, probably, than one would realistically have expected. Beaten only by a length and a neck. But still third.

Victor Briggs unsmilingly watched me pull the saddle off his second stamping, tossing, hepped-up horse. I wrapped the girths around the saddle and paused for a moment face to face with him. He said nothing at all, nor did I. We looked with equal blankness into each other's eyes for a space of seconds, and then I went on, past him, away to the scales.

When I had changed and come out again, he was no-where in sight. I had needed two winners to save my job, and got none. Recklessness wasn't enough. He wanted winners. If he couldn't have certain winners, he'd want certain losers. Like before. Like three years ago. Like when I and my soul were young.

With a deep feeling of weariness I went to meet Marie Millace in the appointed bar.

12

She was sitting in an armchair deep in conversation with another woman, whom I found to my surprise to be Lady White.

"I'll come back later," I said, preparing to retreat.

"No, no," Lady White said, standing up. "I know Marie wants to talk to you." She smiled with all her own troubles showing in lines of anxiety, her eyes screwed up as if in permanent pain. "She tells me you've been so helpful."

"Nothing," I said, shaking my head.

"Not what she says."

The two women smiled and kissed cheeks, and said goodbye, and Lady White with a nod and another vague smile for me made her way out of the bar. I watched her go; a thin defeated lady trying to behave as if the whole racing world were not aware of her discomfiture, and not altogether succeeding.

"We were at school together," Marie Millace said. "We shared a bedroom, in our last year there. I'm very fond of her."

"You know about . . . er . . . ?"

"About Dana den Relgan? Yes." She nodded. "Would you like a drink?"

"Let me get you one."

I fetched a gin and tonic for her and some Coke for me, and sat in the armchair Lady White had left.

The bar itself, an attractive place of bamboo furniture and green and white colors, was seldom crowded and often, as on that day, almost empty. Tucked away up on the stands far away from the parade ring and the bookmakers, it was a better place for talking than for following the horses, and as such was also warm where most of the stands were not. Semi-invalids tended to spend a lot of time there, with nephews and nieces scurrying backward and forward with Tote tickets.

Marie Millace said, "Wendy . . . Wendy White . . . was asking me if I thought her husband's affair with Dana den Relgan would just blow over. But I don't know. I couldn't tell her. How could I tell her? I said I was sure it would . . ." She paused, and when I didn't answer, said, "Do you think it will?"

"Not for a while, I wouldn't think."

She gloomily swilled the ice around in her drink. "Wendy says he's been away with her. He took her to some friends overnight. He told Wendy he was going to shoot, which she finds boring. She hasn't gone with him to shooting parties for years. But he took Dana den Relgan with him this week, and Wendy says when the party went out with the guns, her husband and Dana den Relgan stayed in the house. I suppose I shouldn't be telling you all this. She heard it from someone who was there. You're not to repeat what I've just said. You won't, will you?"

"Of course not."

"It's so awful for Wendy," Marie Millace said. "She thought it was all over long ago."

"All over? I thought it had just started."

She sighed. "Wendy says her husband fell like a ton of bricks for this Dana creature months ago, but then the wretched girl faded off the scene and didn't go racing at all, and Wendy thought that he'd stopped seeing her. And now she's back in full view and it's obvious to everyone, Wendy says, that her husband is more overpoweringly in love than ever, and also *proud* of it. I'm so sorry for Wendy. It's all so horrid." She looked genuinely sympathetic, and yet her troubles, by any standard, were much worse.

"Do you know Dana den Relgan yourself?" I asked.

"No, not at all. George knew her, I think. Or at least he knew her by sight. He knew everyone. He said when we were in St. Tropez last summer that he thought he'd seen her there one afternoon, but I don't know if he meant it; he was laughing when he said it."

I drank some Coke and asked her conversationally if she and George had enjoyed St. Tropez, and if they had been there often. Yes they had loved it, and no, only once. George as usual had spent most of the time glued to his camera, but he and Marie had lain on their balcony looking out to sea every afternoon and had tanned marvelously . . .

"Anyway," she said, "that's not what I wanted to talk to you about. I wanted to thank you for your kindness and ask you about that exhibition you suggested . . . and about how I might make some money out of those photographs. Because . . . and I know it's a sordid subject . . . I'm going to need . . . er . . ."

"Everyone needs," I said comfortingly. "But didn't George leave things like insurance policies?"

"Yes. Some. And I'll have the money for the house, though not its full value, unfortunately. But it won't be enough to live on, not with inflation and everything."

"Didn't George," I asked delicately, "have any . . . well . . . savings . . . in any separate bank accounts?"

Her friendly expression began to change to suspicion. "Are you asking me the same sort of things as the police?"

"Marie . . . think of the burglaries, and your face, and the arson."

"He wasn't," she said explosively. "George wouldn't . . . I told you before. Don't you believe me?"

I sighed and didn't answer, and asked her if she knew which friend George had stopped for a drink with, on his way back from Doncaster.

"Of course I know. He wasn't a friend. Barely an acquaintance. A man called Lance Kinship. George rang me from Doncaster in the morning, as he often did when he stayed away overnight, and he mentioned he'd be half an hour or so late as he was calling at this man's house, as it was on his way home. This Lance Kinship wanted George to take some pictures of him working. He's a film director, or something. George said he was a pernicious self-deluding little egotist, but if he flattered him he'd pay well. That was almost the last thing he said to me." She took a deep breath and tried to control the tears which stood suddenly in her eyes. "I'm so sorry . . ." She sniffed and straightened her face with an effort, fishing in her pocket for a handkerchief.

"It's natural to cry," I said. It was only three weeks, after all, since George had died.

"Yes, but . . ." She tried to smile. "Not at the races." She wiped the edge of the handkerchief along under her lower eyelids and sniffed again. "The very last thing he said," she said, trying too hard, "was to ask me to buy some Ajax window cleaner. It's stupid, isn't it? I mean, except for saying 'see you,' the last thing George ever said to me was, 'Get some Liquid Ajax, will you?' and I don't even know . . ." She gulped. The tears were winning. "I don't even know what he wanted it for."

"Marie . . ." I held my hand out towards her and she gripped it as fiercely as at the hospital.

"They say you always remember the last thing that someone you love says to you . . ." Her lips quivered hopelessly.

"Don't think about it now," I said.

"No."

She wiped her eyes again and held onto my hand, but presently the turmoil subsided and she loosened her grip and gave a small laugh of embarrassment: and I asked her if there had been an autopsy.

"Oh . . . alcohol, do you mean? Yes, they tested his blood. They said it was below the limit . . . he'd only had two small whiskies with that Kinship. The police asked him . . . Lance Kinship . . . after I told them about George planning to stop there. He wrote to me, you know, saying he was sorry. But it wasn't his fault. I'd told George over and over to be careful. He often got dozy when he'd been driving a long way."

I told her how it happened that Lance Kinship had asked me to take photographs that George had been going to do, and she was more interested than I had expected.

"George always said you'd wake up one day and pinch his market." She produced a wavery smile to make it the joke it had undoubtedly been. "I wish he knew. I wish . . . oh dear, oh dear."

We just sat for a while until the fresh tears subsided, and she apologized again for them, and again I said one would expect them.

I asked for her address so that I could put her in touch with an agent for George's work, and she said she was staying with some friends who lived near Steve. She didn't know, she said forlornly, where she would be going from there. Because of the arson she had no clothes except the few ones she was wearing. No furniture. Nothing to make a home of. Worse . . . much worse . . . she had no photograph of George.

By the time I left Marie Millace, the fifth race had been run. I went straight out to the car to fetch Lance Kinship's pictures, and returned towards the weighing room to find Jeremy Folk standing outside the door on one leg.

"You'll fall over," I said.

"Oh . . . er . . ." He put the foot down gingerly, as if to

stand on two legs made him more positively there. "I thought . . . er . . ."

"You thought if you weren't here I might not do what you want."

"Er . . . yes."

"You may well be right."

"I came here by train," he said contentedly, "so can you take me with you to St. Albans?"

"I guess I'll have to."

Lance Kinship, seeing me there, came over to collect his prints. I introduced him and Jeremy to each other out of habit, and added for Jeremy's sake that it was at Lance Kinship's house that George Millace had taken his last drink.

Kinship, untucking the flap of the stiffened envelope, gave each of us a sharp glance followed by a sorrowful shake of the head.

"A great fellow, George," he said. "Too bad."

He pulled the pictures out of the envelope and looked through them with his eyebrows rising even higher above his spectacle frames.

"Well, well," he said. "I like them. How much do you want?"

I mentioned a figure which I thought exorbitant, but he merely nodded, pulled out a stuffed wallet, and paid me there and then in cash.

"Reprints?" he said.

"Certainly. They'd be less."

"Get me two sets," he said. "Right?"

As before, the last "t" of "right" stuck somewhere in his throat.

"Complete sets?" I said surprised. "All of them?"

"Sure. All of them. Very nice, they are. Want to see?"

He flicked them invitingly at Jeremy, who said he'd like to see them very much; and he too inspected them with his eyebrows rising.

"You must be," he said to Kinship, "a director of great note."

Kinship positively beamed and tucked his pictures back into the envelope. "Two more sets," he said. "Right?"

"Right."

He nodded and walked away, and before he'd gone ten paces he was pulling the pictures out again to show them to someone else.

"He'll get you a lot of work if you don't look out," Jeremy said, watching.

I didn't know whether or not I wanted to believe him, and in any case my attention was caught by something much more extraordinary. I stood very still and stared.

"Do you see," I said to Jeremy, "those two men over there, talking?"

"Of course I see them."

"One of them is Bart Underfield, who trains in Lambourn. And the other is one of the men in that photograph of the French cafe. That's Elgin Yaxley . . . come home from Hong Kong."

Three weeks after George's death, two weeks after the burning of his house; and Elgin Yaxley was back on the scene.

I had jumped to conclusions before, but surely this time it was reasonable to suppose that Elgin Yaxley believed the incriminating photograph had safely gone up in smoke. Reasonable to suppose, watching him standing there expansively smiling and full of confidence, that he felt freed and secure. When a blackmailer and all his possessions were cremated, his victims rejoiced.

Jeremy said, "It can't be coincidence."

"No."

"He looks pretty smug."

"He's a creep."

Jeremy glanced at me. "You've still got that photo?"

"I sure have."

We stood for a while looking on while Elgin Yaxley clapped Bart Underfield on the back and smiled like a crocodile and Bart Underfield looked happier than he had since the trial.

"What will you do with it?"

"Just wait, I suppose," I said, "to see what happens."

"I think I was wrong," Jeremy said thoughtfully, "to say you should burn all those things in the box."

"Mm," I smiled faintly. "Tomorrow I'll have a go at the blue oblongs."

"So you've worked out how?"

"Well, I hope so. Have to see."

"How, then?"

He looked genuinely interested, his eyes switching from their customary scanning of the neighborhood to a steady ten seconds in my direction.

"Um . . . do you want a lecture on the nature of light, or just the proposed order of events?"

"No lecture."

"OK. Then I think if I enlarge the orange negatives through blue light onto high-contrast black-and-white paper I might get a picture."

He blinked. "In black and white?"

"With luck."

"How do you get blue light?"

"That's rather where the lecture comes in," I said. "Do you want to watch the last race?"

We had a slight return of angular elbow movements and of standing on one leg, all on account, I guessed, of squaring the solicitorial conscience with the condoning of gambling.

I had done him an injustice, however. When we were watching on the stands for the race to start he said, "I did . . . ah . . . in point of fact . . . er . . . watch you ride . . . this afternoon."

"Did you?"

"I thought . . . it, ah, might be instructive."

"And how did it grab you?"

"To be honest," he said, "rather you than me."

He told me, as we drove towards St. Albans, about his researches into the television company.

"I got them to show me the credits, as you suggested, and I asked if they could put me in touch with anyone who worked on the play at Pine Woods Lodge. It was only a single play, by the way. The unit was there for only about six weeks."

"Not very promising," I said.

"No. Anyway, they told me where to find the director. Still working in television. Very dour and depressing man, all grunts and heavy moustache. He was sitting on the side of a road in Streatham watching some electricians holding a union meeting before they went on strike and refused to light the scene he wanted to shoot in a church porch. His mood, in a word, was vile."

"I can imagine."

"I'm afraid," Jeremy said regretfully, "that he wasn't much help. Thirteen years ago? How the hell did I expect him to remember one crummy six weeks thirteen years ago? How the hell did I expect him to remember some crummy girl with a crummy brat? And much more to that effect. The only positive thing he said was that if he'd been directing there would have been no crummy hangers on anywhere near Pine Woods Lodge. He couldn't stand outsiders hanging about when he was working, and would I, too, please get the hell out."

"Pity."

"After that I tracked down one of the main actors in the play, who is temporarily working in an art gallery, and got much the same answer. Thirteen years? Girl with small child? Not a chance."

I sighed. "I had great hopes of the television lot."

"I could carry on," Jeremy said. "They aren't difficult

to find. I just rang up a few agents to get the actor."

"It's up to you, really."

"I think I might."

"How long were the musicians there?" I said.

Jeremy fished out a by now rather worn-looking piece of paper, and consulted it.

"Three months, give or take a week."

"And after them?"

"The religious fanatics." He grimaced. "I don't suppose your mother was religious?"

"Heathen."

"It's all so long ago."

"Mm." I said. "Why don't we try something else? Why not publish Amanda's photograph in the *Horse and Hound*, and ask specifically for an identification of the stable. Those buildings are probably still standing, and looking just the same."

"Wouldn't a big enough picture cost a lot?"

"Not compared with private detectives." I reflected. "I think the *Horse and Hound* charges for space, not for what you put in it. Photographs cost no more than words. So I could make a good sharp black-and-white print of Amanda . . . and we could at least see."

He sighed. "OK, then. But I can see the final expenses of this search costing more than the inheritance."

I glanced at him. "Just how rich is she . . . my grandmother?"

"She may be broke, for all I know. She's incredibly secretive. I dare say her accountant has some idea, but he makes a clam look sloppy."

We reached St. Albans and detoured around to the nursing home; and, while Jeremy read old copies of *The Lady* in the waiting room, I talked upstairs with the dying old woman.

Sitting up, supported by pillows, she watched me walk into her room. The strong harsh face was still full of stubborn life, the eyes as unrelentingly fierce. She said not something gentle like "Hallo" or "Good evening," but merely "Have you found her?"

"No."

She compressed her mouth. "Are you trying?"

"Yes and no."

"What does that mean?"

"It means I've used some of my spare time looking for her but not my whole life."

She stared at me with narrowed eyes, and presently I sat in the visitor's armchair and continued to stare back.

"I went to see your son," I said.

Her face melted for a passing moment into an unguarded and revealing mixture of rage and disgust, and with a sense of surprise I saw the passion of her disappointment. I had already understood that a non-marrying non-child-producing son had essentially robbed her not of daughter-in-law and grandchildren as such, to whom on known form she might anyway have behaved tyrannically, but of continuation itself; but I certainly hadn't realized that her search for Amanda sprang from obsession and not pique.

"Your genes to go on," I said slowly. "Is that what you want?"

"Death is pointless otherwise."

I thought that life itself was pretty pointless, but I didn't say so. One woke up alive, and did what one could, and died. Perhaps she was in fact right . . . that the point of life was for genes to go on. Genes surviving, through generations of bodies.

"Whether you like it or not," I said, "your genes may go on through me."

The idea still displeased her. The muscles tightened along her jaw, and it was in a hard unfriendly voice that at length she said, "That young solicitor thinks I should tell you who your father was."

I stood up at once, unable to stay calm. Although I had come to find out, I now didn't want to. I wanted to escape.

To leave the room. Not to hear. I felt nervous in a way I hadn't done for years, and my mouth was sticky and dry.

"Don't you want to know?" she demanded.

"No."

"Are you afraid?" She was scornful. Sneering.

I simply stood there, not answering, wanting to know and not wanting, afraid and not afraid: in an absolute muddle.

"I have hated your father since before you were born," she said bitterly. "I can hardly bear even now to look at you, because you're like him . . . like he was at your age. Thin . . . and physical . . . and with the same eyes."

I swallowed, and waited, and felt numb.

"I loved him," she said, spitting the words out as if they themselves offended her. "I doted on him. He was thirty and I was forty-four. I'd been a widow for five years . . . I was lonely. Then he came. He lived with me . . . and we were going to marry. I adored him. I was stupid."

She stopped. There really was no need to go on. I knew all the rest. All the hatred she had felt for me all those years was finally explained. So simply explained . . . and understood . . . and forgiven. Against all expectations what I suddenly felt for my grandmother was pity.

I took a deep breath. I said, "Is he still alive?"

"I don't know. I haven't spoken to him or heard of him since."

"And what . . . was his name?"

She stared at me straightly, nothing in her own persistent hatred being changed a scrap. "I'm not going to tell you. I don't want you seeking him out. He ruined my life. He bedded my seventeen-year-old daughter under my own roof and he was after my money. That's the sort of man your father was. The only favor I'll do you is not to tell you his name. So be satisfied."

I nodded. I made a vague gesture with one hand and said awkwardly, "I'm sorry."

Her scowl if anything deepened.

"Now find Amanda for me," she said. "That solicitor said you would, if I told you. So go away and do it." She closed her eyes and looked immediately more ill, more vulnerable. "I don't like you," she said. "So go away."

"Well?" Jeremy said, downstairs.

"She told me."

"The milkman?"

"Near enough." I relayed to him the gist of it, and his reaction was the same as mine.

"Poor old woman."

"I could do with a drink," I said.

13

In printing color photographs one's aim was usually to produce a result that looked natural, and this was nowhere near as easy as it sounded. Apart from trifles like sharp focus and the best length and brightness of exposure, there was the matter of color itself, which came out differently on each make of film, and on each type of photographic printing paper, and even on paper from two boxes of the same type from the same manufacturer: the reason for this being that the four ultra-thin layers of emulsion laid onto color printing paper varied slightly from batch to batch. In the same way that it was almost impossible to dye two pieces of cloth in different dye baths and produce an identical result, so it was with light-sensitive emulsions.

To even this out and persuade all colors to look natural, one used color filters—pieces of colored glass inserted between the bright light on the enlarger and the negative. Get the mixture of filters right, and in the finished print blue eyes came out blue and cherry lips, cherry.

In my enlarger, as on the majority, the three filters were the same colors as the colors of negatives, yellow, magenta and cyan. Using all three filters together produced gray, so one used only two at once, and those two, as far as my sort of photographs were concerned, were always yellow and magenta. Used in delicate balance they could produce skin colors that were neither too yellow nor too pink for human faces, and it was to a natural looking skin color that one normally geared one's prints.

However, if one put a square of magenta-colored glass on a square of yellow-colored glass and shone a light through both together, one saw the result as red.

Shine a light through yellow and cyan, and you got green. And through magenta and cyan . . . a pure royal blue.

I had been confused when Charlie had first shown me, because mixing colored light produced dramatically different results from mixing colored paints. Even the primary colors were different. Forget paint, Charlie had said. This is light. You can't make blue by mixing other colored paints, but you can with light.

"Cyan?" I'd said. "Like cyanide?"

"Cyanide turns you blue," he said. "Cyan is a Greek word for blue. *Kyanos*. Don't forget. Cyan is greeny blue, and not surprisingly you get it by mixing blue light with green."

"You do?" I'd said doubtfully, and he had shown me the six colors of light, and mixed them for me before my eyes until I got their relationship fixed in my head forever, until they were as basic in my brain as the shape of letters.

In the beginning were red, green, and blue. I went into my darkroom on that fateful Sunday morning and adjusted the filters in the head of the enlarger so that the light which shone through the negatives would be that unheard-of combination for normal printing: full cyan and full magenta filtration, producing a deep clear blue.

I was going to print George's blank color negatives onto black-and-white paper, which would certainly rid me of the blue of the oblongs: but all I might get instead were gray oblongs.

Black-and-white printing paper was sensitive only to blue light (which was why one could print in black and white in red safe-light). I thought that if I printed the blank-looking negatives through heavy pure blue filtration I might get a greater contrast between the yellow dye image on the negative and the orange mask covering it. Make the image, in fact, emerge from its surroundings.

I had a feeling that whatever was hidden by the mask would not itself be sharply black and white anyway . . . because if it had been it would have been visible through and in spite of the blue. What I was looking for would in itself be some sort of gray.

I set out the trays of developer and stop bath and fixer, and put all of the first thirty-six unblotched negatives into a contact-printing frame. In this way the negative was held directly against the printing paper when the light was passed through it, so that the print, when finished, was exactly the same size as the negative. The frame merely held all the negatives conveniently so that all thirty-six could be printed at once onto one eight-by-ten-inch sheet of paper.

Getting the exposure time right was the biggest difficulty, chiefly because the heavy blue filtration meant that the light getting to the negatives was far dimmer than I was used to. I wasted about six shots in tests, getting useless results from gray to black, all the little oblongs still stubbornly looking as if there was nothing on them to see, whatever I did.

Finally in irritation I cut down the exposure time to far below what it was reasonable to think right, and came up with a print that was almost entirely white. I stood in the dim red light watching the white sheet lie in the developer with practically nothing happening except that the frame numbers of the negatives very palely appeared, followed by faint lines showing where the edges of the negatives had been.

Sighing with frustration I left it in the developer until

nothing else emerged, and then feeling depressed dipped it in the stop bath and then fixed it and washed it, and switched on the bright lights.

Five of the oblongs were not entirely white. Five of the little oblongs, scattered at random through the thirty-six, bore very pale gray geometric shapes.

I had found them.

I could feel myself smiling with ridiculous joy. George had left a puzzle, and I had almost solved it. If I was going to take his place, it was right that I should.

If I . . . My God, I thought. Where did thoughts come from? I had no intention of taking his place. No conscious intention. That thought had come straight from the sub-conscious, unbidden, unwanted.

I shivered slightly and felt vaguely alarmed, and without any smile at all wrote down the frame numbers of the five gray-patterned prints. Then I wandered around the house for a while doing mindless jobs like tidying the bedroom and shaking out the beanbags and stacking a few things in the dishwasher. Made a cup of coffee and sat down in the kitchen to drink it. Considered walking down to the village to fetch a Sunday paper, and instead went compulsively back to the darkroom.

It made all the difference knowing which negatives to look at, and roughly what to look for.

I took the first one numerically, which happened to be number seven, and enlarged it to the full size of the ten-by-eight-inch paper. A couple more bad guesses at exposure times left me with unclear dark gray prints, but in the end I came up with one which developed into mid-gray on white; I took it out of the developer as soon as it had reached its peak of contrast, and stopped it and fixed it and washed it, and carried it out to the daylight in the kitchen.

Although the print was still wet, one could see exactly what it was. One could read it without difficulty. A typewritten letter starting, "Dear Mr. Morton" and ending "Yours sincerely, George Millace."

A letter typed onto white paper with an old grayish ribbon, so that the typing itself looked pale gray. Pale gray, but distinct.

The letter said:

Dear Mr. Morton,

I am sure you will be interested in the enclosed two photographs. As you will see, the first one is a picture of your horse Amber Globe running poorly in your colors in the two-thirty race at Southwell on Monday, May 12th.

As you will also see, the second picture is of your horse Amber Globe winning the four o'clock race at Fontwell on Wednesday, August 27th.

If you look closely at the photographs you will see that they are not of the same horse. Alike but not identical.

I am sure that the Jockey Club would be interested in this difference. I will ring you shortly, however, with an alternative suggestion.

Yours sincerely,
George Millace

I read it through about six times, not because I didn't take it in the first time, but simply as an interval for assimilation and thought.

There were some practical observations to be made, which were that the letter bore no heading and no date and no handwritten signature. There was an assumption to be drawn that the other four pale gray geometric patterns would also turn out to be letters; and that what I had found was George's idiosyncratic filing system.

Beyond those flat thoughts lay a sort of chaos: a feeling of looking into a pit. If I enlarged and read the other letters, I could find that I knew things which would make "waiting to see what happens" impossible. I might feel, as I did in the case of the gray-smudge lovers, that doing nothing was weak and wrong. If I learned all George's secrets, I would have to accept the moral burden of deciding what to do about them . . . and of doing it.

To postpone the decision I went upstairs to the sitting room and looked through the form books to find out in which year Amber Globe had won at Fontwell on August 12th; it had been four years previously.

I looked up Amber Globe's career from start to finish, and what it amounted to on average was three or four poorer showings followed by an easy win at high odds, this pattern being repeated twice a season for four years. Amber Globe's last win had been the one on August 12th, and from then on he had run in no more races at all.

A supplementary search showed that the trainer of Amber Globe did not appear in the list of trainers for any subsequent years, and had probably gone out of business. There was no way of checking from those particular books whether "Dear Mr. Morton" had subsequently owned or run any more horses, although such facts would be stored in central official racing records.

Dear Mr. Morton and his trainer had been running two horses under the name of Amber Globe, switching in the good one for the big gambles, letting the poor one lengthen the odds. I wondered if George had noticed the pattern and gone deliberately to take his photographs; or whether he had taken the photographs merely in the course of work, and then had noticed the difference in the horses. There was no way of knowing or even guessing, as I hadn't found the two photographs in question.

I looked out of the window at the Downs for a while, and wandered around a bit fingering things and doing nothing much, waiting for the arrival of a comfortable certainty that knowledge did not involve responsibility. I waited in vain. I knew that it did. The knowledge was

downstairs, and I would have to acquire it. I had come
too far to want to stop.

Unsettled, fearful, but with a feeling of inevitability, I
went down to the darkroom and printed the other four
negatives one by one, and read the resulting letters in the
kitchen. With all five in the drier I sat for ages staring
into space, thinking disjointed thoughts.

George had been busy. The sly malice of George's
mind spoke out as clearly as if I could hear his voice.
George's ominous letters must have induced fear and de-
spondency in colossal proportions.

The second of them said:

Dear Bonnington Ford,
   I am sure you will be interested in the enclosed
series of photographs, which, as you will see, are
a record of you entertaining in your training stables on Sunday afternoons a person who has been
"warned off." I don't suppose I need to remind
you that the racing authorities would object
strongly to this continuous association, even to
the extent of reviewing your license to train.
   I could of course send copies of these photographs to the Jockey Club. I will ring you shortly,
however, with an alternative suggestion.
                                        Yours sincerely,
                                        George Millace

Bonnington Ford was a third-rate trainer who by general consensus was as honest and trustworthy as a pick-
pocket at Aintree, and he trained in a hollow in the Downs
at a spot where any passing motorist could glance down
into his yard. It would have been no trouble at all for
George Millace, if he had wanted to, to sit in his car at
that spot and take telephoto pictures at his leisure.

Again I hadn't found the photographs in question, so
there was nothing I could do about that particular letter,

even if I had wanted to. George hadn't even mentioned the name of the disqualified person. I was let off any worrying choice.

The last three letters were a different matter, one in which the dilemma sharply raised its head: where did duty lie, and how much could one opt out.

Of these three letters the first said:

Dear Elgin Yaxley,

I am sure you will be interested in the enclosed photograph. As you will see, it clearly contradicts a statement you recently made on oath at a certain trial.

I am sure that the Jockey Club would be interested to see it, and also the police, the judge, and the insurance company. I could send all of them copies simultaneously.

I will ring you shortly, however, with an alternative suggestion.

Yours sincerely,
George Millace

The one next to it on the film roll would have driven the nails right in. It said:

Dear Elgin Yaxley,

I am happily able to tell you that since I wrote to you yesterday there have been further developments.

Yesterday I also visited the farmer upon whose farm you boarded your unfortunate steeplechasers, and I showed him in confidence a copy of the photograph, which I sent to you. I suggested that there might be a full further enquiry, during which his own share in the tragedy might be investigated.

He felt able to respond to my promise of silence with the pleasing information that your five good horses were not after all dead. The five horses which died had been bought especially and cheaply by him (your farmer friend) from a local auction, and it was these which were shot by Terence O'Tree at the appointed time and place. Terence O'Tree was not told of the substitution.

Your farmer friend also confirmed that when the veterinary surgeon had given your good horses their anti-tetanus jabs and had left after seeing them in good health, you yourself arrived at the farm in a horsebox to supervise their removal.

Your friend understood you would be shipping them out to the Far East, where you already had a buyer.

I enclose a photograph of his signed statement to this effect.

I will ring you shortly with a suggestion.

Yours sincerely,
George Millace

The last of the five prints was different from the others in that its letter was handwritten, not typed, but as it had apparently been written in pencil, it was still of the same pale gray.

It said:

Dear Elgin Yaxley,

I bought the five horses that T. O'Tree shot. You fetched your own horses away in a horsebox, to export them to the East. I am satisfied with what you paid me for this service.

Yours faithfully,
David Parker

I thought of Elgin Yaxley as I had seen him the previous day at Ascot, smirking complacently and believing himself safe.

I thought of right and wrong, and justice. Thought of Elgin Yaxley as the victim of George Millace, and of the insurance company as the victim of Elgin Yaxley. Thought of Terence O'Tree who had gone to jail, and David Parker, who hadn't.

I couldn't decide what to do.

After a while I got up stiffly and went back to the darkroom. I put all of the magenta-splashed set of negatives into the contact-printing frame and made a nearly white print: and this time there were not five little oblongs with gray blocks, but fifteen.

With a hollow feeling of horror I switched off all the lights, locked the doors, and walked up the road to my briefing with Harold.

"Pay attention," Harold said sharply.

"Er . . . yes."

"What's the matter?"

"Nothing."

"I'm talking about Coral Key at Kempton on Wednesday, and you're not listening."

I dragged my attention back to the matter in hand.

"Coral Key," I said. "For Victor Briggs."

"That's right."

"Has he said anything . . . about yesterday?"

Harold shook his head. "We had a drink after the race, but if Victor doesn't want to talk, you can't get a word out of him, and all he uttered were grunts. But until he tells me you're off his horses, you're still on them."

He gave me a glass and a can of Coke and poured a large whisky for himself.

"I haven't much for you this week," he said. "Nothing Monday or Tuesday. Pebble was going to run at Leicester but there's some heat in his leg . . . There's just Coral Key on Wednesday, Diamond Buyer and the mare Friday, and two on Saturday, as long as it doesn't rain. Have you any outside rides lined up?"

"A novice 'chaser at Kempton on Thursday."

"I hope it can bloody jump."

I went back to the quiet cottage and made prints from the fifteen magenta-splashed negatives, getting plain white-and-gray results as before, as the blotchy shapes were filtered out along with the blue.

To my relief they were not fifteen threatening letters: only the first two of them finished with the promise of alternative suggestions.

I had expected one on the subject of the lovers, and it was there. It was the second one which left me breathless and weakly laughing in the kitchen: and certainly it put me in a better frame of mind for any revelations to come.

The last thirteen prints, however, turned out to be George's own notes of where and when he had taken his incriminating pictures, and on what film, and at which exposures, and on what dates he had sent the frightening letters. I guessed he had kept his records in this form because it had turned out to be easy for him, and had seemed safer than leaving such damaging material lying legibly around on paper.

As a backup to the photographs and letters they were fascinating, but they all failed to say what the "alternative suggestions" had been. There was no record of what monies George had extorted, nor of any bank, safe deposit, or hiding place where he could have stashed the proceeds. Even to himself, George on this subject had been reticent.

I went late to bed and couldn't sleep, and in the morning made some telephone calls.

One to the editor of the *Horse and Hound*, whom I knew, begging him to include Amanda's picture in that week's issue, emphasizing that time was short. He said dubiously that he would print it if I got it to his office that morning, but after that it would be too late.

"I'll be there," I said. "Two columns wide, photograph seven centimeters deep, with some wording top and bottom. Say eleven centimeters altogether. On a nice right-hand page near the front where no one can miss it."

"Philip!" he protested, but then sighed audibly, and I knew he would do it. "That camera of yours . . . If you've got any racing pics I might use, bring them along. I'll have a look anyway. No promises, mind, but a look. It's people I want, not horses. Portraits. Got any?"

"Well . . . yes."

"Good. Soon as possible, then. See you."

I telephoned to Marie Millace for Lord White's home number, and then I telephoned Old Driven Snow at his home in the Cotswolds.

"You want to see me?" he said. "What about?"

"About George Millace, sir."

"Photographer? Died recently?"

"Yes, sir. His wife is a friend of Lady White."

"Yes, yes," he said, impatiently. "I could see you at Kempton, if you like."

I asked if I could call on him at his home instead, and although he wasn't overpoweringly keen, he agreed to my taking half an hour of his time at five o'clock the next day. With slightly sweating palms I replaced the receiver and said "phew" and thought that all I had to do to back out was to ring him again and cancel.

After that I telephoned to Samantha, which was a great deal easier, and asked if I could take her and Clare out to dinner. Her warm voice sounded pleased.

"Tonight?" she said.

"Yes."

"I can't go. But I'm sure Clare can. She'd like it."

"Would she?"

"Yes, you silly man. What time?"

I said I would pick her up at about eight, and Samantha said fine and how was the search for Amanda going, and

I found myself talking to her as if I'd known her all my life. As indeed, in a way, I had.

I drove to London to the *Horse and Hound* offices and fixed with the editor to print Amanda's picture captioned *"Where is this stable? Ten pounds for the first person— and particularly for the first child—who can telephone Philip Nore to tell him."*

"Child?" said the editor, raising his eyebrows and adding my telephone number. "Do they read this paper?"

"Their mothers do."

"Subtle stuff."

He said, looking through the folder I'd brought of racing faces, that they were starting a series on racing personalities, and he wanted new pictures that hadn't already appeared all over the place, and he could use some of mine, if I liked.

"Er . . . yes."

"Usual rates," he said casually, and I said fine; and only after a pause did I ask him what the usual rates were. Even to ask, it seemed to me, was a step nearer to caring as much for the income as for the photographs themselves. Usual rates were a commitment. Usual rates meant joining the club. I found it disturbing. I accepted them, all the same.

Samantha was out when I went to fetch Clare.

"Come in for a drink first," Clare said, opening the door wide. "It's such a lousy evening."

I stepped in out of the wind and cold rain of late November and we went not downstairs to the kitchen but into the long gently lit ground floor sitting room, which stretched from the front to the back of the house. I looked around, seeing its comfort, but feeling no familiarity.

"Do you remember this room?" Clare said.

I shook my head.

"Where's the bathroom?" she said.

I answered immediately, "Up the stairs, turn right, blue ba . . ."

She laughed. "Straight from the subconscious."

"It's so odd."

There was a television set in one corner with a program of talking heads, and Clare walked over and switched it off.

"Don't, if you're in the middle of watching," I said.

"It was just another antidrug lecture. All these pontificating so-called experts. How about that drink? What would you like? There is some wine . . ." She held up a bottle of white Burgundy, opened, so we settled on that.

"Some smug little presenter was saying," she said, pouring into the glasses, "that one in five women take tranquilizers, but only one in ten men. Implying that poor little women are so much less able to deal with life, the feeble little dears." She handed me a glass. "Makes you laugh."

"Does it?"

She grinned. "I suppose it never occurs to the doctors who write out the prescriptions that the poor feeble little women sprinkle those tranquilizers all over their husbands' dinner when he comes home from work."

I laughed.

"They do," she said. "The ones with great hulking bastards who knock them about, and the ones who don't like too much sex . . . they mix the nice tasteless powder into the brute's meat and potatoes, and lead a quiet life."

"It's a great theory."

"Fact," she said.

We sat in a couple of pale velvet armchairs sipping the cool wine, she, in a scarlet silk shirt and black trousers, making a bright statement against the soft coloring of the room. A girl given to positive statements. A girl of decision and certainty and mental energy. Not at all like the gentle undemanding girls I occasionally took home.

"I saw you racing on Saturday," she said. "On television."

"I didn't think you were interested."

"Of course I am, since I saw your photos." She drank a mouthful. "You do take some frightful risks."

"Not always like Saturday." She asked why not, and rather to my surprise, I told her.

"But my goodness," she said indignantly, "that's not fair."

"Life's not fair. Too bad."

"What a gloomy philosophy."

"Not really. Take what comes, but hope for the best."

She shook her head. "Go out looking for the best." She drank and said, "What happens if you're really smashed up by one of those falls?"

"You curse."

"No, you fool. To your life, I mean."

"Mend as fast as possible and get back in the saddle. While you're out of it, some other jockey is pinching your rides."

"Charming," she said. "And what if it's too bad to mend?"

"You've got a problem. No rides, no income. You start looking at want ads."

"And what happens if you're killed?"

"Nothing much," I said.

"You don't take it seriously," she complained.

"Of course not."

She studied my face. "I'm not used to people who casually risk their lives most days of the week."

I smiled at her. "The risk is less than you'd think. But if you're really unlucky, there's always the Injured Jockeys' Fund."

"What's that?"

"The racing industry's private charity. It looks after the widows and orphans of dead jockeys and gives succor to badly damaged live ones, and makes sure no one pops off in old age for want of a lump of coal."

"Can't be bad."

We went out a little later and ate in a small restaurant determinedly decorated as a French peasant kitchen with scrubbed board tables, rushes on the floor, and dripping candles stuck in wine bottles. The food turned out to be as bogus as the surroundings, never having seen the light of anyone's pot au feu. Clare, however, seemed not to mind and we ate microwaved veal in a blanket white sauce, trying not to remember the blanquettes in France, where she too had been frequently, though for holidays, not racing.

"You race in France?"

"After Christmas, if it freezes here, there's always the chance of some rides at Cagnes sur Mer . . . down on the south coast."

"It sounds marvelous."

"It's still winter. And still work. But yes, not bad."

She returned to the subject of photographs, and said she would like to come down to Lambourn again to go through the Jockey's Life file.

"Don't worry if you want to change your mind," I said.

"Of course I don't." She looked at me in seeming alarm. "You haven't sold any to anyone else, have you? You did say you wouldn't."

"Not those."

"What, then?"

I told her about the *Horse and Hound*, and about Lance Kinship, and how odd I found it that all of a sudden people seemed to be wanting to buy my work.

"I would think," she said judiciously, "that the word has gone around." She finished her veal and sat back, her face serious with thought. "What you need is an agent."

I explained about having to find one for Marie Millace anyway, but she brushed that aside.

"Not *any* agent," she said. "I mean me."

She looked at my stunned expression and smiled. "Well?" she said. "What does any agent do? He knows the markets and sells the goods. Your goods will sell . . . obviously. So I'll learn pretty damn quick what the markets are, that I don't know already. The sports side of it, I mean. And what if I got you commissions for illustrations for other books . . . on any subject . . . would you do them?"

"Yes, but . . ."

"No buts," she said. "There's no point in taking super photos if no one sees them."

"But there are thousands of photographers."

"Why are you so defeatist?" she said. "There's always room for one more."

The candlelight shone on the intent expression and lay in apricot shadows under cheekbone and chin. Her gray eyes looked steadily at a future I still shied away from. I wondered what she'd say if I said I wanted to kiss her, when her thoughts were clearly more practical.

"I could try," she said persuasively. "I'd like to try. Will you let me? If I'm no good, I'll admit it."

She'll bully you into things, Samantha had said.

Take what comes, and hope for the best.

I stuck to my old philosophy and said, "All right," and she said "Great" as if she meant it: and later, when I delivered her to her doorstep and kissed her, she didn't object to that either.

14

Four times on Tuesday morning I lifted the telephone to cancel my appointment with Lord White. Once I got as far as hearing the bell ring at the other end. Four times I put the receiver down and decided I would have to go. I would have liked to go with more certainty that I was doing right; but anyway, I went.

Lord White's house in Gloucestershire turned out to be a weathered stone pile with more grandeur than gardeners. Noble windows raised their eyebrows above drifts of unswept leaves. A stubble of fawn stalks indicated lawn. A mat of dead weeds glued the gravel together. I rang the front doorbell and wondered about the economics of barony.

The third Baron White received me in a small sitting room, which gave onto a view of straggly rosebushes and an unclipped hedge. Inside, everything was of venerable antiquity, dusted and gleaming. Holes in the chintz chair covers had been patched. Less money than was needed, I diagnosed briefly, but still enough to keep at bay a three-bedroom apartment.

Lord White shook hands and offered me a chair in a mixture of puzzlement and civility, waiting for me to say

why I had come; and although I'd spent the whole journey
inventing possible openings, I found it an agony to begin.

"Sir . . ." I said. "I'm sorry . . . very sorry, sir . . . but
I'm afraid what I've come about may be a great shock to
you."

He frowned slightly. "About George Millace?" he said.
"You said it was something about George Millace."

"Yes . . . about some photographs he took."

I stopped. Too late, I wished fervently that I hadn't
come. I should after all have adhered to the lifetime habit
of noninvolvement, of wait and see. I should never have
set out to use George's wicked arsenal. But I had. I was
there. I had made the decision and acted on it. What I
was there for . . . had to be done.

My errand was to give pain. Purposely to hurt. To go
against all the instincts of compassion I owed to Samantha
and Charlie and Margaret and Bill. To serve as a wrecker,
with a brutal celluloid axe.

"Get on with it, Nore," Lord White said comfortably,
unsuspecting.

With foreboding I opened the large envelope I carried.
I pulled out the first of the three pictures of the lovers,
and put it into his outstretched hand: and for all that I
thought he was behaving foolishly over Dana den Relgan,
I felt deeply sorry for him.

His first reaction was of extreme anger. How dared I,
he said, standing up and quivering, how dared I bring him
anything so filthy and *disgusting*?

With the greatest difficulty, I thought; but he wouldn't
have appreciated it. I took the second and third photographs out of the envelope and rested them picture side
down on the arm of my chair.

"As you will see," I said, and my voice was hoarse,
"the others are if anything worse."

I reckoned it took him a lot of courage to pick up the
other two pictures. He looked at them in desparate silence,
and slowly sank down again in his chair.

His face told of his anguish. Of his disbelief. Of his horror.

The man making love to Dana was Ivor den Relgan.

"They say," Lord White said, "that they can fake pictures of anything." His voice shook. "Cameras do lie."

"Not this one," I said regretfully.

"It can't be true."

I took from the envelope a print of the letter George Millace had written, and gave it to him. He had difficulty in bringing himself to read it, so physically shaking was his distress.

The letter, which I knew by heart, read:

Dear Ivor den Relgan,

I am sure you will be interested in the enclosed photographs, which I was happily able to take a few days ago in St. Tropez.

As you will see, they show you in a compromising position with the young lady who is known as your daughter. (It is surely unwise to do this sort of thing on hotel balconies without making sure that one cannot be seen by telephoto lenses?)

There seem to be two possibilities here.

One. Dana den Relgan is your daughter, in which case this is incest.

Two. Dana den Relgan is not your daughter, in which case why are you pretending she is? Can it have anything to do with the ensnaring of a certain member of the Jockey Club? Are you hoping for entry to the Club, and other favors?

I could of course send these photographs to the Lord in question. I will ring you shortly, however, with an alternative suggestion.

Yours sincerely,
George Millace

Lord White became much older before my eyes, the glow that loving had given him shrinking grayly back into deepening wrinkles. I looked away. Looked at my hands, my feet, the spindly rosebushes outside. Anywhere but at that devastated man.

After a very long time he said, "Where did you get these?"

"George Millace's son gave me a box with some things of his father's in it, after his father died. These photos were in it."

He suffered through another silence, and said, "Why did you bring them to me? For the sake of causing me . . . mortification?"

I swallowed and said as flatly as possible, "You won't really have noticed, sir, but people are worried about how much power has been given recently to Ivor den Relgan."

He shuddered slightly at the name but raised the blue eyes to give me a long unfriendly inspection.

"And you have taken it upon yourself to try to stop it?"

"Sir . . . yes."

He looked grim, and as if seeking refuge in anger he said authoritatively, "It's none of your business, Nore."

I didn't answer at once. I'd had enough trouble in persuading myself that it *was* my business to last a lifetime. But in the end, diffidently, I said, "Sir, if you are certain in your own mind that Ivor den Relgan's sudden rise to unheard-of power is nothing whatever to do with your affection for Dana den Relgan, then I do most abjectly beg your pardon."

He merely stared.

I tried again. "If you truly believe that racing would benefit by Ivor den Relgan's appointing paid stewards, I apologize."

"Please leave," he said rigidly.

"Yes, sir."

I stood up and walked over to the door, but when I

reached it I heard his voice from behind me.

"Wait. Nore . . . I must think."

I turned, hovering. "Sir," I said, "you're so respected . . . and liked . . . by everyone. It's been no fun to watch what's been happening."

"Will you please come back and sit down?" His voice was still stern, still full of accusation and judgment. Still full of defense.

I returned to the armchair, and he went and stood by the window with his back to me, looking out to the dead roses.

His thoughts took time. So would mine have done, in the same situation. The result of them was a deep change in his voice in both pitch and content, for when he finally spoke again he sounded not shattered nor furious, but normal. He spoke, however, without turning around.

"How many people," he said, "have seen these pictures?"

"I don't know how many George Millace showed them to," I said. "As for me, they've been seen only by one friend. He was with me when I found them. But he doesn't know the den Relgans. He doesn't often go racing."

"So you didn't consult with anyone before you came here?"

"No, sir."

Another long pause. I was good, anyway, at waiting. The house around us was very quiet: holding its breath, I thought fancifully, as I, in a way, held mine.

"Do you intend," he said quietly, "to make jokes about this on the racecourse?"

"No." I was horrified. "I do not."

"And would you . . ." He paused, but went on. "Would you expect any reward, in service . . . or cash . . . for this silence?"

I stood up as if he had actually hit me, not delivered his thrust from six paces with his back turned.

"I would not," I said. "I'm not George Millace. I think . . . I think I'll go now." And go I did, out of the room, out of the house, out of his weedy domain, impelled by a severe hurt to the vanity.

On Wednesday nothing much happened; less, in fact, than expected, as I was met when I went to ride out first lot with the news that Coral Key wouldn't be running that day at Kempton after all.

"Bloody animal got cast in its box during the night," Harold said. "I woke and heard him banging. God knows how long he'd been down; he was halfway exhausted. It won't please Victor."

With the riding fee down the drain it wasn't worth-while spending money on petrol to go spectating at the races, so I stayed at home and did Lance Kinship's re-prints.

Thursday I set off to Kempton with only one ride, thinking it was a very thin week on the earning front; but almost as soon as I'd stepped through the gate I was grabbed by a fierce little man who said his guv'nor was looking for me, and if I wanted his spare rides I should shift my arse.

I shifted, and got the rides just before the trainer in question thought I wouldn't get there in time and gave them to someone else.

"Very annoying," he said, puffing as if breathless, though I gathered he had been standing still waiting for me for fifteen minutes. "My fellow said yesterday he'd no ill effects from a fall he'd had. And then this morning, cool as you please, he rings to say he's got flu."

"Well . . . er . . ." I swallowed a laugh. "I don't suppose he can help it."

"Damned inconsiderate."

His horses turned out to have better lungs than their master, but were otherwise no great shakes. I got one of them round into third place in a field of six, and came down on the other two fences from home; a bit of a crash but nothing broken in either him or me.

The third horse, the one I'd gone originally to ride, wasn't much better: a clumsy underschooled baby of a horse with guts about equal to his skill. I took him round carefully in the novice 'chase to try to teach him his job, and got no thanks from the trainer who said I hadn't gone fast enough to keep warm.

"There were six or seven behind us," I said mildly.

"And six or seven in front."

I nodded. "He needs time." And patience, and weeks and months of jumping practice. He probably wouldn't get either, and I probably wouldn't be offered the mount again. The trainer would go for speed regardless, and the horse would crash at the open ditch, and it would serve the trainer right. Pity the poor horse.

The relief of the afternoon, as far as I was concerned, was the absence of Lord White.

The surprise of the afternoon was the presence of Clare. She was waiting outside the weighing room when I'd changed back into street clothes and was leaving for home.

"Hullo," she said.

"Clare!"

"Just thought I'd come and take a look at the real thing." Her eyes smiled. "Is today typical?"

I looked at the gray windy sky and the thin Thursday crowd, and thought of my three nondescript races.

"Pretty much," I said. "How did you get here?"

"By race train. Very educational. And I've been walking around all afternoon all a-goggle. I never knew people actually *ate* jellied eels."

I laughed. "I've never looked one in the face. Er . . . what would you like? A drink? A cup of tea? A trip to Lambourn?"

She thought it over briefly. "Lambourn," she said. "I can get a train back from there, can't I?"

I drove her to Berkshire with an unaccustomed feeling of contentment. It felt right to have her sitting there in the car. Natural. Probably, I thought, rationalizing, because she was Samantha's daughter.

The cottage was dark and cold, but soon warmed. I went around switching on lights and heat and the kettle for tea. When the telephone rang, I answered it in the kitchen, which was where it happened to be plugged in, and had my eardrum half-shattered by a piercing voice which shrieked, "Am I first?"

"Um," I said, wincing and holding the receiver away from my ear. "Are you first what?"

"First!" A very young voice. A child. Female. "I've been ringing every five minutes for *hours*. So am I first? Do say I'm first."

Realization dawned. "Yes," I said. "You're the very first. Have you been reading the *Horse and Hound*? It isn't published until tomorrow . . ."

"It gets to my auntie's bookshop on Thursdays." She sounded as if anyone in their right mind would know things like that. "I collect it for Mummy on my way home from school. And she saw the picture, and told me to ring you. So can I have the ten pounds? Can I really?"

"If you know where the stable is, yes, of course."

"Mummy knows. She'll tell you. You'd better talk to her now, but you won't forget, will you?"

"I won't," I said.

There were some background voices and clinks of the receiver at the far end, and then a woman's voice, pleasant and far less excited.

"Are you the Philip Nore who rides in National Hunt races?"

"Yes," I said.

It seemed to be enough of a reference, because she said without reservation, "I do know where that stable is, but I'm afraid you'll be disappointed, because it isn't used for horses any longer. Jane, my daughter, is afraid you won't send her the ten pounds when you know that, but I expect you will."

"I expect so," I agreed, smiling. "Where is it?"

"Not far from here. That's Horley, in Surrey. Near Gatwick airport. The stable's about half a mile from our house. It's still called Zephyr Farm Stables, but the riding school has been closed for years and years."

I sighed. "And the people who kept it?"

"No idea," she said. "I suppose they sold it. Anyway, it's been adapted into living quarters. Do you want the actual address?"

"I guess so," I said. "And yours, too, please."

She read them out to me and I wrote them down, and then I said, "Do you happen to know the name of the people living there now?"

"Huh," she said scornfully. "They're real pests. You won't get far with them, whatever it is you want, I'm afraid. They've got the place practically fortified to ward off furious parents."

"To . . . what?" I said, mystified.

"Parents trying to persuade their children to come home. It's one of those commune things. Religious brainwashing, something like that. They call themselves Colleagues of Supreme Grace. All nonsense. Pernicious nonsense."

I felt breathless.

"I'll send Jane the money," I said. "And thanks very much."

"What is it?" Clare said, as I slowly replaced the receiver.

"The first real lead to Amanda."

I explained about the *Horse and Hound* advertisement, and about the tenants of Pine Woods Lodge.

Clare shook her head. "If these Supreme Grace people know where Amanda is, they won't tell you. You must have heard of them, haven't you? Or others like them? They're all gentle and smiling on the surface, and like steel rat-traps underneath. They lure people my age with friendliness and sweet songs and hook them into Believing, and once they're in the poor slobs never get out. They're in love with their prison. Their parents hardly stand a chance."

"I've heard of something like it. But I've never seen the point."

"Money," Clare said crisply. "All the darling little Colleagues go out with saintly faces and collecting boxes, and rake in the cash."

"To live on?"

"Sure, to live on. And to further the cause, or in other words, to line the pockets of our great leader."

I made the tea and we sat by the table to drink it.

Amanda in a stableyard at Horley; Caroline twenty miles away at Pine Woods Lodge. Colleagues of Supreme Grace at Pine Woods Lodge, Colleagues ditto at Horley. Too close a connection to be a coincidence. Even if I never found out precisely what, there had been a rational sequence of events.

"She's probably not still there," I said.

"But you'll go looking?"

I nodded. "Tomorrow, I think, after racing."

When we'd finished the tea, Clare said she wanted to see the Jockey's Life folder again, so we took it upstairs, and I showed some of the pictures blown up on the wall to amuse her, and we talked of her life and mine and of nothing in particular; and later in the evening we went to the good pub at Ashbury for a steak.

"A great day," Clare said, smiling over the coffee. "Where's the train?"

"Swindon. I'll drive you there . . . or you could stay."

She regarded me levelly. "Is that the sort of invitation I think it is?"

"I wouldn't be surprised."

She looked down and fiddled with her coffee spoon, paying it a lot of attention. I watched the bent dark thinking head and knew that if it took her so long to answer, she would go.

"There's a fast train at ten-thirty," I said. "You could catch it comfortably. Just over an hour to Paddington."

"Philip . . ."

"It's all right," I said easily. "If one never asks, one never gets." I paid the bill. "Come on."

She was distinctly quiet on the six-mile drive to the railway station, and she didn't share her thoughts. Not until I'd bought her a ticket (against her objections) and was waiting with her up on the platform did she give any indication of what was in her mind, and then only obliquely.

"There's a Board meeting in the office tomorrow," she said. "It will be the first I've been to. They made me a director a month ago, at the last one."

I was most impressed, and said so. It couldn't be often that publishing houses put girls of twenty-two on the Board. I understood, also, why she wouldn't stay. Why she might never stay. The regret I felt shocked me with its sudden intensity, because my invitation to her hadn't been a desperate plea but only a suggestion for passing pleasure. I had meant it as a small thing, not a lifetime commitment. My sense of loss, on that railway platform, seemed out of all proportion.

The train came in and she climbed aboard, pausing with the door open to exchange kisses. Brief unpassionate kisses, no advance from Monday on the doorstep.

See you soon, she said, and I said yes. About contracts, she said. A lot to discuss.

"Come on Sunday," I said.

"Let you know. Goodbye."

"Goodbye."

The impatient train ground away, accelerating fast, and I drove home to the empty cottage with a most unaccustomed feeling of loneliness.

* * *

Newbury races, Friday, late November.

Lord White was there, standing under the expanse of glass roof outside the weighing room, talking earnestly to two fellow stewards. He looked the same as always, gray-white hair mostly hidden by trilby, brown covert coat over dark gray suit, air of benign good sense. Hard to imagine him high as a kite on love. Impossible, if one hadn't seen it.

I had to pass near him to reach the weighing-room door. He steadfastly continued his conversation with the stewards, and only through the barest flicker of his eyes in my direction did he show he knew I was there. If he didn't want to talk to me, I didn't mind. Less embarrassing all around.

Inside the weighing room stood Harold, expansively telling a crony about a good place for cut-price new tires. Hardly pausing for breath he told me he'd wait for my saddle if I'd do him a favor and change and weigh quickly, and when I went back to him in colors he was still on about cross-ply and radials. The crony took the opportunity to depart, and Harold, taking my saddle and weightcloth, said with mischievous amusement, "Did you hear that Ghengis Khan got the boot?"

I paid him sharp attention.

"Are you sure?" I said.

Harold nodded. "Old Lanky"—he pointed to the disappearing crony—"was telling me just before you arrived. He says they held an emergency-type meeting of the Jockey Club this morning in London. He was at it. Lord White asked them to cancel plans for a committee chaired by Ivor den Relgan, and as it was old Driven Snow's idea in the first place, they all agreed."

"It's something, anyway," I said.

"Something?" Harold swung towards exasperation. "Is that all you think? It's the best about-turn since the Armada."

He stalked off with my saddle, muttering and shaking

his head, and leaving me, had he but known it, in a state of extreme relief. Whatever else my visit to Lord White had done, it had achieved its primary object. At least, I thought gratefully, I hadn't caused so much havoc in a man I liked for nothing at all.

I rode a novice hurdler, which finished second, pleasing the owner mightily and Harold not much, and later a two-mile 'chase on a sensitive mare who had no real heart for the job and had to be nursed. Getting her around at all was the best to be hoped for, a successful conclusion greeted by Harold with a grunt. As we had also finished fourth I took it for a grunt of approval, but one could never be sure.

When I was changing back into street clothes a racecourse official stepped into the big bustling jockeys' room and shouted down the length of it, "Nore, you're wanted."

I finished dressing and went out into the weighing room, and found that the person who was waiting was Lord White.

"I want to talk to you," he said. "Come over here into the stewards' room . . . and close the door, will you?"

I followed him into the room off the weighing room used by the stewards for on-the-spot enquiries, and, as he asked, shut the door. He stood behind one of the chairs which surrounded the big table, grasping its back with both hands as if it gave him a shield, a barrier, the rampart of a citadel. "I regret," he said formally, "what I imputed to you on Tuesday."

"It's all right, sir."

"I was upset . . . but it was indefensible."

"I do understand, sir."

"What do you understand?"

"Well . . . that when someone hurts you, you want to kick them."

He half smiled. "Poetically put, if I may say so."

"Is that all, sir?"

"No, it isn't." He paused, pondering. "I suppose you've heard that the committee is canceled?"

I nodded.

He drew a sober breath. "I want to request den Relgan's resignation from the Jockey Club. The better to persuade him, I am of a mind to show him those photographs, which of course he has seen already. I think, however, that I need your permission to do so, and that is what I am asking."

Talk about leverage, I thought; and I said, "I've no objection. Please do what you like with them."

"Are they . . . the only copies?"

"Yes," I said, which in fact they were. I didn't tell him I also had the negatives. He would have wanted me to destroy them, and my instincts were against it.

He let go of the chair back as if no longer needing it, and walked around me to the door. His face, as he opened it, bore the firm familiar blameless expression of pre-Dana days. The cruel cure, I thought, had been complete.

"I can't exactly thank you," he said civilly, "but I'm in your debt." He gave me a slight nod and went out of the room: transaction accomplished, apology given, dignity intact. He would soon be busy persuading himself, I thought, that he hadn't felt what he'd felt, that his infatuation hadn't existed.

Slowly I followed, satisfied on many counts, on many levels, but not knowing if he knew it. The profoundest gifts weren't always those explicitly given.

From Marie Millace I learned more.

She had come to Newbury to see Steve ride now that his collarbone had mended, though she confessed, as I steered her off for a cup of coffee, that watching one's son race over fences was an agony.

"All jockeys' wives say it's worse when their sons start," I said. "Daughters too, I dare say."

We sat at a small table in one of the bars, surrounded

by people in bulky overcoats which smelled of cold damp
air and seemed to steam slightly in the warmth. Marie
automatically stacked to one side the debris of cups and
sandwich wrappers left by the last customers, and
thoughtfully stirred her coffee.

"You're looking better," I said.

She nodded. "I feel it."

She had been to a hairdresser, I saw, and had bought
some more clothes. Still pale, with smudged grieving
eyes. Still fragile, inclined to sound shaky, tears under
control but not far. Four weeks away from George's
death.

She sipped the hot coffee and said, "You can forget
what I told you last week about the Whites and Dana den
Relgan."

"Can I?"

She nodded. "Wendy's here. We had coffee earlier on.
She's very much happier."

"Tell me about it," I said.

"Are you interested? I'm not prattling on?"

"Very interested," I assured her.

"She said that last Tuesday, sometime on Tuesday, her
husband found out something he didn't like about Dana
den Relgan. She doesn't know what. He didn't tell her.
But she said he was like a zombie all evening, white and
staring and not hearing a word that was said to him. She
didn't know what was the matter, not then, and she was
quite frightened. He locked himself away alone all
Wednesday, but in the evening he told her his affair with
Dana was over, and that he'd been a fool, and would she
forgive him."

I listened, amazed that women so easily relayed that
sort of gossip, and pleased they did.

"And after that?" I said.

"Aren't men extraordinary?" Marie Millace said. "After that he began to behave as if the whole thing had never
happened. Wendy says that now he has confessed and

apologized, he expects her to go on as before, as if he'd never gone off and slept with the wretched girl."

"And will she?"

"Oh, I expect so. Wendy says his trouble was the common one among men of fifty or so, wanting to prove to themselves they're still young. She understands him, you see."

"So do you," I said.

She smiled with sweetness. "Goodness, yes. You see it all the time."

When we'd finished the coffee I gave her a short list of agents that she might try, and said I'd give any help I could. After that I told her I'd brought a present for her. I had been going to give it to Steve to give to her, but as she was there herself, she could have it: it was in my bag in the changing room.

I fetched out and handed to her a ten-by-eight-inch cardboard envelope which said "Photographs—Do Not Bend" along its borders.

"Don't open it until you're alone," I said.

"I *must*," she said, and opened it there and then.

It contained a photograph I'd taken once of George. George holding his camera, looking towards me, smiling his familiar sardonic smile. George in color. George in a typically George-like pose, one leg forward with his weight back on the other, head back, considering the world a bad joke. George as he'd lived.

There and then in full public view Marie Millace flung her arms round me and hugged me as if she would never let go, and I could feel her tears trickling down my neck.

15

Zephyr Farm Stables was indeed fortified like a stockade, surrounded by a seven-foot-high stout wooden fence and guarded by a gate that would have done credit to Alcatraz. I sat lazily in my car across the street from it, waiting for it to open.

I waited while the cold gradually seeped through my anorak and numbed my hands and feet. Waited while a few intrepid pedestrians hurried along the narrow path beside the fence without giving the gate a glance. Waited in the semisuburban street on the outskirts of Horley, where the streep lamps faltered to a stop and darkness lay beyond.

No one went in or out of the gate. It stayed obstinately shut, secretive and unfriendly, and after two fruitless hours I abandoned the chilly vigil and booked in to a local hotel.

Enquiries brought a sour response. Yes, the receptionist said, they did sometimes have people staying there who were hoping to persuade their sons and daughters to come home from Zephyr Farm Stables. Hardly any of them ever managed it, because they were never allowed to see their children alone, if at all. Proper scandal, said the receptionist, and the law can't do a thing about it. All over eighteen, they are, see? Old enough to know their own minds. Phooey.

"I just want to find out if someone's there," I said.

She shook her head and said I didn't have a chance.

I spent the evening drifting around hotels and pubs talking about the Colleagues to a succession of locals propping up the bars. The general opinion was the same as the receptionist's: anything or anyone I wanted from Zephyr Farm Stables, I wouldn't get.

"Do they ever come out?" I asked. "To go shopping, perhaps?"

Amid a reaction of rueful and sneering smiles I was told that yes indeed the Colleagues did emerge, always in groups, and always collecting money.

"They'll sell you things," one man said. "Try to sell you bits o' polished stone and such. Just beggin' really. For the cause, they say. For the love of God. Bunk, I say. I tell 'em to be off to church, and they don't like that, I'll tell ye."

"Ever so strict, they are," a barmaid said. "No smokes, no drinks, no sex. Can't see what the nitwits see in it myself."

"They don't do no harm," someone said. "Always smiling."

Would they be out collecting in the morning, I asked. And if so, where?

"In the summer they hang about the airport all the time, scrounging from people going on holiday and sometimes picking someone up for themselves . . . recruits, like . . . but your best bet would be in the center of town. Right here. Saturday . . . they're sure to be here. Sure to be."

I thanked them all, and went to bed, and in the morning parked as near to the center as possible and wandered about on foot.

By ten o'clock the town was bustling with its morning trade, and I'd worked out that I would have to leave by eleven-thirty at the latest to get back to Newbury, and even that was cutting it a bit fine. The first race was at twelve-thirty because of the short winter days, and although I wasn't riding in the first two, I had to be there an hour before the third, or Harold would be dancing mad.

I saw no groups of collecting Colleagues. No groups at all. No chanting people with shaven heads and bells, or anything like that. All that happened was that a smiling girl touched my arm and asked if I would like to buy a pretty paperweight.

The stone lay on the palm of her hand, wedge-shaped, greeny-brown and polished.

"Yes," I said. "How much?"

"It's for charity," she said. "As much as you like." She produced in her other hand a wooden box with a slit in the top but with no names of charities advertised on its sides.

"What charity?" I asked pleasantly, fishing for my wallet.

"Lots of good causes," she said.

I sorted out a pound note, folded it, and pushed it through the slit.

"Are there many of you collecting?" I asked.

She turned her head involuntarily sideways, and I saw from the direction of her eyes that there was another girl offering a stone to someone waiting at a bus stop, and on the other side of the road, another. All pretty girls in ordinary clothes, smiling.

"What's your name?" I asked.

She broadened the smile as if that were answer enough, and gave me the stone. "Thank you very much," she said. "Your gift will do so much good."

I watched her move on down the street, pulling another stone from a pocket in her swirling skirt and accosting a kind-looking old lady. She was too old to be Amanda, I thought, though it wasn't always easy to tell. Especially not, I saw a minute later as I stood in the path of another

stone-seller, in view of the otherwordly air of saintliness
they wore like badges.

"Would you like to buy a paperweight?"

"Yes," I said, and we went through the routine again.

"What's your name?" I asked.

"Susan," she said. "What's yours?"

I in my turn gave her the smile and the shake of the
head, and moved on.

In half an hour I bought four paperweights. To the
fourth girl I said, "Is Amanda out here this morning?"

"Amanda? We haven't got a . . ." She stopped, and her
eyes, too, went on a giveaway trek.

"Never mind," I said, pretending not to see. "Thanks
for the stone."

She smiled the bright empty smile and moved on, and
I waited a short while until I could decently drift in front
of the girl she'd suddenly glanced at.

She was young, short, smooth-faced, curiously blank
about the eyes, and dressed in an anorak and swirling
skirt. Her hair was medium brown, like mine, but straight,
not slightly curling, and there was no resemblance that I
could see between our faces. She might or she might not
be my mother's child.

The stone she held out to me was dark blue with black
flecks, the size of a plum.

"Very pretty," I said. "How much?"

I got the stock reply, and gave her a pound.

"Amanda," I said.

She jumped. She looked at me doubtfully. "My name's
not Amanda."

"What then?"

"Mandy."

"Mandy what?"

"Mandy North."

I breathed very slowly, so as not to alarm her, and
smiled, and asked her how long she had lived at Zephyr
Farm Stables.

"All my life," she said limpidly.

"With your friends?"

She nodded. "They're my guardians."

"And you're happy?"

"Yes, of course. We do God's work."

"How old are you?"

Her doubts returned. "Eighteen . . . yesterday . . . but I'm not supposed to talk about myself . . . only about the stones."

The childlike quality was very marked. She seemed not exactly to be mentally retarded, but in the old sense, simple. There was no life in her, no fun, no awakening of womanhood. Beside the average teenager she was like a sleepwalker.

"Have you any more stones then?" I asked.

She nodded and produced another one from her skirt. I admired it and agreed to buy it, and said while picking out another note, "What was your mother's name, Mandy?"

She looked scared. "I don't know. You mustn't ask things like that."

"When you were little did you have a pony?"

For an instant her blank eyes lit with an uncrushable memory, and then she glanced at someone over my left shoulder, and her simple pleasure turned to red-faced shame.

I half turned. A man stood there; not young, not smiling. A tough-looking man a few years older than myself, very clean, very neatly dressed and very annoyed.

"No conversations, Mandy," he said to her severely. "Remember the rule. Your first day out collecting, and you break the rule. The girls will take you home now. You'll be back on housework, after this. Go along, they're waiting over there." He nodded sharply to where a group of girls waited together, and watched as she walked leaden-footed to join them. Poor Mandy in disgrace. Poor Amanda. Poor little sister.

"What's your game?" the man said to me. "The girls say you've bought stones from all of them. What are you after?"

"Nothing," I said. "They're pretty stones."

He glared at me doubtfully, and he was joined by another similar man who walked across after talking to the now departing girls.

"This guy was asking the girls their names," he said. "Looking for Amanda."

"There's no Amanda."

"Mandy. He talked to her."

They both looked at me with narrowed eyes, and I decided it was time to leave. They didn't try to stop me when I headed off in the general direction of the parking lot. They didn't try to stop me, but they followed along in my wake.

I didn't think much about it, and turned into the short side road which led to the parking lot. Glancing back to see if they were still following I found not only that they were, but that there were now four of them. The two new ones were young, like the girls.

It seemed too public a place for much to happen; and I suppose by many standards nothing much did. There were three more of them loitering around the parking lot entrance, and all seven of them encircled me outside, before I got there. I pushed one of them to get him out of the way, and got shoved in return by a forest of hands. Shoved sideways along the road a few steps and against a brick wall. If any of the Great British Public saw what was happening, they passed by on the other side of the road.

I stood looking at the seven Colleagues. "What do you want?" I said.

The second of the two older men said, "Why were you asking for Mandy?"

"She's my sister."

It confounded the two elders. They looked at each other. Then the first one decisively shook his head. "She's got no family. Her mother died years ago. You're lying. How could you possibly think she's your sister?"

"We don't want you nosing around, making trouble," the second one said. "If you ask me, he's a reporter."

The word stung them all into reconciling violence with their strange religion. They banged me against the wall a shade too often, and also pushed and kicked a shade too hard, but apart from trying to shove all seven away like a rugger scrum there wasn't a great deal I could physically do to stop them. It was one of those stupid sorts of scuffles in which no one wanted to go too far. They could have half-killed me easily if they'd meant to, and I could have hurt them more than I did. Escalation seemed a crazy risk when all they were truly delivering was a warning, so I pushed against their close bodies and hacked at a couple of shins, and that was that.

I didn't tell them the one thing which would have saved me the drubbing: that if they could prove that Mandy was indeed my sister she would inherit a fortune.

Harold watched my arrival outside the weighing room with a scowl of disfavor.

"You're bloody late," he said. "And why are you limping?"

"Twisted my ankle."

"Are you fit to ride?"

"Yes."

"Huh."

"Is Victor Briggs here?" I said.

"No, he isn't. You can stop worrying. Sharpener's out to win, and you can ride him in your usual way. None of those crazy damn-fool heroics. Understood? You look after Sharpener or I'll belt the hide off you. Bring him back whole."

I nodded, smothering a smile, and he gave me another extensive scowl and walked off.

"Honestly, Philip," said Steve Millace, wandering past. "He treats you like dirt."

"No . . . just his way."

"I wouldn't stand for it."

I looked at the easy belligerence in the overyoung face and realized that he didn't really know about affection's coming sometimes in a rough package.

"Good luck, today," I said neutrally, and he said, "Thanks," and went on into the weighing room. He would never be like his father, I thought. Never as bright, as ingenious, as perceptive, as ruthless or as wicked.

I followed Steve inside and changed into Victor Briggs' colors, feeling the effects of the Colleagues' attentions as an overall ache. Nothing much. A nuisance. Not enough, I hoped, to make any difference to my riding.

When I went outside I found Elgin Yaxley and Bart Underfield, who were slapping each other on the shoulder and looking the faintest bit drunk. Elgin Yaxley peeled off and rolled away, and Bart, turning with an extravagant lack of coordination, bumped into me.

"Hullo," he said, giving a spirits-laden cough. "You'll be the first to know. Elgin's getting some more horses. They're coming to me, of course. We'll make Lambourn sit up. Make the whole of racing sit up." He gave me a patronizing leer. "Elgin's a man of ideas."

"He is indeed," I said dryly.

Bart remembered he didn't much like me and took his good news off to other, more receptive ears. I stood watching him, thinking that Elgin Yaxley would never kill another horse for the insurance. No insurance company would stand for it twice. But Elgin Yaxley believed himself undetected . . . and people didn't change. If their minds ran to fraud once, they would again. I didn't like the sound of Elgin Yaxley's having ideas.

The old dilemma still remained. If I gave the proof of Elgin Yaxley's fraud to the police or the insurance company, I would have to say how I came by the photograph.

From George Millace . . . who wrote threatening letters. George Millace, husband of Marie, who was climbing back with frail handholds from the wreck of her life. If justice depended on smashing her deeper into soul-wrecking misery, justice would have to wait.

Sharpener's race came third on the card. Not the biggest event of the day, which was the fourth race, a brandy-sponsored Gold Cup, but a well-regarded two-mile 'chase. Sharpener had been made favorite because of his win at Kempton and with some of the same *joie de vivre* he sailed around most of Newbury's long oval in fourth place. We lay third at the third-to-last fence, second at the second-to-last, and jumped to the front over the last. I sat down and rode him out with hands and heels, and my God, I thought, I could do with the muscle-power I lost in Horley.

Sharpener won and I was exhausted, which was ridiculous. Harold, beaming, watched me fumble feebly with the girth buckles in the winners' enclosure. The horse, stamping around, almost knocked me over.

"You only went two miles," Harold said. "What the hell's the matter with you?"

I got the buckles undone and pulled off the saddle, and began in fact to feel a trickle of strength flow again through my arms. I grinned at Harold and said, "Nothing . . . It was a damn good race. Nice shape."

"Nice shape be buggered. You won. Any race you win is a nice bloody shape."

I went in to be weighed, leaving him surrounded by congratulations and sportswriters; and while I was sitting on the bench by my peg waiting to get my strength back I decided what to do about Elgin Yaxley.

I had grown a habit, over the past two weeks, of taking with me in the car not only my favorite two cameras but also the photographs I seemed to keep on needing. Lance Kinship's reprints were there, although he himself hadn't turned up, and so were the four concerning Yaxley. Straight after the big race I went out and fetched them.

The second horse I was due to ride for Harold was a novice hurdler in the last race, and because there had been so many entries in the novice hurdle that they'd split it into two divisions, the last race on that day was the seventh, not the sixth. It gave me just enough extra time for what I wanted.

Finding Elgin Yaxley wasn't so difficult, it was detaching him from Bart Underfield that gave the trouble.

"Can I talk to you for a moment?" I said to Yaxley.

"You're not having the rides on our horses," Bart said bossily. "So don't waste time asking."

"You can keep them," I said.

"What do you want, then?"

"I want to give Mr. Yaxley a message." I turned to Yaxley. "It's a private message, for your ears only."

"Oh, very well." He was impatient. "Wait for me in the bar, Bart."

Bart grumbled and fussed, but finally went.

"Better come over here," I said to Elgin Yaxley, nodding towards a patch of grass by the entrance gate, away from the huge big-race crowd with their stretched ears and curious eyes. "You won't want anyone hearing."

"What the devil *is* all this?" he said crossly.

"A message from George Millace," I said.

His sharp features grew rigid. The small moustache he wore bristled. The complacency vanished into a furious concentration of fear.

"I have some photographs," I said, "which you might like to see."

I handed him the cardboard envelope. It seemed easier this second time, I thought, to deliver the chop. Maybe I was becoming hardened . . . or maybe I simply didn't like Elgin Yaxley. I watched him open the envelope with no pity at all.

He first went pale, and then red, and great drops of

sweat stood out like blisters on his forehead. He checked through the four pictures and found the whole story was there, the cafe meeting and George's two letters, and the damning note from the farmer, David Parker. The eyes he raised to me were sick and incredulous, and he had difficulty finding his voice.

"Take your time," I said. "I expect it's a shock."

His mouth moved as if practicing, but no words came out.

"Any number of copies," I said, "could go off to the insurance company and the police and so on."

He managed a strangled groan.

"There's another way," I said.

He got his throat and tongue to shape a single hoarse unedifying word. *"Bastard."*

"Mm," I said. "There's George Millace's way."

I'd never seen anyone look at me with total hatred before, and I found it unnerving. But I wanted to find out just what George had extracted from at least one of his victims, and this was my best chance.

I said flatly, "I want the same as George Millace."

"No." It was more a wail than a shout. Full of horror; empty of hope.

"Yes, indeed," I said.

"But I can't afford it. I haven't got it."

The anxiety in his eyes was almost too much for me, but I spurred on my flagging resolution with the thought of five shot horses, and said again, "The same as George."

"Not ten," he said wildly. "I haven't got it."

I stared at him.

He mistook my silence and gabbled on, finding his voice in a flood of begging, beseeching, cajoling words.

"I've had expenses, you know. It hasn't all been easy. Can't you let me alone? Let me off, won't you? George said once and for all . . . and now *you* . . . Five, then," he said in the face of my continued silence. "Will five do? That's enough. I haven't got any more. I haven't."

I stared once more, and waited.

"All right, then. All *right*." He was shaking with worry and fury. "Seven and a half. Will that do? It's all I've got, you bloodsucking leech . . . you're worse than George Millace . . . bastard *blackmailers* . . ."

While I watched he fumbled into his pockets and brought out a checkbook and a pen. Clumsily supporting the checkbook on the photograph envelope, he wrote the date and a sum of money, and signed his name. Then with shaking fingers he tore the slip of paper out of the book and stood holding it.

"Not Hong Kong," he said.

I didn't know at once what he meant, so I took refuge in more staring.

"Not Hong Kong. Not there again. I don't like it." He was beseeching again, begging for crumbs.

"Oh . . ." I hid my understanding in a cough. "Anywhere," I said. "Anywhere out of Britain."

It was the right answer, but gave him no comfort. I stretched out my hand for the check.

He gave it to me, his hand trembling.

"Thank you," I said.

"Rot in hell."

He turned and stumbled away, half running, half staggering, utterly in pieces. Serve him right, I thought callously. Let him suffer. It wouldn't be for long.

I meant to tear up his check when I'd looked to see how much he thought my silence was worth: how much he'd paid George. I meant to, but I didn't. When I looked at that check, something like a huge burst of sunlight happened in my head, a bright expanding delight of awe and comprehension.

I had used George's own cruelty. I had demanded to be given what he himself had demanded. His alternative suggestion for Elgin Yaxley.

I had it. All of it.

Elgin Yaxley was going off into exile, and I held his

check for seven thousand five hundred pounds.

It was made out not to me, or to Bearer, or even to the estate of George Millace, but to the Injured Jockeys' Fund.

16

I walked around for a while trying to find the particular ex-jockey who had become one of the chief administrators of the fund, and at length tracked him down in the private entertainment box of one of the television companies. There was a crowd in there, but I winkled him out.

"Want a drink?" he said, holding up his glass.

I shook my head. I was wearing colors, breeches, boots and an anorak. "More than my life's worth, boozing with you lot before racing."

He said cheerfully, "What can I do for you?"

"Take a check," I said, and gave it to him.

"Phew," he said, looking at it. "And likewise *wow*."

"Is it the first time Elgin Yaxley's been so generous?"

"No, it isn't," he said. "He gave us ten thousand a few months ago, just before he went abroad. We took it of course, but some of the trustees wondered if it wasn't conscience money. I mean . . . he'd just been paid a hundred thousand by the insurance company for those horses of his that were shot. The whole business looked horribly fishy, didn't it?"

"Mm." I nodded. "Well . . . Elgin Yaxley's going

abroad again, so he says, and he gave me this check for you. So will you take it?"

He smiled. "If his conscience is troubling him again, we might as well benefit." He folded the check, tucked it away and patted the pocket which contained it.

"Have you had any other huge checks like that?" I enquired conversationally.

"People leave big amounts in their wills, sometimes, but no . . . not many like Elgin Yaxley."

"Would Ivor den Relgan be a generous supporter?" I asked.

"Well, yes, he gave us a thousand at the beginning of the season. Some time in September. Very generous."

I pondered. "Do you keep lists of the people who donate?"

He laughed. "Not all of them. Thousands of people contribute over the years. Old-age pensioners. Children. Housewives. Anyone you can think of." He sighed. "We never seem to have enough for what we need to do, but we're always grateful for the smallest help . . . and you know all that."

"Yes. Thanks anyway."

"Any time."

He went back to the convivial crowd and I returned to the weighing room and got myself and my saddle weighed out for the last race.

I was as bad as George, I thought. Identically as bad. I had extorted money by threats. It didn't seem so wicked, now that I'd done it myself.

Harold in the parade ring said sharply, "You're looking bloody pleased with yourself."

"Just with life in general."

I'd ridden a winner. I'd almost certainly found Amanda. I'd discovered a lot more about George. Sundry kicks and punches on the debit side, but who cared? Overall, not a bad day.

"This hurdler," Harold said severely, "is the one who

wrecked the schooling session last Saturday. I know you weren't on him ... it wasn't your fault ... but you just mind he gets a good clear view of what he's got to jump. Understand? Go to the front and make the running, so he's got a clear view. He won't last the trip, but it's a big field and I don't want him being jostled and blinded in the pack early on. Got it?"

I nodded. There were twenty-three runners, almost the maximum allowed in this type of race. Harold's hurdler, walking edgily around the parade ring, was already sweating with nervous excitement, and he was an animal, I knew from experience, who needed a soothing phlegmatic approach.

"Jockeys, please mount," came the announcement, and I and the hurdler in a decently quiet way got ourselves together and down to the start.

I was thinking only of bowling along in front out of trouble, and when the tapes went up, off we set. Over the first, leading as ordered; good jump, no trouble. Over the second, just out in front; passable jump, no trouble. Over the third ...

In front, as ordered, at the third. Rotten, disastrous jump, all four feet seeming to tangle in the hurdle instead of rising over it: exactly the mess he'd made over the schooling hurdle at home.

He and I crashed to the turf together, and twenty-two horses came over the hurdle after us.

Horses do their very best to avoid a man or a horse on the ground, but with so many, so close, going so fast, it would have been a miracle if I hadn't been touched. One couldn't ever tell at those times just how many galloping hooves connected: it always happened too fast. It felt like being rolled like a rag doll under a stampede.

It had happened before. It would happen again. I lay painfully on my side looking at a close bunch of grass, and thought it was a damn silly way to be earning one's living. I almost laughed. I've thought that before, I thought. Every time I'm down here on the mud, I think it.

A lot of First Aid hands arrived to help me up. Nothing seemed to be broken. Thank God for strong bones. I wrapped my arms around my body, as if hugging would lessen the hurt.

The horse had got up and decamped, unscathed. I rode back to the stands in an ambulance, demonstrated to the doctor that I was basically in one piece, and winced my slow way into ordinary clothes.

When I left the weighing room, most people had gone home, but Harold was standing there with Ben, his traveling head lad.

"Are you all right?" Harold demanded.

"Yeah."

"I'll drive you home," he said. "Ben can take your car."

I looked at the generous worry in both of their faces, and didn't argue. Dug into my pocket, and gave Ben my keys.

"That was a hell of a fall," Harold said, driving out of the gates. "A real brute."

"Mm."

"I was glad to see you stand up."

"Is the horse all right?"

"Yes, clumsy bugger."

We drove in companionable silence towards Lambourn. I felt beaten up and shivery, but it would pass. It always passed. Always would, until I got too old for it. I'd be too old in my mind, I thought, before my body gave out.

"If Victor Briggs comes down here again," I said, "would you tell me?"

He glanced at me sideways. "You want to see him? Won't do any good, you know. Victor just does what he wants."

"I want to know . . . what he wants."

"Why not leave well enough alone?"

"Because it isn't well. I've left it alone . . . it doesn't work. I want to talk to him . . . and don't worry, I'll be diplomatic. I don't want to lose this job. I don't want you to lose Victor's horses. Don't worry. I know all that. I want to talk to him."

"All right," Harold said doubtfully. "When he comes, I'll tell him."

He stopped his car beside my front door.

"You're sure you're all right?" he said. "You look pretty shaken. Nasty fall. Horrid."

"I'll have a hot bath . . . get the stiffness out. Thanks for the lift home."

"You'll be fit for next week? Tuesday at Plumpton?"

"Absolutely," I said.

It was already getting dark. I went around in the cottage drawing the curtains, switching on lights, heating some coffee. Bath, food, television, aspirins, bed, I thought, and pray not to feel too sore in the morning.

Ben parked my car in the carport, gave me the keys through the back door and said goodnight.

Mrs. Jackson, the horsebox driver's wife from next door, came to tell me the tax assessor had called.

"Oh?" I said.

"Yes. Yesterday. Hope I did right, letting him in, like. Mind you, Mr. Nore, I didn't let him out of my sight. I went right around with him, like. He was only in here a matter of five minutes. He didn't touch a thing. Just counted the rooms. Hope it's all right. He had papers from the council, and such."

"I'm sure it's fine, Mrs. Jackson."

"And your telephone," she said. "It's been ringing and ringing. Dozens of times. I can hear it through the wall, you know, when everything's quiet. I didn't know if you'd want me to answer it. I will, any time, you know, if you want."

"Kind of you," I said. "I'll let you know if I do."

She gave me a bright nod and departed. She would

have mothered me if I'd let her, and I guessed she would have been glad to let the tax man in, as she liked looking around in my house. Nosy, friendly, sharp-eyed neighbor, taker in of parcels and dispenser of gossip and advice. Her two boys had broken my kitchen window once with their football.

I telephoned to Jeremy Folk. He was out: would I care to leave a message? Tell him I found what we were look- ing for, I said.

The instant I put the receiver down, the bell rang. I picked it up again, and heard a child's breathless voice. "I can tell you where that stable is. Am I the first?"

I regretfully said not. I also passed on the same bad news to ten more children within the next two hours. Sev- eral of them checked disappointedly to make sure I'd been told the right place—Zephyr Farm Stables? And several said did I know it had been owned for years and years by some Jesus freaks? I began asking them if they knew how the Colleagues had chanced to buy the stables, and even- tually came across a father who did.

"Us and the people who kept the riding school," he said, "we were pretty close friends. They wanted to move to Devon, and were looking for a buyer for their place, and these fanatics just turned up one day with suitcases full of cash, and bought it on the spot."

"How did the fanatics hear of it? Was it advertised?"

"No . . ." He paused, thinking. "Oh, I remember . . . it was because of one of the children who used to ride the ponies. Yes, that's right. Sweet little girl. Mandy some- thing. Always there. She used to stay with our friends for weeks on end. I saw her often. There was something about her mother being on the point of death, and the religious people looking after her. It was through the mother that they heard the stables were for sale. They were in some ruin of a house at the time, I think, and wanted somewhere better."

"You don't remember the mother's name, I suppose."

"Sorry, no. Don't think I ever knew it, and after all these years . . ."

"You've been tremendously helpful," I said. "I'll send your Peter the ten pounds, even though he wasn't first."

The father's voice chuckled. "That'll please him."

I took his address, and also the name of the people who had owned the stables, but Peter's father said he had lost touch with them over the years and no longer knew where they lived.

Jeremy could find them, I thought, if he needed to. After I'd bathed and eaten I unplugged the telephone from the kitchen and carried it up to the sitting room, where for another hour it interrupted the television. God bless the little children, I thought, and wondered how many thousands were going to ring up. None of them had ever been inside the high wooden walls; it was always their mummies and daddies who had ridden there when they were young.

By nine o'clock I was thoroughly tired of it. Despite the long hot soak my deeply bruised muscles were beginning to stiffen; and the best place to take them was bed. Get it over with, I thought. It was going to be lousy. It always was, for about twenty-four hours, after so many kicks. If I went to bed I could sleep through the worst.

I unplugged the telephone and went down to the bathroom in shirtsleeves for a scratch round the teeth; and the front doorbell rang.

Cursing, I went to see who had called.

Opened the door.

Ivor den Relgan stood there, holding a gun.

I stared at the pistol, not believing it.

"Back up," he said. "I'm coming in."

It would be untrue to say I wasn't afraid. I was certain he was going to kill me. I felt bodiless. Floating. Blood racing.

For the second time that day I saw into the eyes of hatred, and the power behind den Relgan's paled Elgin

Yaxley's into petulance. He jerked the lethal black weapon towards me, insisting I retreat, and I took two or three steps backward, hardly feeling my feet.

He stepped through my door and kicked it shut behind him.

"You're going to pay," he said, "for what you've done to me."

Be careful, Jeremy had said.

I hadn't been.

"George Millace was bad," he said. "You're worse."

I wasn't sure I was actually going to be able to speak, but I did. My voice sounded strange: almost squeaky.

"Did you . . ." I said, ". . . burn his house?"

His eyes flickered. His naturally arrogant expression, which had survived whatever Lord White had said to him, wasn't going to be broken up by any futile last minute questions. In adversity his air of superiority had if anything intensified, as if belief in his own importance, were the only thing left.

"Burgled, ransacked, burned," he said furiously. "And you had the stuff all the time. You . . . you *rattlesnake*."

I had destroyed his power base. Taken away his authority. Left him metaphorically as naked as on his St. Tropez balcony.

George, I thought, must have used the threat of those photographs to stop den Relgan angling to be let into the Jockey Club. I'd used them to get him thrown out.

He'd had some sort of standing, of credibility, before, in racing men's eyes. Now he had none. Never to be in was one thing. To be in and then out, quite another.

George hadn't shown those photographs to anyone but den Relgan himself.

I had.

"Get back," he said. "Back there. Go on."

He made a small waving movement with the pistol. An automatic. Stupid thought. What did it matter?

"My neighbors'll hear the shot," I said hopelessly.

He sneered and didn't answer. "Back past that door."

It was the door to the darkroom, solidly shut. Even if I could jump in there alive . . . no sanctuary. No lock. I stepped past it.

"Stop," he said.

I'd have to run, I thought wildly. Had at least to try. I was already turning on the ball of one foot when the kitchen door was smashed open.

I thought for a split second that somehow den Relgan had missed me and the bullet had splintered some glass, but then I realized he hadn't fired. There were people coming into the house from the back. Two people. Two bustling burly young men . . . with nylon stocking masks over their faces.

"Take him," den Relgan said, pointing with his gun.

I thought "*Christ* . . ."

A flash of Marie's battered face lit in my memory, and her voice: "like bulls . . . white . . . young . . . stockings over their faces . . ."

They were rushing, banging against each other, fast, eager, infinitely destructive.

I tried to fight them.

I tried.

God almighty, I thought. Not three times in one day. How could I explain to them . . . ? Blood vessels were already severed and bleeding under my skin . . . too many muscle fibers already crushed and torn . . . too much damage already done. How could I explain . . . and if I had, it wouldn't have made any difference. Pleased them, if anything.

Thoughts scattered and flew away. I couldn't see, couldn't yell, could hardly breathe. They wore roughened leather gloves, which tore my skin, and the punches to my face knocked me silly. When I fell on the ground, they used their boots. On limbs, back, stomach, head.

I drifted off altogether.

When I came back, it was quiet. I was lying on the

white-tiled floor with my cheek in a pool of blood. In a dim way I wondered whose blood it was.

Drifted off again.

It's my blood, I thought.

Tried to open my eyes. Something wrong with the eyelids. Oh well, I thought, I'm alive. Drifted off again.

He didn't shoot me, I thought. Did he shoot me? I tried to move, to find out. Bad mistake.

When I tried to move, my whole body went into a sort of rigid spasm. Locked tight in a monstrous cramp from head to foot, I gasped with the crushing, unexpected agony of it. Worse than fractures, worse than dislocations, worse than anything . . .

Screaming nerves, I thought. Telling my brain to seize up. Saying too much was injured, too much was smashed, nothing must move. Too much was bleeding inside.

Christ, I thought. Leave go. Let me go. I won't move. I'll just lie here. Let me go.

After a long time the spasm did pass, and I lay in relief in a flaccid heap. Too weak to do anything but pray that the cramp wouldn't come back. Too shattered to think much at all.

The thoughts I did have, I could have done without. Thoughts like people who died of ruptured internal organs . . . kidneys, liver, spleen. Thoughts like, what exactly did I have wrong with me, to cause such a fierce reaction? Thoughts like den Relgan coming back to finish the job.

Den Relgan's midworld voice: "You'll pay for what you've done to me . . ."

Pay in cuts and internal hemorrhage and wretched pain. Pay in fear that I was lying there dying. Bleeding inside. Bleeding to death. The way people beaten to death died.

Ages passed.

If any of those things were ruptured, I thought . . . liver, kidneys, spleen . . . and pouring out blood, I would be showing the signs of it. Shallow breathing, fluttering pulse, thirst, restlessness, sweat. None of that seemed to be happening.

I took heart after a while, knowing that at least I wasn't getting worse. Maybe if I moved gently, cautiously, it would be all right.

Far from all right. Back into a rigid locked spasm, as bad as before.

It had taken only the intention to move. Only the outward message. The response had been not movement, but cramp. I dare say it was the body's best line of defense, but I could hardly bear it.

It lasted too long, and went away slowly, tentatively, as if threatening to come back. I won't move, I promised. I won't move . . . just let go . . . let me go.

The lights in the cottage were on, but the heating was off. I grew very cold; literally congealing. Cold stopped things bleeding, I thought. Cold wasn't all bad. Cold would contract all those leaking internal blood vessels and stop the red stuff trickling out into where it shouldn't be. Hemorrhage would be finished. Recovery could start.

I lay quiet for hours, waiting. Sore but alive. Increasingly certain of staying alive. Increasingly certain I'd been lucky.

If nothing fatal had ruptured, I could deal with the rest. Familiar country. Boring, but known.

I had no idea of the time. Couldn't see my watch. Suppose I move my arm, I thought. Just my arm. Might manage that, if I'm careful.

It sounded simple. The overall spasm stayed away, but the specific message to my arm produced only a twitch. Crazy. Nothing was working. All circuits jammed.

After another long while I tried again. Tried too hard. The cramp came back, taking my breath away, holding me in a vise, worst now in my stomach, not so bad in my arms, but rigid, fearful, frightening, lasting too long.

I lay on the floor all night and well on into the morning. The patch of blood under my head got sticky and dried. My face felt like a pillow puffed up with gritty lumps. There were splits in my mouth, which were sore, and I could feel with my tongue the jagged edges of broken teeth.

Eventually I lifted my head off the floor.

No spasm.

I was lying in the back part of the hall, not far from the bottom of the stairs. Pity the bedroom was right up at the top. Also the telephone. I might get some help . . . if I could get up the stairs.

Gingerly I tried moving, dreading what could happen. Moved my arms, my legs, tried to sit up. Couldn't do it. My weakness was appalling. My muscles were trembling. I moved a few inches across the floor, still half lying down. Got as far as the stairs. Hip on the hall floor, shoulders on the stairs, head on the stairs, arms failing with weakness . . . the spasms came back.

Oh Christ, I thought, how much more?

In another hour I'd got my haunch up three steps and was again rigid with cramp. Far enough, I thought numbly. No farther. It was certainly more comfortable lying on the stairs than on the floor, as long as I stayed still.

I stayed still. Gratefully, wearily, lazily still. For ages.

Somebody rang the front doorbell.

Whoever it was, I didn't want them. Whoever it was would make me move. I no longer wanted help, but just peace. Peace would mend me, given time.

The bell rang again. Go away, I thought. I'm better alone.

For a while I thought I'd got my wish, but then I heard someone at the back of the house, coming in through the back door. The broken back door, open to a touch.

Not den Relgan, I thought abjectly. Don't let it be den Relgan . . . not him.

It wasn't, of course. It was Jeremy Folk.

It was Jeremy, coming in tentatively, saying, "Er . . ."

and "Are you there?" and "Philip?" and standing still with shock when he reached the hall.

"Jesus Christ," he said blankly.

I said, "Hello."

"Philip." He leaned over me. "Your face . . ."

"Yeah."

"What shall I do?"

"Nothing," I said. "Sit down . . . on the stairs." My mouth and tongue felt stiff. Like Marie's, I thought. Just like Marie.

"But what happened? Did you have a fall at the races?"

He did sit down, on the bottom stair by my feet, folding his own legs into ungainly angles.

"Yeah." I said. "A fall."

"But . . . the blood. You've got blood . . . all over your face. In your hair. Everywhere."

"Leave it," I said. "It's dry."

"Can you see?" he said. "Your eyes are . . ." He stopped, reduced apparently to silence, not wanting to tell me.

"I can see out of one of them," I said. "It's enough."

He wanted of course to move me, wash the blood off, make things more regular. I wanted to stay just where I was, without having to argue. Hopeless wish. I persuaded him to leave me alone only by confessing to the cramps.

His horror intensified. "I'll get you a doctor."

"Just shut up," I said. "I'm all right. Talk if you like, but don't *do* anything."

"Well . . ." He gave in. "Do you want anything? Tea, or anything?"

"Find some champagne. Kitchen cupboard."

He looked as if he thought I was mad, but champagne was the best tonic I knew for practically all ills. I heard the cork pop and presently he returned with two tumblers. He put mine on the stair by my left hand, near my head.

Oh well, I thought. May as well find out. The cramps would have to stop sometime. I stiffly moved the arm and fastened the hand round the chunky glass, and tried to connect the whole thing to my mouth; and I got at least three reasonable gulps before everything seized up.

It was Jeremy, that time, who was frightened. He took the glass I was dropping and had a great attack of the dithers, and I said "Just wait," through my teeth. The spasm finally wore off, and I thought perhaps it hadn't been so long or so bad that time, and that things really were getting better.

Persuading people to leave one alone always took more energy than one wanted to spend for the purpose. Good friends tired one out. For all that I was grateful for his company, I wished Jeremy would stop fussing and be quiet.

The front doorbell rang yet again, and before I could tell him not to, he'd gone off to answer it. My spirits sank even lower. Visitors were too much. The visitor was Clare, come because I'd invited her.

She knelt on the stairs beside me and said, "This isn't a fall, is it? Someone's done this to you, haven't they? Beaten you up?"

"Have some champagne," I said.

"Yes. All right."

She stood up and went to fetch a glass, and argued on my behalf with Jeremy.

"If he wants to lie on the stairs, let him. He's been injured countless times. He knows what's best."

My God, I thought. A girl who understands. Incredible.

She and Jeremy sat in the kitchen introducing themselves and drinking my booze, and on the stairs things did improve. Small exploratory stretchings produced no cramps. I drank some champagne. Felt sore but less ill. Felt that some time soon I'd sit up.

The front doorbell rang.

An epidemic.

Clare walked through the hall to answer it. I was sure she intended to keep whoever it was at bay, but she found it impossible. The girl who had called wasn't going to be stopped on the doorsteps. She pushed into the house physically past Clare's protestations, and I heard her heels clicking at speed towards me down the hall.

"I must see," she said frantically. "I must know if he's alive."

I knew her voice. I didn't need to see the distraught beautiful face seeking me, seeing me, freezing with shock.

Dana den Relgan.

17

"**O**h my *God*," she said.

"I am," I said in my swollen way, "alive."

"He said it would be . . . a toss up."

"Came down heads," I said.

"He didn't seem to care. Didn't seem to realize . . . If they'd killed you . . . what it would mean. He just said no one saw them, they'd be arrested, so why worry?"

Clare demanded, "Do you mean you know who did this?"

Dana gave her a distracted look. "I have to talk to him. Alone. Do you mind?"

"But he's . . ." She stopped, and said, "Philip?"

"It's all right."

"We'll be in the kitchen," Clare said. "Just shout."

Dana waited until she had gone, and then perched beside me on the stairs, half sitting, half lying, to bring her head near to mine. I regarded her through the slit of my vision, seeing her almost frantic and deadly anxiety and not knowing its cause. Not for my life, since she could now see it was safe. Not for my silence, since her very presence was an admission that could make things worse. The gold-flecked hair fell softly forward, almost touching me. The sweet scent she was wearing reached my perception even through a battered nose. The silk of her blouse brushed my hand. Her voice was soft with its cosmopolitan accent . . . and beseeching.

"Please," she said. *"Please . . ."*

"Please . . . what?"

"How can I ask you?" Even in trouble, I thought, she had a powerful attraction. I'd only seen it before, not felt it, but now, with the full wattage switched my way, I found myself thinking that I would help her, if I could.

She said persuadingly, "Please give me . . . what I wrote for George Millace."

I lay without answering, closing the persevering eye. She misread my inaction, which was in truth born of ignorance, and rushed into a flood of impassioned begging.

"I know you'll be thinking . . . how can I ask you, when Ivor's done this to you . . . how can I expect the slightest favor . . . or mercy . . . or kindness." Her voice was a jumble of shame and despair and anger and cajoling, every emotion rising separately like a wave and subsiding before the next. Asking a favor from someone her father . . . husband? . . . lover? . . . had mauled halfway to extinction, wasn't the easiest of errands, but she was having a pretty good stab at it. "Please, please, I beg of you, give it back."

"Is he your father?" I said.

"No." A breath; a whisper; a sigh.

"What, then?"

"We have . . . a relationship."

You don't say, I thought dryly.

She said, "Please, please give me the cigarettes."

The what? I had no idea what she meant.

Trying not to mumble, trying to make my slow tongue lucid, I said, "Tell me about your . . . relationship . . . with den Relgan . . . and about . . . your relationship with . . . Lord White."

"If I tell you, will you give it to me? Please, *please*, will you?"

She took my silence to mean that at least she could hope. She scurried into explanations, the words falling over themselves here and there, and here and there coming in faltering pauses: and all of it, apologetic and self-excusing, a distinct flavor of "poor little me, I've been used, none of it's my fault."

I opened the slit eye, to watch.

"I've been with him two years ... not married, it's never been like that ... not domestic, just ..."

Just for sex, I thought.

"You talk like him," I said.

"I'm an actress." She waited a shade defiantly for me to dispute it, but indeed I couldn't. A pretty good actress, I would have said. Equity card? I thought sardonically, and couldn't be bothered to ask.

"Last summer," she said, "Ivor came one day spilling over with a brilliant idea. So pleased with himself ... if I'd cooperate, he'd see I didn't suffer ... I mean, he meant ..." She stopped there, but it was plain what he meant. Won't suffer financially ... A neat euphemism for a hefty bribe.

"He said there was a man at the races wanting to flirt. He used not to take me to the races, not until then. But he said, would I go with him and pretend to be his daughter, and see if I could get the man to flirt with *me*. It was a laugh, you see. Ivor said this man had a reputation like snow, and he wanted to play a joke on him ... Well, that's what he said. He said the man was showing all the signs of wanting a sexual adventure ... looking at pretty girls in that special way that they do, patting their arms, you know what I mean."

I thought, how odd it must be to be a pretty girl, to find it normal for middleaged men to be on the lookout for sex, to expect them to pat one's arms.

"So you went," I said.

She nodded. "He was a sweetie . . . John White. It was easy. I mean . . . I liked him. I just smiled . . . and liked him . . . and he . . . well . . . I mean, it was true what Ivor had said, he was on the lookout, and there I was."

There she was, I thought, beautiful and not too dumb, and trying to catch him. Poor Lord White, hooked because he wanted to be. Fooled by his foolish age, his nostalgia for youth.

"Ivor wanted to use John, of course. I saw it . . . it was plain, but I didn't see all that harm in it. I mean . . . why not? Everything was going fine until Ivor and I went to St. Tropez for a week." The pretty face clouded with remembered rage. "And that beastly photographer wrote to Ivor . . . saying lay off Lord White, or else he'd show him those pictures of us . . . Ivor and me . . . Ivor was livid, I've never seen him so angry . . . not until this week."

Each of us, I supposed, thought of the fury we'd witnessed that week in den Relgan.

"Does he know you're here?" I said.

"My God, no." She looked horrified. "He doesn't know . . . He hates drugs . . . It's all we have rows about . . . George Millace made me write that list . . . said he'd show the pictures to John if I didn't . . . I *hated* George Millace . . . but you . . . you'll give it back to me, won't you? Please . . . please . . . you must see . . . it would ruin me with anyone who matters. I'll pay you. I'll pay you . . . if you'll give it to me."

Crunch time, I thought.

"What do you expect . . . me to give to you?" I said.

"The packet of cigarettes, of course. With the writing on it."

"Yes . . . why did you write on a cigarette packet?"

"I wrote on the wrapping with the red felt pen . . . George Millace said write the list and I said I wouldn't whatever he did and he said write it then with this pen on the cellophane wrapper round these cigarettes and you can pretend you haven't done it, because how could anyone

take seriously a scrawl on wrapping paper." She stopped
suddenly and said with awakening suspicion. "You have
got it, haven't you? George Millace gave it to you . . .
with the pictures . . . didn't he?"

"What did you write?"

"My God," she said. "You haven't got it. You haven't
and I've come here . . . I've told you . . . it's all for nothing. You haven't got it . . ." She stood up abruptly, beauty
vanishing in fury. "You beastly *shit*. Ivor should have
killed you. Should have made sure. I hope you *hurt*."

She had her wish, I thought calmly. I felt surprisingly
little resentment about den Relgan's tit for tat. I'd clobbered his life, he'd clobbered my body. I'd come off the
better, I thought, on the whole. My troubles would pass.

"Be grateful," I said.

She was too angry, however, at what she had given
away. She whisked off through the hall in her silks and
her scent, and slammed out of the front door. The air in
her wake quivered with feminine impact. Just as well, I
thought hazily, that the world wasn't full of Dana den
Relgans.

Clare and Jeremy came out of the kitchen.

"What did she want?" Clare said.

"Something I . . . haven't got."

They began asking what in general was happening, but
I said "Tell you . . . tomorrow," and they stopped. Clare
sat beside me on the stairs and rubbed one finger over my
hand.

"You're in a poor way, aren't you?" she said.

I didn't want to say yes. I said, "What's the time?"

"Half past three . . . getting on for four." She looked at
her watch. "Twenty to four."

"Have some lunch," I said. "You and Jeremy."

"Do you want any?"

"No."

They heated some soup and some bread and kept life
ticking over. It's the only day, I thought inanely, that I've

ever spent lying on the stairs. I could smell the dust in the carpet. I ached all over, incessantly, with a grinding stiff soreness, but it was better than the cramps; and movement was becoming possible. Movement soon, I thought, would be imperative. A sign that things were returning to order. I needed increasingly to go to the bathroom.

I sat up on the stairs, my back propped against the wall. Not so bad. Not so bad. No spasms.

A perceptible improvement in function in all muscles. The memory of strength no longer seemed remote. I could stand up, I thought, if I tried.

Clare and Jeremy appeared enquiringly, and without pride I used their offered hands to pull myself upright.

Tottery, but upright.

No cramps.

"Now what?" Clare said.

"A pee."

They laughed. Clare went off to the kitchen and Jeremy said something, as he gave me an arm for support across the hall, about washing the pool of dried blood off the floor.

"Don't bother," I said.

"No trouble."

I hung onto the towel rail in the bathroom a bit and looked into the glass over the washbasin, and saw the state of my face. Swollen, misshapen landscape. Unrecognizable. Raw in patches. Dark red in patches. Caked with dried blood; hair spiky with it. One eye lost in puffy folds, one showing a slit. Cut, purple mouth. Two chipped front teeth.

Give it a week, I thought, sighing. Boxers did it all the time from choice, silly buggers.

Emptying the bladder brought an acute awareness of heavy damage in the abdomen but also reassurance. No blood in the urine. My intestines might have caught it, but not once had those feet, equine or human, landed squarely with exploding force over a kidney. I'd been lucky. Exceptionally lucky and thanked God for it.

I ran some warm water into the washbasin and sponged off some of the dried blood. Wasn't sure, on the whole, that it was any improvement, either in comfort or visibly. Where the blood had been were more raw patches and clotted cuts. Gingerly I patted the washed bits dry with a tissue. Leave the rest, I thought.

There was a heavy crash somewhere out in the hall.

I pulled open the bathroom door to find Clare coming through from the kitchen, looking anxious.

"Are you all right?" she said. "You didn't fall?"

"No . . . Must be Jeremy."

Unhurriedly we went forward towards the front of the house to see what he'd dropped . . . and found Jeremy himself face down on the floor. Half in and half out of the darkroom door. The bowl of water he'd been carrying spilled wetly all around him, and there was a smell . . . a strong smell of bad eggs. A smell I knew. I . . .

"Whatever . . ." Clare began.

Dear Christ, I thought, and it was a prayer, not a blasphemy. I caught her fiercely around the waist and dragged her to the front door. Opened it. Pushed her outside.

"Stay there," I said urgently. "Stay outside. It's gas."

I took a deep lungful of the dark wintry night air and turned back. Felt so feeble . . . so desperate. Bent over Jeremy, grabbed hold of his wrists, one in each hand, and pulled.

Pulled and dragged him over the white tiles, pulling him, sliding him, feeling the deadly tremors in my weak arms and legs. Out of the darkroom, through the hall, to the front door. Not far. Not more than ten feet. My own lungs were bursting for air . . . but not that air . . . not rotten eggs.

Clare took one of Jeremy's arms and pulled with me, and between us we dragged his unconscious form out into the street. I twitched the door shut behind me, and I knelt on the cold road, retching and gasping and feeling utterly useless.

Clare was already banging on the house next door, returning with the schoolmaster who lived there.

"Breathe . . . into him," I said.

"Mouth to mouth?" I nodded. "Right, then." He knelt down beside Jeremy, turned him over, and without question began efficient resuscitation, knowing the drill.

Clare herself disappeared but in a minute was back.

"I called the ambulance," she said, "but they want to know what gas. There's no gas in Lambourn, they say. They want to know . . . what to bring."

"A respirator." My own chest felt leaden. Breathing was difficult. "Tell them . . . it's sulphur. Some sort of sulphide. Deadly. Tell them to hurry."

She looked agonized, and ran back into the schoolmaster's house, and I leaned weakly on my knees against the front wall of my own house and coughed and felt incredibly ill. From the new troubles, not the old. From the gas.

Jeremy didn't stir. Dear God, I thought. Dear Christ, let him live.

The gas in my darkroom had been meant for me, not for him. Must have been in there, waiting for me, all the hours I'd spent lying outside in the hall.

I thought incoherently: Jeremy, *don't die.* Jeremy, it's my fault. *Don't die.* I should have burned George Millace's rubbish . . . not used it . . . not brought us so near to death.

People came out from all the cottages, bringing blankets and shocked eyes. The schoolmaster went on with his task, though I saw from his manner, from glimpses of his face, that he thought it was useless.

Don't die.

Clare felt Jeremy's pulse. Her own face looked ashen.

"Is he . . . ?" I said.

"A flutter."

Don't die.

The schoolmaster took heart and tirelessly continued.
I felt as if there was a constricting band round my ribs,
squeezing my lungs. I'd taken only a few breaths of gas
and air. Jeremy had breathed pure gas. And Clare . . .

"How's your chest?" I asked her.

"Tight," she said. "Horrid."

The crowd around us seemed to be swelling. The ambulance arrived, and a police car, and Harold, and a doctor, and what seemed like half of Lambourn.

Expert hands took over from the schoolmaster and
pumped air in and out of Jeremy's lungs: and Jeremy
himself lay like a log while the doctor examined him and
while he was lifted onto a stretcher and loaded into the
ambulance.

He had a pulse. Some sort of pulse. That was all they
would say. They shut the doors on him, and drove him
to Swindon.

Don't die, I prayed. Don't let him die. It's my fault.

A fire engine arrived with men in breathing apparatus.
They went round to the back of the cottage carrying
equipment with dials, and eventually came out through
my front door into the street. What I heard of their reports
to the policemen suggested that there shouldn't be any
close investigation until the toxic level inside the cottage
was within limits.

"What gas is it?" one of the policemen asked.

"Hydrogen sulphide."

"Lethal?"

"Extremely. Paralyzes the breathing. Don't go in until
we give the all clear. There's some sort of source in there,
still generating gas."

The policeman turned to me. "What is it?" he said.

I shook my head. "I don't know."

He had asked earlier what was wrong with my face.

"Fell in a race."

Everyone had accepted it. Battered jockeys were commonplace in Lambourn. The whole circus moved up the road to Harold's house, and events became jumbled.

Clare telephoned twice to the hospital for news of Jeremy.

"He's in intensive care . . . very ill. They want to know his next of kin."

"Parents," I said despairingly. "In St. Albans." The number was in my house, with the gas.

Harold did some work with directory enquiries and got through to Jeremy's father.

Don't die, I thought. Bloody well live . . . Please live.

Policemen tramped in and out. An inspector came, asking questions. I told him, and Clare told him, what had happened. I didn't know how hydrogen sulphide had got into my darkroom. It had been a sheer accident that it had been Jeremy who breathed it. I didn't know why anyone should want to put gas in my darkroom. I didn't know who.

The inspector said he didn't believe me. No one had death traps like that set in their houses without knowing why. I shook my head. Talking was still a trial. I'd tell him why, I thought, if Jeremy died. Otherwise not.

How had I known so quickly that there was gas? My reaction had been instantaneous, Clare had said. Why was that?"

"Sodium sulphide . . . used to be used in photographic studios. Still sometimes used . . . but not much . . . because of the smell. I didn't have any. It wasn't . . . mine."

"Is it a gas?" the inspector asked, puzzled.

"No. Comes in crystals. Very poisonous. Comes in sepia toner kits. Kodak makes one called T-7A, I think."

"But you knew it *was* a gas."

"Because of Jeremy passing out. And I breathed it . . . it felt . . . wrong. You can make gas . . . using sodium sulphide . . . I just knew it was gas . . . I don't know how I knew . . . I just knew."

"How do you make hydrogen sulphide gas from sodium sulphide crystals?"

"I don't know."

He was insistent that I should answer, but I truthfully didn't know. And now, sir, he said, about your injuries. Your obvious discomfort and weakness. The state of your face. Are you sure, sir, that these were the result of a fall in a horse race? Because they looked to him, he had to say, more like the result of a severe human attack. He'd seen a few in his time, he said.

A fall, I said.

The inspector asked Harold, who looked troubled but answered forthrightly, "A wicked fall, inspector. Umpteen horses kicked him. If you want witnesses . . . about six thousand people were watching."

The inspector shrugged but looked disillusioned. Maybe he had an instinct, I thought, which told him I'd lied on some counts. When he'd gone, Harold said, "Hope you know what you're doing. Your face was OK when I left you, wasn't it?"

"Tell you one day," I said, mumbling.

He said to Clare, "What happened?" but she too shook her head in exhaustion and said she didn't know anything, didn't understand anything, and felt terrible herself. Harold's wife gave us comfort and food and eventually beds; and Jeremy at midnight was still alive.

Several rotten hours later Harold came into the little room where I sat in bed. Sat because I could breathe better that way, and because I couldn't sleep, and because I still ached abominably all over. My young lady, he said, had gone off to London to work and would telephone that evening. The police wanted to see me. And Jeremy? Jeremy was still alive, still unconscious, still critically ill.

The whole day continued wretchedly.

The police went into my cottage, apparently opening doors and windows for the wind to blow through, and the inspector came to Harold's house to tell me the results.

We sat in Harold's office, where the inspector in daylight proved to be a youngish blond man with sensible eyes and a habit of cracking his knuckles. I hadn't taken him in much as a person the evening before, only his air of hostility; and that was plainly unchanged.

"There's a water filter on the tap in your darkroom," he said. "What do you use it for?"

"All water for photographs," I said, "has to be clean."

Some of the worst swelling around my eyes and mouth was beginning to subside. I could see better, talk better: at least some relief.

"Your water filter," the inspector said, "is a hydrogen sulphide generator."

"It can't be."

"Why not?"

"Well . . . I used it all the time. It's only a water softener. You regenerate it with salt . . . like all softeners. It couldn't possibly make gas."

He gave me a long considering stare. Then he went away for an hour, and returned with a box and a young man in jeans and a sweater.

"Now, sir," the inspector said to me with the studied procedural politeness of the suspicious copper, "is this your water filter?"

He opened the box to show me the contents. One Durst filter, with, screwed onto its top, the short rubber attachment which was normally pushed onto the tap.

"It looks like it," I said. "It looks just like it should. What's wrong with it? It couldn't possibly make gas."

The inspector gestured to the young man, who produced a pair of plastic gloves from a pocket and put them on. He then picked up the filter, which was a black plastic globe about the size of a grapefruit, with clear sections top and bottom, and unscrewed it around the middle.

"Inside here," he said, "there's usually just the filter cartridge. But as you'll see, in this particular object, things are quite different. Inside here there are two containers, one above the other. They're both empty now, but this lower one contained sodium sulphide crystals, and this one"—he paused with an inborn sense of the dramatic— "this upper one contained sulphuric acid. There must have been some form of membrane holding the contents of the two containers apart, but when the tap was turned on, the water pressure broke or dissolved the membrane, and the two chemicals mixed. Sulphuric acid and sodium sulphide, propelled by water, a very highly effective sulphide generator. It would have gone on pouring out gas even if the water was turned off. Which it was, presumably by Mr. Folk."

There was a long, meaningful, depressing silence.

"So you can see, sir," the inspector said, "it couldn't in any way have been an accident."

"No," I said dully. "But I don't know, I truthfully don't know, who could have put such a thing there. They would have to have known what sort of filter I had, wouldn't they?"

"And that you had a filter in the first place."

"Everyone with a darkroom has a filter of some sort."

Another silence. They seemed to be waiting for me to tell them, but I didn't know. It couldn't have been den Relgan: why should be bother with such a device when one or two more kicks would have finished me? It couldn't have been Elgin Yaxley: he hadn't had time. It couldn't have been any of the other people George Millace had written his letters to. Two of them were old history, gone and forgotten. One of them was still current, but I'd done nothing about it, and hadn't told the man concerned that the letter existed. It wouldn't anyway be him. He would certainly not kill me.

All of which left one most uncomfortable explanation— that somebody thought I had something I didn't have. Someone who knew I'd inherited George Millace's black-mailing package and who knew I'd used some of it and who wanted to stop me using any more of it.

George Millace had definitely had more in that box than I'd inherited. I didn't have, for instance, the cigarette packet on which Dana den Relgan had written her drugs list. And I didn't have . . . what else?

"Well, sir," the inspector said.

"No one's been into my cottage since I was using the darkroom on Wednesday. Only my neighbour, and the tax assessor—" I stopped, and they pounced on it.

"What tax assessor?"

Ask Mrs. Jackson, I said, and they said yes they would.

"She said he didn't touch anything."

"But he could have seen what type of filter . . ."

"Is it my own filter?" I asked. "It does look like it."

"Probably," the younger man said. "But our man would have had to see it for the dimensions. Then he would come back and it would take about thirty seconds, I'd reckon, to take the filter cartridge out and put the packets of chemicals in. Pretty neat job."

"Will Jeremy live?" I said.

The younger man shrugged. "I'm a chemist. Not a doctor."

They went away after a while, taking the filter.

I rang the hospital. No change.

I went to the hospital myself in the afternoon, with Harold's wife driving because she insisted I wasn't fit.

I didn't see Jeremy. I saw his parents. They were abstracted with worry, too upset to be angry. Not my fault, they said, though I was afraid they would think so later. Jeremy was being kept alive by a respirator. His breathing was paralyzed. His heart was beating. His brain was alive.

His mother wept.

"Don't worry so," Harold's wife said, driving home. "He'll be all right."

She had persuaded the nurse, whom she knew, to get

me to have some stitches in my face. The result felt stiffer than ever.

"If he dies . . ."

"He won't die," Harold's wife said.

The inspector telephoned to say I could go back to the cottage, but not into the darkroom: the police had sealed it.

I wandered slowly around my home feeling no sort of ease. Physically wretched, morally pulverized, neck-deep in guilt.

There were signs everywhere that the police had searched. Hardly surprising, I supposed. They hadn't come across the few prints I still had of George Millace's letters, which were locked in the car. They had left undisturbed on the kitchen dresser the box with the blank-looking negatives.

I opened it. It still contained, besides the puzzles I'd solved, the one that I hadn't. The black light-proof envelope, which contained what looked like a piece of clear plastic and two unused sheets of typing paper.

Perhaps I thought, perhaps it's because I have these that the gas trap was set.

But what . . . *what* did I have?

It was no good, I thought: I would have to find out . . . and pretty fast, before whoever it was had another go at killing me, and succeeded.

18

I begged a bed again from Harold's wife, and in the morning telephoned again to Swindon hospital.

Jeremy was alive. No change.

I sat in Harold's kitchen drinking coffee, suicidally depressed.

Harold answered his ringing telephone for about the tenth time that morning and handed the receiver to me.

"It's not an owner, this time," he said. "It's for you."

It was Jeremy's father. I felt sick.

"We want you to know . . . he's awake."

"Oh . . ."

"He'll still on the respirator. But they say that by now if he'd been going to die, he'd have gone. He's still very ill, but they say he'll recover. We thought you'd like to know."

"Thank you," I said.

The reprieve was almost more unbearable than the anxiety. I gave the reciver to Harold and said Jeremy was better, and went out into the yard to look at the horses. Even in the fresh air I felt stifled. In relief, overthrown. I stood in the wind waiting for the internal storm to abate, and gradually felt an incredible sense of release. I had literally been freed. Let off a life sentence. Screw you, Jeremy, I thought, dishing out such a fright.

Clare telephoned.

"He's all right. He's awake," I said.

"Thank God."

"Can I ask you a favor?" I said. "Can I dump myself on Samantha for a night or two?"

"As in the old days?"

"Until Saturday."

She swallowed a laugh and said why not, and when did I want to come.

"Tonight," I said. "If I may."

"We'll expect you for supper."

Harold wanted to know when I thought I'd be fit to race.

I would get some physiotherapy from the Clinic for Injuries in London, I said. By Saturday I'd be ready.

"Not by the look of you."

"Four days. I'll be fit."

"Mind you are, then."

I felt distinctly unfit still for driving, but less than inclined to sleep alone in my cottage. I did some minimal packing, collected George's rubbish box from the kitchen, and set off to Chiswick, where despite wearing sunglasses I got a horrified reception. Black bruises, stitched cuts, three-day growth of beard. Hardly a riot.

"But it's *worse*," Clare said, staring closely.

"Looks worse, feels better." A good job, I thought, that they couldn't see the rest of me. My whole belly was black with the decaying remains of internal abdominal bleeding. The damage, I'd concluded, which had set off the spasms.

Samantha was troubled. "Clare said someone had punched you, but I never thought . . ."

"Look," I said, "I could go somewhere else."

"Don't be silly. Sit down. Supper's ready."

They didn't talk much or seem to expect me to. I wasn't good company. Too drastically feeble. I asked with the coffee if I might telephone to Swindon.

"Jeremy?" Clare said.

I nodded.

"I'll do it. What's the number?"

I told her, and she got through, and consulted.

"Still on the respirator," she said, "but progress maintained."

"If you're tired," Samantha said calmly, "go to bed."

"Well . . ."

They both came upstairs. I walked automatically, without thinking, into a small bedroom next door to the bathroom.

They both laughed. "We wondered if you would," Samantha said.

Clare went to work and I spent most of Wednesday dozing in the swinging basket chair in the kitchen. Samantha came in and out, went to her part-time job in the morning, shopped in the afternoon. I waited in a highly peaceful state for energy of any sort to return to brain or limbs and reckoned I was fortunate to have a day like that to mend in.

Thursday took me to the Clinic for Injuries for two long sessions of electric treatment, massage and exercise, with two more sessions promised for Friday.

Between the sessions I telephoned four photographers and one acquaintance who worked on a specialist magazine, and found no one who knew how to raise pictures from plastic or typing paper. Don't waste my time, old boy, the specialist said wearily.

When I got back to Chiswick the sun was low on the winter horizon, and in the kitchen Samantha was cleaning the french windows.

"They always look so filthy when the sun shines on

them," she said, busily rubbing with a cloth. "Sorry if it's cold in here, but I won't be long."

I sat in the basket chair and watched her shake liquid cleaner out of a white plastic bottle. She finished the outside of the doors and came in, pulling them after her, fastening the bolts. The plastic bottle stood on a table beside her.

AJAX, it said, in big letters.

I frowned at it, trying to remember. Where had I heard the word Ajax?

I stood up out of the swinging chair and walked over for a closer look. "Ajax Window Cleaner," it said in smaller red letters on the white plastic, "With Ammonia." I picked the bottle up and shook it. Liquid. I put my nose to the top, and smelled the contents. Soapy. Sweet scented. Not pungent.

"What is it?" Samantha said. "What are you looking at?"

"This cleaner . . ."

"Yes?"

"Why would a man ask his wife to buy him some Ajax?"

"What a question," Samantha said. "I've no idea."

"Nor did she have," I said. "She didn't know why."

Samantha took the bottle out of my hands and continued with her task. "You can clean any sort of glass with it," she said. "Bathroom tiles. Looking glass. Quite useful stuff."

I went back to the basket chair and swung in it gently. Samantha cast me a sideways glance, smiling.

"You looked like death two days ago," she said.

"And now?"

"Now one might pause before calling the undertaker."

"I'll shave tomorrow," I said.

"Who punched you?" Her voice sounded casual. Her eyes and attention were on the window. It was, all the same, a serious question. A seeking not for a simple one-

word answer, but for commitment to herself. A sort of
request for payment for shelter unquestioningly given. If
I didn't tell her, she wouldn't persist. But if I didn't tell
her, we had already gone as far as we ever would in our
relationship.

What did I want, I thought, in that house that now
increasingly felt like home? I have never wanted a family:
I'd wanted no loving ties. No suffocating emotional de-
pendents. So if I nested comfortably, deeply into the lives
lived in that house, wouldn't I feel impelled in a short
while to break-out with wild flapping freedom-seeking
wings? Did anyone ever fundamentally change?

Samantha read into my silence what I expected, and
her manner did subtly alter, not to one of unfriendliness,
but to a cut-off intimacy. Before she'd finished the window, I'd become her guest, not her . . . her what? Her son,
brother, nephew . . . part of her.

She gave me a bright surface smile and put the kettle
on for tea.

Clare returned from work with gaiety carefully layered
over tiredness, and she too, though not asking, was waiting.

I found myself, halfway through supper, telling them
about George Millace. In the end it was no great hard
decision. No cut-and-dried calculation. I just naturally told
them.

"You won't approve," I said. "I carried on where
George left off."

They listened with their forks in the air, taking mouth-
fuls at long intervals, eating peas and lasagne slowly.

"So you see," I said at the end. "It isn't finished yet.
There's no going back or wishing I hadn't started . . . I
don't know that I do wish that . . . but I asked to come
here for a few days because I didn't feel safe in the cottage, and I'm not going back there to live permanently
until I know who tried to kill me."

Clare said, "You might never know."

"Don't say that," Samantha said sharply. "If he doesn't find out . . ." She stopped.

I finished it for her, "I'll have no defense."

"Perhaps the police . . ." Clare said.

"Perhaps."

We passed the rest of the evening more in thoughtfulness than depression, and the news from Swindon was good. Jeremy's lungs were coming out of paralysis. Still on the respirator, but a significant improvement during the past twenty-four hours. The prim voice reading the written bulletin sounded bored. Could I speak to Jeremy himself yet, I asked. They'd check. The prim voice came back; not in intensive care: try on Sunday.

I spent a long time in the bathroom on Friday morning scraping off beard and snipping out unabsorbed ends of the fine transparent thread the nurse had used in her stitching. She'd done a neat job, I had to confess. The cuts had all healed, and would disappear probably without scars. All the swelling, also, had gone. There were still the remains of black bruises turning yellow, and still the chipped teeth, but what finally looked out of the mirror was definitely a face, not a nightmare.

Samantha looked relieved over the reemergence of civilization and insisted on telephoning to her dentist. "You need caps," she said, "and caps you'll have." And caps I had, late that afternoon. Temporaries, until porcelain jobs could be made.

Between the two sessions in the clinic I drove north out of London to Basildon in Essex, where a British firm manufactured photographic printing paper. I went instead of telephoning because I thought they would find it less easy to say they had no information if I was actually there; and so it proved.

They did not, they said in the front office politely, know of any photographic material which looked like plastic or typing paper. Had I brought the specimens with me?

No, I had not. I didn't want them examined in case they were sensitive to light. Could I see someone else?

Difficult, they said.

I showed no signs of leaving. Perhaps Mr. Christopher could help me, they suggested at length, if he wasn't too busy.

Mr. Christopher turned out to be about nineteen with an antisocial haircut and chronic catarrh. He listened, however, attentively.

"This paper and this plastic've got no emulsion on them?"

"No, I don't think so."

He shrugged. "There you are, then."

"There I am where?"

"You got no pictures."

I sucked at the still broken teeth and asked him what seemed to be a nonsensical question.

"Why would a photographer want ammonia?"

"Well, he wouldn't. Not for photographs. No straight ammonia in any developer or bleach or fix, that I know of."

"Would anyone here know?" I asked.

He gave me a pitying stare, implying that if he didn't know, no one else would.

"You could ask," I said persuasively. "Because if there's a process which does use ammonia, you'd like to know, wouldn't you?"

"Yeah. I reckon I would."

He gave me a brisk nod and vanished, and I waited a quarter of an hour, wondering if he'd gone off to lunch. He returned, however, with a gray elderly man in glasses who was none too willing but delivered the goods.

"Ammonia," he said, "is used in the photographic sections of engineering industries. It develops what the public call blueprints. More accurately, of course, it's the diazo process."

"Please," I said humbly and with gratitude, "could you describe it to me."

"What's the matter with your face?" he said.

"Lost an argument."

"Huh."

"Diazo process," I said. "What is it?"

"You get a drawing—a line drawing, I'm talking about—from the designer. Say of a component in a machine. A drawing with exact specifications for manufacture. Are you with me?"

"Yes."

"The industry will need several copies of the master drawing. So they make blueprints of it. Or rather, they don't."

"Er . . ." I said.

"In blueprints," he said severely, "the paper turns blue, leaving the design in white. Nowadays the paper turns white and the lines develop in black. Or dark red."

"Please, go on."

"From the beginning?" he said. "The master drawing, which is of course on translucent paper, is pinned and pressed tightly by glass over a sheet of diazo paper. Diazo paper is white on the back and yellow or greenish on the side covered with ammonia-sensitive dye. Bright carbon arclight is shone onto the master drawing for a measured length of time. This light bleaches out all the dye on the diazo paper underneath except for the parts under the lines on the master drawing. The diazo paper is then developed in hot ammonia fumes, and the lines of dye emerge, turning dark. Is that what you want?"

"Indeed it is," I said with awe. "Does diazo paper look like typing paper?"

"Certainly it can, it it's cut down to that size."

"And how about a piece of clear-looking plastic?"

"Sounds like a diazo film," he said calmly. "You don't

need hot ammonia fumes for developing that. Any form
of cold liquid ammonia will do. But be careful. I said
carbon arclight, because that's the method that's used in
engineering, but of course a longer exposure to sunlight
or any other form of light would also have the same effect.
If the piece of film you have looks clear, it means that
most of the yellow-looking dye has already been bleached
out. If there is a drawing there, you must be careful not
to expose it to too much more light."

"How much more light is too much?" I said anxiously.

He pursed his lips. "In sunlight, you'd have lost any
trace of dye forever in thirty seconds. In normal room
light, five to ten minutes."

"It's in a light-proof envelope."

"Then you might be lucky."

"And the sheets of paper? They look white on both
sides."

"The same applies," he said. "They've been exposed
to light. You might have a drawing there, or you might
not."

"How do I make hot ammonia fumes, to find out?"

"Simple," he said, as if everyone would know items
like that. "Put some ammonia in a saucepan and heat it.
Hold the paper over the top. Don't get it wet. Just steam
it."

"Would you," I said carefully, "like some champagne
for lunch?"

I returned to Samantha's house at about six o'clock with
a cheap saucepan, two bottles of Ajax, an anesthetized top
lip, and a set of muscles that had been jerked, pressed and
exercised into some sort of resurrection. I also felt dead
tired, which wasn't a good omen for fitness the next day,
when, Harold had informed me on the telephone, two
'chasers would be awaiting my services at Sandown Park.

Samantha had gone out. Clare, with work scattered all

over the kitchen table, gave me a fast assessing scrutiny
and suggested a large brandy.

"It's in the cupboard with the salt and flour and herbs.
Cooking brandy. Pour me some, too, would you?"

I sat at the table with her for a while, sipping the re-
pulsive stuff neat and feeling a lot better for it. Her dark
head was bent over the book she was working on, the
capable hand stretching out now and again for the glass,
the mind engrossed in her task.

"Would you live with me?" I said.

She looked up; abstracted, faintly frowning, question-
ing.

"Did you say . . . ?"

"Yes. I did," I said. "Would you live with me?"

Her work at last lost her attention. With a smile in her
eyes, she said, "Is that an academic question or a positive
invitation?"

"Invitation."

"I couldn't live in Lambourn," she said. "Too far to
commute. You couldn't live here. Too far from the
horses."

"Somewhere in between."

She looked at me wonderingly. "Are you serious?"

"Yes."

"But we haven't . . ." She stopped, leaving a clear
meaning.

"Been to bed."

"Well . . ."

"In general," I said, "what do you think?"

She took refuge and time with sips from her glass. I
waited for what seemed a small age.

"I think," she said finally, "why not give it a try?"

I smiled from intense satisfaction.

"Don't look so smug," she said. "Drink your brandy
while I finish this book."

She bent her head down again but didn't read far.

"It's no good," she said. "How can I work? Let's get the supper."

Cooking frozen fish fillets took ages because of her trying to do it with my arms around her waist and my chin on her hair. I didn't taste the stuff when we ate it. I felt extraordinarily light-headed. I hadn't deeply hoped she would say yes, and still less had I expected the incredible sense of adventure since she had. To have someone to care about seemed no longer a burden to be avoided, but a positive privilege.

Amazing, I thought dimly; the whole thing's amazing. Was this what Lord White had felt for Dana den Relgan?

"What time does Samantha get back?" I said.

Clare shook her head. "Too soon."

"Will you come with me tomorrow?" I said. "To the races . . . and then stay somewhere together afterwards?"

"Yes, I will."

"Samantha won't mind?"

She gave me an amused look. "No, I don't think so."

"Why do you laugh?"

"She's gone to the pictures. I asked her why she had to go on your last night here. She said she wanted to see the film. I thought it odd, but I believed her. She saw more than I did."

"My God," I said. *"Women."*

While she tried again to finish her work, I fetched the rubbish box and took out the black light-proof envelope.

I borrowed a flat glass dish from a cupboard. Took the piece of plastic film from the envelope. Put it in the dish. At once poured liquid Ajax over it. Held my breath.

Almost instantly dark brownish-red lines became visible. I rocked the dish, sloshing the liquid across the plastic surface, conscious that all of the remaining dye had to be covered with ammonia before the light bleached it away.

It was no engineering drawing, but handwriting.

It looked odd.

As more and more developed, I realized that from the reading point of view the plastic was wrong side up.

Turned it over. Sloshed more Ajax over it, tilting it back and forth until I could read the revealed words, as clear as when they'd been written.

They were, they had to be, what Dana den Relgan had written on the cigarette packet.

Heroin, cocaine, marijuana. Quantities, dates, prices paid, suppliers. No wonder she had wanted it back.

Clare looked up from her work.

"What have you found?"

"What the Dana girl who came last Sunday was wanting."

"Let's see." She came across and looked into the dish, reading. "That's pretty damning, isn't it?"

"Mm."

"But how did it turn up like this?"

I said appreciatively, "Crafty George Millace. He got her to write on cellophane wrapping with a red-felt tip pen. She felt safer that way, because cigarette packet wrapping is so fragile, so destructible . . . and I expect the words themselves looked indistinct, over the printed packet. But from George's point of view all he wanted was solid lines on transparent material, to make a diazo print."

I explained to her all that I'd learned in Basildon. "He must have cut the wrapping off carefully, pressed it flat under glass on top of this piece of diazo film, and exposed it to light. Then with the drugs list safely recorded, it wouldn't matter if the wrapping came to pieces. And the list was hidden, like everything else."

"He was an extraordinary man."

I nodded. "Extraordinary. Though mind you he didn't mean anyone else to have to solve his puzzles. He made them only to please himself and to save the records from angry burglars."

"In which he succeeded."

"He sure did."

"What about all your photographs?" she said in sudden alarm. "All the ones in the filing cabinet. Suppose—"

"Calm down," I said. "Even if anyone stole them or burned them, they'd miss all the negatives. The butcher has those down the road in his freezer room."

"Maybe all photographers," she said, "are obsessed."

It wasn't until much later that I realized that I hadn't disputed her classification. I hadn't even *thought*, "I'm a jockey."

I asked her if she'd mind if I filled the kitchen with the smell of boiling ammonia.

"I'll go and wash my hair," she said.

When she'd gone, I drained the Ajax out of the dish into the saucepan and added to it what was left in the first bottle, and while it heated opened the french windows so as not to asphyxiate. Then I held the first of the sheets of what looked like typing paper over the simmering cleaner, and watched George's words come alive as if they'd been written in secret ink. The ammonia content clearly evaporated quickly, because it took the whole second bottle to get results with the second sheet, but it too grew words like the first.

Together they constituted one handwritten letter in what I had no doubt was George's own writing. He must himself have written on some sort of transparent material. It could have been anything: a plastic bag, tracing paper, a piece of glass, film with all the emulsion bleached off, anything. When he'd written, he had put his letter over diazo paper and exposed it to light, and immediately stored the exposed paper in the light-proof envelope.

And then what? Had he sent his transparent original? Had he written it again on ordinary paper? Had he typed it? No way of knowing. But one thing was certain: in some form or other he had dispatched his letter.

I had heard of the results of its arrival.

I could guess, I thought, who wanted me dead.

19

Harold met me with some relief on the verandah outside the weighing room at Sandown.

"You at least look better . . . have you passed the doctor?"

I nodded. "He signed my card." He'd no reason not to. By his standards a jockey who took a week off because he'd been kicked was acting more self-indulgently than usual. He'd asked me to a bendstretch, and nodded me through.

"Victor's here," Harold said.

"Did you tell him?"

"Yes, I did. He says he doesn't want to talk to you on a racecourse. He says he wants to see his horses work on the Downs. He's coming on Monday. He'll talk to you then. And, Philip, you bloody well be careful what you say."

"Mm," I said noncommittally "How about Coral Key?"

"What about him? He's fit."

"No funny business?"

"Victor knows how you feel," Harold said.

"Victor doesn't care a losing tote ticket how I feel. Is the horse running straight?"

"He hasn't said anything."

"Because I am," I said. "If I'm riding it, I'm riding it straight. Whatever he says in the parade ring."

"You've got bloody aggressive all of a sudden."

"No, just saving you money. You personally. Don't back me to lose, like you did on Daylight. That's all."

He said he wouldn't. He also said there was no point in holding the Sunday briefing if I was talking to Victor on Monday, and that we would discuss next week's plans after that. Neither of us said what was in both our minds. After Monday, would there be any plans?

Steve Millace in the changing room was complaining about a starter letting a race off when he, Steve, hadn't been ready, with the consequence that he was left so flat-footed that the other runners had gone half a furlong before he'd begun. The owner was angry and said he wanted another jockey next time, and, as Steve asked everyone ad infinitum, was it fair?

"No," I said. "Life isn't."

"It should be."

"Better face it," I said smiling. "The best you can expect is a kick in the teeth."

"Your teeth are all right," someone said.

"They've got caps on."

"Pick up the pieces, huh? Is that what you're saying?" I nodded.

Steve said, not following this exchange, "Starters should be fined for letting a race off when the horses aren't pointing the right way."

"Give it a rest," someone said. But Steve as usual was still going on about it a couple of hours later.

His mother, he said when I inquired, had gone to friends in Devon for a rest.

Outside the weighing room Bart Underfield was lecturing one of the more gullible of the reporters on the subject of unusual nutrients.

"It's rubbish giving horses beer and eggs and ridiculous things like that. I never do it."

The reporter refrained from saying—or perhaps he didn't know—that the trainers addicted to eggs and beer were on the whole more successful than Bart. Bart's face when he saw me changed from bossy know-all to tight-lipped spite. He jettisoned the reporter and took two decisive steps to stand in my path, but when he'd stopped me he didn't speak.

"Do you want something, Bart?" I said.

He still didn't say anything. I thought that quite likely he couldn't find words intense enough to convey what he felt. I was growing accustomed, I thought, to being hated.

He found his voice. "You wait," he said with bitter quiet. "I'll get you."

If he'd had a dagger and privacy, I wouldn't have turned my back on him, as I did, to walk away.

Lord White was there, deep in earnest conversation with fellow stewards, his gaze flicking over me quickly as if wincing. He would never, I supposed, feel comfortable when I was around. Never be absolutely sure that I wouldn't tell. Never like my knowing what I knew.

He would have to put up with it for a long time, I thought. One way or another the racing world would always be my world, as it was his. He would see me, and I him, week by week, until one of us died.

Victor Briggs was waiting in the parade ring when I went out to ride Coral Key. A heavy brooding figure in his broad-brimmed hat and long navy overcoat: unsmiling, untalkative, gloomy. When I touched my cap to him politely, there was no response of any sort, only the maintenance of an expressionless stare.

Coral Key was an oddity among Victor Briggs' horses, a six-year-old novice 'chaser bought out of the hunting field when he had begun to show promise in point-to-points. Great horses in the past had started that way, like Oxo and Ben Nevis, which had both won the Grand National, and although Coral Key was unlikely to be of that class, it seemed to me that he, too, had the feel of good things to come. There was no way that I was going to mess up his early career, whatever my instructions. In my mind and very likely in my attitude I dared his owner to say he didn't want him to try to win.

He didn't say it. He said nothing at all about anything. He simply watched me unblinkingly, and kept his mouth shut.

Harold bustled about as if movement itself could dispel the atmosphere existing between his owner and his jockey; and I mounted and rode out to the course feeling as if I'd been in a strong field of undischarged electricity.

A spark . . . an explosion . . . might lie ahead. Harold sensed it. Harold was worried to the depths of his own explosive soul.

It might be the last race I ever rode for Victor Briggs. I lined up at the start thinking that it was no good speculating about that; that all I should be concentrating on was the matter in hand.

A cold windy cloudy day. Good ground underfoot. Seven other runners, none of them brilliant. If Coral Key jumped as he had when I'd schooled him at home, he should have a good chance.

I settled my goggles over my eyes and gathered the reins.

"Come in, now, jockeys," the starter said. The horses advanced towards the tapes in a slow line and as the gate flew up accelerated away from bunched haunches. Thirteen fences; two miles. I would find out pretty soon, I thought ruefully, if I wasn't yet fit.

Important, I thought, to get him to jump well. It was what I was best at. What I most enjoyed doing. There were seven fences close together down the far side of the course. If one met the first of them just right, they all fitted, but a brakes-on approach to the first often meant seven blunders by the end, and countless lengths lost.

From the start there were two fences, then the uphill stretch past the stands, then the top bend, then the downhill fence where I'd stepped off Daylight. No problems on Coral Key: he cleared the lot. Then the sweep around to the seven trappy fences, and if I lost one length getting Coral Key set right for the first, by the end of the seventh I'd stolen ten.

Still it was too soon for satisfaction. Around the long bottom curve Coral Key lay second, taking a breather. Three fences to go and the long hill to home. Between the last two fences I caught up with the leader. We jumped the last fence alongside, nothing between us. Raced up the hill, stretching, flying, doing everything I could.

The other horse won by two lengths.

Harold said, "He ran well," a shade apprehensively, patting Coral Key in the unsaddling enclosure; and Victor Briggs said nothing.

I pulled the saddle off and went in to weigh. There wasn't any way that I could think of that I could have won the race. The other horse had had enough in hand to beat off my challenge. He'd been stronger than Coral Key, and faster. I hadn't felt weak. I hadn't thrown anything away in jumping mistakes. I just hadn't won.

I had needed a strong hand for talking to Victor Briggs; and I hadn't got it.

When life kicks you in the teeth, get caps.

I won the other 'chase, the one that didn't matter so much except to the owners, a junketing quartet of businessmen.

"Bloody good show," they said, beaming. "Bloody well ridden."

I saw Victor Briggs watching from ten paces away, balefully staring. I wondered if he knew how much I'd have given to have those two results reversed.

Clare said, "I suppose the wrong one won?"

"Yeah."

"How much does it matter?"

"I'll find out on Monday."

"Well . . . let's forget it."

"Shouldn't be difficult," I said. I looked at the trim dark coat, the long polished boots. Looked at the large gray eyes and the friendly mouth. Incredible, I thought, to have someone like that waiting for me outside the weighing room. Quite extraordinarily different from going home alone. Like a fire in a cold house. Like sugar on strawberries.

"Would you mind very much," I said, "if we made a detour for me to call on my grandmother?"

The old woman was markedly worse.

No longer propped more or less upright, she sagged back without strength on the pillows; and even her eyes seemed to be losing the struggle, with none of the beady aggression glittering out.

"Did you bring her?" she said.

Still no salutation, no preliminaries. Perhaps it was a mistake to expect changes in the mind to accompany changes in the body. Perhaps my feelings for her were different and all that remained immutable was her hatred for me.

"No," I said. "I didn't bring her. She's lost."

"You said you would find her."

"She's lost."

She gave me a feeble cough, the thin chest jerking. Her eyelids closed for a few seconds and opened again. A weak hand twitched at the sheet.

"Leave your money to James," I said.

With a faint outer echo of persistent inner stubbornness, she shook her head.

"Leave some to charity, then," I said. "Leave it to a dog's home."

"I hate dogs." Her voice was weak. Not her opinions.

"How about lifeboats?"

"Hate the sea. Makes me sick."

"Medical research?"

"Hasn't done me much good, has it?"

"Well," I said slowly, "how about leaving it to a religious order of some sort."

"You must be mad. I hate religion. Cause of trouble. Cause of wars. Wouldn't give them a penny."

I sat down unbidden in the armchair.

Amanda was lost within her religion. Indoctrinated, cared for, perhaps loved: and fourteen formative years couldn't be undone. Wrenching her out forcibly (even if one were able to) would inflict incalculable psychological damage. For her own sake one would have to leave her in peace, however stunted and alien that peace might seem. If one day she sought change of her own accord, so much the better. Meanwhile, it remained only to see that she was provided for.

"Can I do anything for you?" I asked. "Besides, of course, finding Amanda. Can I fetch anything? Is there anything you want?"

My grandmother raised a faint sneer. "Don't think you can soft soap me into leaving any money to you, because I'm not going to."

"I'd give water to a dying cat," I said. "Even if it spat in my face."

Her mouth opened and stiffened with affront.

"How dare you?"

"How dare you still think I'd shift a speck of dust for your money?"

The mouth closed into a thin line.

"Can I fetch you anything?" I said again, levelly. "Is there anything you want?"

She didn't answer for several seconds. Then she said, "Go away."

"Well, I will, in a minute," I said. "But I want just to suggest something else." I waited a fraction, but as she didn't immediately argue I continued. "In case Amanda is ever found, why don't you set up a trust for her? Tie up the capital tight with masses of excellent trustees. Make it so that she couldn't ever get her hands on the money herself, nor could anyone who was perhaps after her fortune. Make it impossible for anyone but Amanda herself to benefit, with an income paid out only at the direction of the trustees."

She watched me with half-lowered eyelids.

"Wherever she is," I said, "Amanda is still only seventeen or eighteen. Too young to inherit a lot of money without strings. Leave it to her with strings like steel hawsers."

"Is that all?"

"Mm."

She lay quiet, immobile.

I waited. I had waited all my life for something other than malevolence from my grandmother. I could wait forever.

"Go away," she said.

I stood up and said, "Very well."

Walked to the door. Put my hand on the knob.

"Send me some roses," my grandmother said.

We found a flower shop still open in the town, though they were sweeping out, ready to close.

"Doesn't she realize it's December?" Clare said. "Roses will cost a fortune."

"If you were dying, and you wanted roses, do you think you'd care?"

"Maybe not."

All they had in the flower shop were fifteen very small pink buds on very long thin stems. Not much call for roses. These were left over from a wedding.

We drove back to the nursing home and gave them to a nurse to deliver at once, with a card enclosed saying I'd get some better ones next week.

"She doesn't deserve it," Clare said.
"Poor old woman."

We stayed in a pub by the Thames which had old beams
and good food and bedroom windows looking out to bare
willows and sluggish brown water.

No one knew us. We signed in as Mr. and Mrs. and
ate a slow dinner, and went unobtrusively to bed. Not the
first time she'd done it, she said: did I mind? Preferred it,
I said. No fetishes about virgins? No kinks at all, that I
knew of. Good, she said.

It began in friendship and progressed to passion. Ended
in breathlessness and laughter, sank to murmurs and sleep.
The best it had ever been for me. I couldn't tell about
her, but she showed no hesitation about a repeat program
in the morning.

In the afternoon, in peaceful accord, we went to see
Jeremy.

He was lying in a high bed in a room of his own, with
a mass of breathing equipment to one side. He was,
though, breathing for himself. Precariously, I guessed,
since a nurse came in to check on him every ten minutes
while we were there, making sure that a bell-push remained under his fingers the whole time.

He looked thinner than ever and grayly pale, but there
had been no near-execution in his brain. The eyes were
as intelligent as ever, and the silly-ass manner appeared
strongly as a defense against the indignities of his position.

I tried to apologize for what he'd suffered. He wouldn't
have it.

"Don't forget," he said. "I was there because I wanted
to be. No one exactly twisted my arm." He gave me a
traveling inspection. "Your face looks OK. How do you
heal so fast?"

"Always do."

"Always . . ." He gave a weak laugh. "Funny life you lead. Always healing."

"How long will you be in here?"

"Three or four days."

"Is that all?" Clare said, surprised. "You look . . . er . . ."

He looked whiter than the pillow his head lay on. He nodded, however, and said, "I'm breathing much better. Once there's no danger the nerves will pack up again, I can go. There's nothing else wrong."

"I'll take you home if you need transport," I said.

"Might hold you to that."

We didn't stay very long because talking clearly tired him, but just before we went he said, "You know, that gas was so quick. Not slow, like gas at the dentist. I'd no time to do anything. It was like breathing a brick wall."

Into a short reflective silence Clare said, "No one would have lived if they'd been there alone."

"Makes you think, what?" said Jeremy cheerfully.

As we drove back towards the pub Clare said, "You didn't tell him about Amanda."

"Plenty of time."

"He came down last Sunday because he'd got your message that you'd found her. He told me while we were in the kitchen. He said your phone was out of order, so he came."

"I'd unplugged it."

"Odd how things happen."

"Mm."

Our second night was a confirmation of the first. Much the same, but new and different. A tingling, fierce, gentle, intense, turbulent time. A matter, it seemed, as much to her liking as mine.

"Where's this depression one's supposed to get?" she said, very late. "Post what's-it."

"Comes in the morning, when you go."

"That's hours off yet."

"So it is."

The morning came, as they do. I drove her to a station to catch a train, and went on myself to Lambourn.

When I got there, before going to Harold's, I called at my cottage. All seemed strangely unfamiliar, as if home was no longer the natural embracing refuge it should be. I saw for the first time the bareness, the emotional chill which had been so apparent to Jeremy on his first visit. It no longer seemed to fit with myself. The person who had made that home was going away, receding in time. I felt oddly nostalgic, but there was no calling him back. The maturing change had gone too far.

Shivering a little I spread out on the kitchen table a variety of photographs of different people, and then I asked my neighbor Mrs. Jackson to come in and look at them.

"What am I looking for, Mr. Nore?"

"Anyone you've seen before."

Obliging she studied them carefully one by one, and stopped without hesitation at a certain face.

"How extraordinary!" she exclaimed. "That's the council man who came about the taxes. The one I let in here. Ever so sarcastic, the police were about that, but as I told them, you don't *expect* people to say they're tax assessors if they aren't."

"You're sure he's the one?"

"Positive," she said, nodding. "He had that same hat on, and all."

"Then would you write on the back of the photo, for me, Mrs. Jackson?" I gave her a felt pen that would write boldly and blackly on the photographic paper, and dictated the words for her, saying that this man had called at the house of Philip Nore posing as a tax assessor on Friday, November 27th.

"Is that all?" she asked.

"Sign your name, Mrs. Jackson. And would you mind repeating the whole message on the back of this other photograph?"

With concentration she did so. "Are you giving these to the police?" she said. "I don't want them bothering me again really. Will they come back again with their questions?"

"I shouldn't think so," I said.

20

Victor Briggs had come in his Mercedes, but he went up to the Downs with Harold in the Land Rover. I rode up on a horse. The morning's work got done to everyone's reasonable satisfaction, and we all returned variously to the stable.

When I rode into the yard, Victor Briggs was standing by his car, waiting. I slid off the horse and gave it to one of the lads to see to.

"Get in the car," Victor said.

No waster of words, ever. He stood there in his usual clothes, gloved as always against the chilly wind, darkening the day. If I could see auras, I thought, his would be black.

I sat in the front passenger seat, where he pointed, and he slid himself in beside me, behind the steering wheel. He started the engine, released the brake, put the automatic gear into drive. The quiet hunk of metal eased out of Lambourn, going back to the Downs.

He stopped on a wide piece of grass verge from where one could see half of Berkshire. He switched off the engine, leaned back in his seat, and said, "Well?"

"Do you know what I'm going to say?" I asked.

"I hear things," he said. "I hear a lot of things."

"I know that."

"I heard that den Relgan set his goons on you."

"Did you?" I looked at him with interest. "Where did you hear that?"

He made a small tight movement of his mouth, but he did answer. "Gambling club."

"What did you hear?"

"True, isn't it?" he said. "You still had the marks on Saturday."

"Did you hear any reasons?"

He produced the twitch that went for a smothered smile.

"I heard," he said, "that you got den Relgan chucked out of the Jockey Club a great deal faster than he got in."

He watched my alarmed surprise with another twitch, a less successful effort this time at hiding amusement.

"Did you hear how?" I said.

He said with faint regret. "No. Just that you'd done it. The goons are talking. Stupid bone-headed bull-muscle. Den Relgan's heading for trouble, using them. They never keep their mouths shut."

"Are they . . . um . . . out for general hire?"

"Chuckers out at a gaming club. Muscle for hire. As you say."

"They beat up George Millace's wife. Did you hear that too?"

After a pause he nodded, but offered no comment.

I looked at the closed expression, the dense whitish skin, the black shadow of beard. A secretive, solid, slow-moving man with a tap into a world I knew little of. Gaming clubs, hired bully-boys, underworld gossip.

"The goons said they left you for dead," he said. "A week later, you're winning a race."

"They exaggerated," I said dryly.

I got a twitch but also a shake of the head. "One of

them was scared. Rattled. Said they'd gone too far with
the boots."

"You know them well?" I said.

"They talk."

There was another pause, then I said without emphasis,
"George Millace sent you a letter."

He moved in his seat, seeming almost to relax,
breathing out in a long sigh. He'd been waiting to know,
I thought. Patiently waiting. Answering questions. Being
obliging.

"How long have you had it?" he said.

"Three weeks."

"You can't use it." There was a faint tremor of triumph
in the statement. "You'd be in trouble yourself."

"How did you know I'd got it?" I said.

He blinked. The mouth tightened. He said slowly, "I
heard you had George Millace's . . ."

"George Millace's what?"

"Files."

"Ah," I said. "Nice anonymous word, files. How did
you hear I had them? Who from?"

"Ivor," he said. "And Dana. Separately."

"Will you tell me?"

He thought it over, giving me a blank inspection, and
then said grudgingly. "Ivor was too angry to be discreet.
He said too much about you—such as poisonous creep.
He said you were fifty times worse than George Millace.
And Dana, another night, she said did I know you had
copies of some blackmailing letters George Millace had
sent, and were using them. She asked if I could help her
to get hers back."

I smiled in my turn. "What did you say?"

"I said I couldn't help her."

"When you talked to them," I said, "was it in gaming
clubs?"

"It was."

"Are they your gaming clubs?"

"None of your business," he said.

"Well," I said, "why not tell me?"

He said after a pause, "I have two partners. Four gaming clubs. The clientele in general don't know I'm a proprietor. I move around. I play. I listen. Does that answer your question?"

I nodded. "Yes, thank you. Are those goons your goons?"

"I employ them," he said austerely, "as chuckers out. Not to smash up women and jockeys."

"A little moonlighting, was it? On the side?"

He didn't answer directly. "I have been expecting," he said, "that you would demand something from me if you had that letter. Something more than answers."

I thought of the letter, which I knew word for word:

Dear Victor Briggs,
  I am sure you will be interested to know that I have the following information. You did on five separate occasions during the past six months conspire with a bookmaker to defraud the betting public by arranging that your odds-on favorites should not win their races.

There followed a list of the five races, complete with the sums Victor had received from his bookmaker friend. The letter continued:

  I hold a signed affidavit from the bookmaker in question.
  As you see, all five of these horses were ridden by Philip Nore, who certainly knew what he was doing.
  I could send this affidavit to the Jockey Club, in which case you would both be warned off. I will telephone you soon, however, with an alternative suggestion.

The letter had been sent more than three years earlier. For three years Victor Briggs had run his horses straight. When George Millace died, a week to the day, Victor Briggs had gone back to the old game. Had gone back to find that his vulnerable jockey was no longer reliable.

"I didn't want to do anything about the letter," I said. "I didn't mean to tell you I had it. Not until now."

"Why not? You wanted to ride to win. You could have used it to make me agree. You'd been told you'd lose your job anyway if you wouldn't ride as I wanted. You knew I couldn't face being warned off. Yet you didn't use the letter for that. Why not?"

"I wanted to make you run the horses straight for their own sakes."

He gave me another of the long uninformative stares.

"I'll tell you," he said at last. "Yesterday I added up all the prize money I'd won since Daylight's race at Sandown. All those seconds and thirds, as well as Sharpener's wins. I added up my winnings from betting, win and place. I made more money in the past month with you riding straight than I did with you stepping off Daylight." He paused, waiting for a reaction, but, catching it from him, I simply stared back. "I've seen," he went on, "that you weren't going to ride any more crooked races. I've understood that. I know you've changed. You're a different person. Older. Stronger. If you go on riding for me, I won't ask you again to lose a race." He paused once more. "Is that enough? Is that what you want to hear?"

I looked away from him, out across the windy landscape.

"Yes."

After a bit he said, "George Millace didn't demand money, you know. At least . . ."

"A donation to the Injured Jockeys?"

"You know the lot, don't you?"

"I've learned," I said. "George wasn't interested in ex-

torting money for himself. He extorted—" I searched for
the word "—frustration."

"From how many?"

"Seven, that I know of. Probably eight, if you ask your
bookmaker."

He was astonished.

"George Millace," I said, "enjoyed making people
cringe. He did it to everybody in a mild way. To people
he could catch out doing wrong, he did it with gusto. He
had alternative suggestions for everyone—disclosure, or
do what George wanted. And what George wanted, in
general, was to frustrate. To stop Ivor den Relgan's power
play. To stop Dana taking drugs. To stop other people
doing other things."

"To stop me," Victor said with a hint of dry humor,
"from being warned off." He nodded. "You're right, of
course. When George Millace telephoned, I was expecting
a straight blackmail. Then he said all I had to do was
behave myself. Those were his words. As long as you
behave, Victor, he said, nothing will happen. He called
me Victor. I'd never met him. Knew who he was, of
course, but that was all. Victor, he said, as if I were a
little pet dog, as long as we're a good boy, nothing will
happen. But if I suspect anything, Victor, he said, I'll
follow Philip Nore around with my motorized telephotos
until I have him bang to rights, and then Victor, you'll
both be for the chop."

"Do you remember word for word what he said, after
all this time?" I asked, surprised.

"I recorded him. I was expecting his calls. I wanted
evidence of blackmail. All I got was a moral lecture and
a suggestion that I give a thousand pounds to the Injured
Jockeys' Fund."

"And was that all? Forever?"

"He used to wink at me at the races," Victor said.

I laughed.

"Yes, very funny," he said. "Is that the lot?"

"Not really. There's something you could do for me, if you would. Something you know, and could tell me. Something you could tell me in future."

"What is it?"

"About Dana's drugs."

"Stupid girl. She won't listen."

"She will soon. She's still saveable. And besides her . . ."

I told him what I wanted. He listened acutely. When I'd finished I got the twitch of a throttled smile.

"Beside you," he said, "George Millace was a beginner."

Victor drove off in his car and I walked back to Lambourn over the Downs.

An odd man, I thought. I'd learned more about him in half an hour than I had in seven years, and still knew next to nothing. He had given me what I'd wanted, though. Given it freely. Given me my job without strings for as long as I liked, and help in another matter just as important. It hadn't all been, I thought, because of my having that letter.

Going home in the wind, out on the bare hills, I thought of the way things had happened during the past few weeks. Not about George and his bombshells, but of Jeremy and Amanda.

Because of Jeremy's persistence, I'd looked for Amanda, and because of looking for Amanda I had now met a grandmother, an uncle, a sister. I knew something at least of my father. I had a feeling of origin that I hadn't had before.

I had people. I had people like everyone else had. Not necessarily loving or praiseworthy or successful, but *there*. I hadn't wanted them, but now that I had them they sat quietly in the mind like foundation stones.

Because of looking for Amanda I had found Samantha, and with her a feeling of continuity, of belonging. I saw the pattern of my childhood in a different perspective, not as a chopped up kaleidoscope, but as a curve. I knew a place where I'd been, and a woman who'd known me, and they seemed to lead smoothly now towards Charlie.

I no longer floated on the tide.

I had roots.

I reached the point on the hill from where I could see down to the cottage, the brow that I looked up to from the sitting room windows. I stopped there. I could see most of Lambourn, stretched out. Could see Harold's house and the yard. Could see the whole row of cottages, with mine in the center.

I'd belonged in that village, been part of it, breathed its intrigues for seven years. Been happy, miserable, normal. It was what I'd called home. But now in mind and spirit I was leaving that place, and soon would in body as well. I would live somewhere else, with Clare. I would be a photographer.

The future lay inside me; waiting, accepted. One day fairly soon I'd walk into it.

I would race, I thought, until the end of the season. Five or six more months. Then in May or June, when summer came, I'd hang up my boots: retire, as every jockey had to, some time or other. I would tell Harold soon, to give him time to find someone else for the autumn. I'd enjoy what was left, and maybe have a last chance at the Grand National. Anything might happen. One never knew.

I still had the appetite, still the physique. Better to go, I supposed, before both of them crumbled.

I went on down the hill without any regrets.

21

Clare came down on the train two days later to sort out what photographs she wanted from the filing cabinet: to make a portfolio, she said. Now that she was my agent, she'd be rustling up business. I laughed. It was serious, she said.

I had no races that day. I'd arranged to fetch Jeremy from the hospital and take him home, and to have Clare come with me all the way. I'd also telephoned to Lance Kinship to say I'd had his reprints ready for ages, and hadn't seen him, and would he like me to drop them in as I was practically going past his house.

That would be fine, he said. Afternoon, earlyish, I suggested, and he said "Right" and left the "t" off. And I'd like to ask you something, I said. "Oh? All right. Anything you like."

Jeremy looked a great deal better, without the gray clammy skin of Sunday. We helped him into the back of my car and tucked a rug around him, which he plucked off indignantly, saying he was no aged invalid but a perfectly viable solicitor.

"And incidentally," he said. "My uncle came down

here yesterday. Bad news for you, I'm afraid. Old Mrs. Nore died during Monday night."

"Oh, no," I said.

"Well, you knew," Jeremy said. "Only a matter of time."

"Yes, but . . ."

"My uncle brought two letters for me to give to you. They're in my suitcase somewhere. Fish them out, before we start."

I fished them out, and we sat in the hospital parking lot while I read them.

One was a letter. The other was a copy of her will.

Jeremy said, "My uncle said he was called out urgently to the nursing home on Monday morning. Your grandmother wanted to make her will, and the doctor there told my uncle there wasn't much time."

"Do you know what's in it?" I asked.

He shook his head. "My uncle just said she was a stubborn old woman to the last."

I unfolded the typewritten sheets.

I, Lavinia Nore, being of sound mind, do hereby revoke all previous wills . . .

There was a good deal of legal guff and some complicated pension arrangements for an old cook and gardener, and then the two final fairly simple paragraphs.

". . . Half the residue of my estate to my son James Nore . . ." ". . . Half the residue of my estate to my grandson Philip Nore, to be his absolutely, with no strings or steel hawsers attached."

"What's the matter?" Clare said. "You look so grim."

"The old witch has defeated me."

I opened the other envelope. Inside there was a letter

in shaky handwriting, with no beginning, and no end.
It said:

*I think you did find Amanda, and didn't tell me
because it would have given me no pleasure.*

Is she a nun?

*You can do what you like with my money. If it
makes you vomit, as you once said . . . then VOMIT.*

Or give it to my genes.

Rotten roses.

I handed the will and the letter to Clare and Jeremy,
who read them in silence. We sat there for a while, thinking, and then Clare folded up the letter, put it in its envelope, and handed it back to me.

"What will you do?" she said.

"I don't know. See that Amanda never starves, I suppose. Look after her, somehow. Apart from that . . ."

"Enjoy it," Jeremy said. "The old woman loved you."

I listened to the irony of his voice and wondered if it
was true. Love or hate. Love and hate. Perhaps she'd felt
both at once when she'd made that will.

We drove from Swindon towards St. Albans, making a
short detour to deliver Lance Kinship's reprints.

"Sorry about this," I said. "But it won't take long."

They didn't seem to mind. We found the house without
much trouble. Typical Kinship country, fake Georgian,
large grandiose front, pillared gateway, meager drive.

I picked the packet of photographs out of the trunk of
the car, and rang the front doorbell.

Lance opened the door himself, dressed today not in
country gent togs but in white jeans, espadrilles and a red
and white horizontally striped T-shirt. International film-
director gear, I diagnosed. All he needed was the mega-
phone.

"Come inside," he said. "I'll pay you for these."

"OK. Can't be long though, with my friends waiting."

He looked briefly towards my car, where Clare and Jeremy's interested faces showed in the windows, and went indoors with me following. He led the way into a large sitting room with expanses of parquet and too much black-lacquered furniture. Chrome and glass tables and art deco lamps.

I gave him the packet of pictures.

"You'd better look at them," I said. "To make sure they're all right."

He shrugged. "Why shouldn't they be?" All the same, he opened the envelope and pulled out the contents.

The top picture showed him looking straight at the camera in his country gent clothes; glasses, trilby hat, air of bossy authority.

"Turn it over," I said.

With raised eyebrows he did so, and read what Mrs. Jackson had written: *This is the tax assessor . . .*

The change in him from one instant to the next was like one person leaving and another entering the same skin. He shed the bumptiously sure-of-himself phony; slid into a mess of unstable ill will. The gaudy clothes which had fitted one character seemed grotesque on the other, like gift wrap around a handgrenade. I saw the Lance Kinship I'd only suspected existed. Not the faintly ridiculous poseur pretending to be what he wasn't, but the tangled psychotic who would do anything at all to preserve the outward show.

It was in his very inadequacy, I supposed, that the true danger lay. In his estrangement from reality. In his theatrical turn of mind, which had allowed him to see murder as a solution to problems.

"Before you say anything," I said, "you'd better look at the other things in that envelope."

With angry fingers he sorted them out. The regular reprints and also the black-and-white glossy reproductions

of Dana den Relgan's drugs list and the letter I'd found
on the diazo paper.

They were for him a fundamental disaster.

He let the pictures of the great film producer fall to the
ground around him like ten-by-eight colored leaves, and
stood holding the three black-and-white sheets in visible
horror.

"She said—" he said hoarsely "—she swore you didn't
have it. She swore you didn't know what she was talking
about."

"She was talking about the drugs you supplied her
with. Complete with dates and prices. That list which you
hold, which is recognizably in her handwriting, for all that
it was originally written on cellophane. And of course, as
you see, your name appears on it liberally."

"I'll kill you," he said.

"No, you won't. You've missed your chance. It's too
late now. If the gas had killed me you would have been
all right, but it didn't."

He didn't say, "What gas?" He said, "It all went wrong.
But it didn't matter. I thought it didn't matter." He looked
down helplessly at the black-and-white prints.

"You thought it didn't matter because you heard from
Dana den Relgan that I didn't have the list. And if I didn't
have the list, then I didn't have the letter. Whatever else I'd
had from George Millace, I didn't after all have the list and
the letter. Is that what you thought? So if I didn't have
them, there was no more need to kill me. Was that it?"

He didn't answer.

"It's far too late to do it now," I said, "because there
are extra prints of those pages all over the place. Another
copy of that picture of you, identified by Mrs. Jackson.
Bank, solicitors, several friends, all have instructions
about taking everything to the police if any accidental
death should befall me. You've a positive interest in keeping me alive from now on."

The implication of what I was saying only slowly sank

in. He looked from my face to the photographs and back again several times, doubtfully.

"George Millace's letter——" he said.

I nodded. George's letter, handwritten, read:

Dear Lance Kinship,

I have received from Dana den Relgan a most interesting list of drugs supplied to her by you over the past few months. I am sure I understand correctly that you are a regular dealer in such illegal substances.

It appears to be all too well known in certain circles that in return for being invited to places which please your ego, you will, so to speak, pay for your pleasure with gifts of marijuana, heroin and cocaine.

I could of course place Dana den Relgan's candid list before the proper authorities. I will telephone you shortly, however, with an alternative suggestion.

Yours sincerely,
George Millace

"It was typed when I got it," Lance Kinship said dully. "I burned it."

"When George telephoned," I said, "did he tell you his alternative suggestion?"

The shock in Lance Kinship began to abate, with enmity growing in its place.

"I'm telling you nothing."

I said, disregarding him, "Did George Millace say to stop supplying drugs and donate to the Injured Jockeys' Fund?"

His mouth opened and snapped shut viciously.

"Did he telephone?" I asked. "Or did he tell you his terms when he called here?"

A tight silence.

"Did you put something from your store cupboard into his whisky?"

"Prove it!" he said with sick triumph.

One couldn't, of course. George had been cremated, with his blood tested only for alcohol. There had been no checks for other drugs. Not for, perhaps, tranquilizers, which were flavorless, and which in sufficient quantity would certainly have sent a driver to sleep.

George, I thought regretfully, had stepped on one victim too many. Had stepped on what he'd considered a worm and never recognized the cobra.

George had made a shattering mistake if he'd wanted for once to see the victim squirm when he came up with his terms. George hadn't dreamed that the inadequate weakling would lethally lash out to preserve his sordid life style, hadn't really understood how fanatically Lance Kinship prized his shoulder-rubbing with a jet set that at best tolerated him. George must have enjoyed seeing Lance Kinship's fury. Must have driven off laughing. Poor George.

"Didn't you think," I said, "that George had left a copy of his letter behind him?"

Form his expression, he hadn't. I supposed he'd acted on impulse. He'd very nearly been right.

"When you heard that George had blackmailed other people, including Dana, is that when you began thinking I might have your letter?"

"I heard—" he said furiously "—I heard . . . in the clubs . . . Philip Nore has the letters . . . he's ruined den Relgan . . . got him sacked from the Jockey Club. Did you think . . . once I knew . . . did you really think I'd wait for you to come around to *me*?"

"Unfortunately," I said slowly, "whether you like it or not, I now have come around to you."

"No."

"Yes," I said. "I'll tell you straight away that like George Millace I'm not asking for money."

He didn't look much reassured.

"I'll also tell you it's your bad luck that my mother died from addiction to heroin."

He said wildly, "But I didn't know your mother."

"No, of course not. But there's no question of your ever having supplied her yourself. It's just that I have a certain long-standing prejudice against drug pushers. You may as well know it. You may as well understand why I want what I want."

He took a compulsive step towards me. I thought of the brisk karate kick he had delivered to den Relgan at Kempton and wondered if in his rope-soled sandals on parquet he could be as effective. Wondered if he had any real skill or whether it was more window-dressing to cover the vacuum.

He looked incongruous, not dangerous. A man not young, not old, thinning on top, wearing glasses and beach clothes indoors in December.

A man who could kill if pushed too far. Kill not by physical contact, when one came to think of it, but in his absence, by drugs and gas.

He never reached me to deliver whatever blind vengeful blow he had in mind. He stepped on one of the fallen photographs, and slid, and went down hard on one knee. The inefficient indignity of it seemed to break up conclusively whatever remained of his confidence, for when he looked up at me, I saw not hatred or defiance, but fear.

I said, "I don't want what George did. I don't ask you to stop peddling drugs. I want you to tell me who supplies you with heroin."

He staggered to his feet, his face aghast. "I can't. I can't."

"It shouldn't be difficult," I said mildly. "You must know where you get it from. You get it in sizeable quantities, to sell, to give away. You always have plenty, I'm told. So you must have a regular supplier, mustn't you? He's the one I want."

The source, I thought. One source supplying several pushers. The drug business was like some monstrous tentacly creature: cut off one tentacle and another grew in its place. The war against drugs would never be won, but it had to be fought, if only for the sake of silly girls who were sniffing their way to perdition. For the sake of the pretty ones. For Dana. For Caroline, my lost butterfly mother, who had saved me from an addiction of my own.

"You don't know—" Lance Kinship seemed to be breathless. "It's impossible. I can't tell you. I'd be dead."

I shook my head. "It will be between the two of us. No one will ever know you told me unless you yourself talk, like den Relgan did in the gaming clubs."

"I can't," he said despairingly.

"If you don't," I said conversationally, "I will first tell the policemen investigating an attempted murder in my house that my neighbor positively identifies you as having posed as a tax assessor. This isn't enough on its own to get you charged, but it could certainly get you *investigated* for access to chemicals and so on."

He looked sick.

"Secondly," I said, "I'll see that it gets known all over the place that people would be unwise to ask you to their parties, despite your little goodies, because they might at any time be raided. Unlawful possession of certain drugs is still an offense, I believe."

"You . . . you . . ."

I nodded. He couldn't find a word bad enough.

"I know where you go, to whose houses. Everyone talks. I've been told. A word in the ear of the drugs squad and you'd be the least welcome guest in Britain."

"I . . . I . . ."

"Yes, I know," I said. "Going to these places is what makes your life worth living. I don't ask you not to go. I don't ask you to stop your gifts. Just to tell me where the heroin comes from. Not the cocaine, not the marijuana, just the heroin. Just the deadly one."

The faintest of crafty looks crept in around his anguished eyes.

"And don't," I said, watching for it, "think you get away with any old lie. You may as well know that what you tell me will go to the drugs squad. Don't worry, buy such a roundabout route that no one will ever connect it with you. But your present supplier may very likely be put out of business. If that happens, you'll be safe from me."

He trembled as if his legs would give way.

"Mind you," I said judiciously, "with one supplier out of business, you might have to look around for another. In a year or so, I might ask you his name."

His face was sweating and full of disbelief. "You mean it will go on . . . and on . . ."

"That's right."

"But you *can't*."

"I think you killed George Millace. You certainly tried to kill me. You very nearly killed my friend. Why should you think I shouldn't want retribution?"

He stared.

"I ask very little," I said. "A few words written down . . . now and then."

"Not in my writing," he said, appalled.

"Certainly, in your writing," I said matter-of-factly. "To get the spelling right, and so on. But don't worry, you'll be safe. I promise you no one will ever find out where the tip-offs come from. No one will ever know they come via me. Neither my name nor yours will ever be mentioned."

"You . . . you're *sure*?"

"Sure."

I produced a small notebook and fiber-tipped pen. "Write now," I said. "Your supplier."

"Not *now*," he said, wavering.

"Why not?" I said calmly. "May as well get it over. Sit down."

He sat by one of his glass and chrome coffee tables, looking totally dazed. He wrote a name and address on the notepad.

"And sign it," I said casually.

"Sign . . ."

"Of course. Just your name."

He wrote: *Lance Kinship*. And then, underneath, with a flourish, added *Film Director*.

"That's great," I said, without emphasis. I picked up the pad, reading what he'd written. A foreign name. An address in London. One tentacle under the axe.

I stored away in a pocket the small document that would make him sweat next year . . . and the next, and the next. The document that I would photograph, and keep safe.

"That's all?" he said numbly.

I nodded. "All for now."

He didn't stand up when I left him. Just sat on his black lacquer chair in his T-shirt and white trousers, stunned into silence, staring at space.

He'd recover his bumptiousness, I thought. Phonies always did.

I went out to where Clare and Jeremy were still waiting, and paused briefly in the winter air before getting into the car.

Most people's lives, I thought, weren't a matter of world affairs, but of the problems right beside them. Not concerned portentously with saving mankind, but with creating local order: in small checks and balances.

Neither my life nor George Millace's would ever sway in the fate of nations, but our actions could change the lives of individuals; and they had done that.

The dislike I'd felt for him alive was irrelevant to the intimacy I felt with him dead. I knew his mind, his intentions, his beliefs. I'd solved his puzzles. I'd fired his guns.

I got into the car.

"Everything all right?" Clare asked.

"Yes," I said.